Dripping wet, he regarded her with a sly grin.

He removed his hat and rubbed his forehead, pretending to ponder. "What was it I said? Something about only having to wait until tonight?"

Samantha gasped. "You wouldn't dare."

"Collect on a winning bet? Oh, yeah, I would."

He entered, shrugged off his coat and tossed it into the corner as she backed into the hut. He strode towards her.

"Is your horse lame?" He crossed his muscled arms.

Samantha's legs grew weak and parts of her body liquefied, but she was able to continue her retreat backwards, though half enjoying the cat-and-mouse game.

"Yes." She stopped, the heel of her boot bumping the stone wall behind her.

"Close quarters, princess. And running outside is not an option. I doubt you'll find the mountain lion very friendly this time of night."

"Thanks for the reminder." She swallowed hard and her voice faltered as she caught a quick breath, the hard beat of her heart making her breathing short and choppy. "Funny, I didn't take you as the friendly sort."

He chuckled, deep in his throat. His voice was sexy—too sexy. "No worries, princess. I won't befriend you any more than you want me to."

Arrogant cattleman. "Awfully sure of yourself, Mr. MacLaine."

He ran one finger along her jawline and tilted her chin up. "Ms. Matthews, would you like to put my abilities to the test?"

A southern belle.
A rugged cattleman.
An ill-fated love.
Neither can forget...
That Montana Summer.

That Montana Summer

by

Sloan Seymour

This is a work of fiction. Names, characters, places, and incidents are either the product of the author's imagination or are used fictitiously, and any resemblance to actual persons living or dead, business establishments, events, or locales, is entirely coincidental.

That Montana Summer

COPYRIGHT © 2008 by Mitsi Bennett

All rights reserved. No part of this book may be used or reproduced in any manner whatsoever without written permission of the author or The Wild Rose Press except in the case of brief quotations embodied in critical articles or reviews.
Contact Information: info@thewildrosepress.com

Cover Art by *Kim Mendoza*

The Wild Rose Press
PO Box 706
Adams Basin, NY 14410-0706
Visit us at www.thewildrosepress.com

Publishing History
Yellow Rose Edition, 2008
Print ISBN 1-60154-231-3

Published in the United States of America

Dedication

To my parents. I love you so much.
To fellow author and friend, Teresa Reasor,
for your endless encouragement and many, many
critiques. The day I met you, I struck gold.
To editor Nan S. for believing in this story.
To Kristoffer for understanding my need to spend
weekends as an introvert in story land.
To all my four-legged animals. You supported me
and didn't even know it.
And to the dialysis and cancer patients under my care.
Your bravery doesn't go unnoticed.

Prologue

"Read it, Dalton."

Mary MacLaine's words rang in his ears. Her pleading expression, so untypical of her, touched him as she firmly placed the book on the desk blotter before him.

"If not for you, then read it for me," she appealed, taking a step back. She stood several feet from the desk, tears filling her eyes while she tucked the red shawl, a present from him, closely around her.

His aunt was like a mother to him, had been since he'd lost his parents as a child. But he didn't know if he could do what she asked. As she turned to leave the room, Dalton rose from behind the large antique mahogany desk, an objection on the tip of his tongue, yet before he could get the words out she leveled a beseeching look at him that kicked the words right back between his teeth.

"Please." And she shut the heavy wooden door between them.

Dalton turned to the patio doors and looked out at the snow-topped mountain ranges looming in the distance, his reflection glimmering in the windows. Five years ago he never would have imagined himself dressed in a formal business suit, not to mention looking out at one of the most lucrative cattle operations in the west. He had built it all with his own two hands.

Yes, five years ago he'd made a risky but wise decision. His investment in the hundred-thousand-acre tract of land adjoining his family's property was now generating plenty of income. For a man in his early thirties he'd done well, and his share of hard times and difficulties was on the decline.

Even his social life was in order. A brief smile crossed his face as he recalled finding Hillary waiting for him in his bed when he retired last night. He hadn't asked how she managed to sneak past his housekeeper. He had been too interested in other pursuits, once he found her there.

He turned to look at the book on his desk blotter. How ironic that just the mention of the author's name had nullified the experience with Hillary. He brushed his hands through his hair, leaving it standing on end. He felt torn and confused, and he didn't enjoy the feeling one bit.

If he opened the book would he read what his heart had wanted to hear five years ago? Or should he keep that chapter of his life closed—forever?

He had moved on with his life. Granted, it had taken several years for him not to think of Samantha on a daily basis. But even now the sound of her laughter still haunted him.

Memories of Sam and the summer they had spent together spun through his head. He remembered how her long, wavy, chestnut hair glistened in the sunlight, tucked behind one ear in what she called a bad habit. How her generous heart-shaped mouth was suited perfectly for kissing. How her playful, mischievous smile as she looked up at him could spark his desire. He could almost feel her standing on tiptoe, stretching against his six-foot frame as she nuzzled the side of his neck.

Dalton stood motionless by the patio doors, once again gazing out at the mountainside as he waited for the hot thrum of desire triggered by the memories to subside.

He strode back to his desk and sat down. "*Blue Bandana* by Samantha Matthews" was written in navy letters across the novel's cover. A small chuckle escaped his lips. The title was appropriate. She was always wearing a blue bandana, either to pull her long tresses back off her face or looped around her neck to keep the dust down. Sometimes she would even use it for a tissue.

The scene depicted on the front cover of the book was a girl, with, of course, a bright blue bandana around her neck, sitting on a horse. They stood atop a mountain ridge, looking down the valley to the ranch below. It was unclear whether the girl was leaving the ranch or just arriving, for her expression was inscrutable.

At a knock on the study door, Dalton grumbled, "Come in."

"Sorry to bother you, Mister MacLaine." The southern drawl of his housekeeper was undiminished by time and space since she'd left home years ago. "I didn't want you to miss your flight."

Dalton sat back in his chair and took a deep breath. He stared at the closed book, recalling the bitterness that had surged through him the day Samantha left. She had never said goodbye. And he had never understood why. Would he find some kind of closure in the hardbound pages? "Gloria, you can cancel my flight for today. I'll be staying here."

"But, Mister MacLaine, are you sure?"

"Yes, I'm sure." He was surprised by his own words. "And I'll be taking my meals in here today, Gloria. And something stiff to drink would be great—whiskey," he said, rubbing his temples.

Dalton could have sworn she wore a satisfied smile on her face as she closed the door.

Outside the door to Dalton's study, one loyal housekeeper and one favorite aunt quietly celebrated the news. Then they thought of locking Dalton in his study, in case he had a change of mind, but they opted against that plan.

Chapter One

"Just when exactly will that atrocious cow stench be letting up? Because I'm quite certain it's been following us since we hit Wyoming." Bethany held the collar of her chic Juicy couture T-shirt over her nose, nestling further down into the back seat of the one-ton dually. "Sam, your dog smells better than this."

From the front cab of the truck, Samantha and Jessica exchanged knowing smirks—then exploded into laughter.

Samantha reached forward and muted the melodic sounds of George Strait blaring into the wind. Spying her other best friend in the rearview mirror, Samantha clarified, "Uh, Bethany, just remember that the term 'mud bath' in Montana has a whole different meaning than the one we're used to. Right, Jess?"

"Afraid so," agreed Jessica from the passenger's seat. "However, the words 'fresh' and 'organic' have never been more true."

"Yuck. I've heard enough. I'll stick to the hot stone massage."

Samantha's and Jessica's eyes met and their jaws dropped. Samantha squealed, then laughed. "Wouldn't go there, either!"

"Ugh. Then please tell me we didn't bring the entire George Strait box set?" Bethany whined.

"Afraid so," answered Jessica, her grin like a Cheshire cat, flashing perfectly aligned small, white teeth.

To Bethany's perturbed reflection, Samantha added, "And Willie, too." She could see her dog Dolly's large paws draped across her friend's lap.

"Oh, dear God!" Bethany racked her brunette bangs off her forehead in mock annoyance. "Just kill me now."

From behind the wheel, Samantha camouflaged a smile by biting her lower lip, knowing they were but a few miles from the ranch. "Don't worry, Beth. We're almost there."

Despite Bethany's manufactured complaints, Samantha was thoroughly enjoying their vacation. She was relieved to be taking this trip, needing a getaway as badly as she needed oxygen. A week spent out west, relaxing, riding, feeling the wind in her hair—speaking of which, by the way, they couldn't have asked for better traveling weather. The clear blue sky was full of white, fluffy clouds, and the temperature was in the low eighties. Back home in Lexington, Kentucky, the temperature had already reached the nineties, and it was only the middle of May.

"In fact," Samantha informed, slowing the truck to make a right-hand turn onto a dirt lane, "we're here."

"Amen," Bethany stated.

Samantha agreed. Two days of driving a truck and pulling a horse trailer were enough. She had found the scenic views as they crossed the country both inspiring and humbling, but she was relieved to have reached their destination.

Surveying the ranch entrance, she found something startling. The address was correct, but the hand-peeled cedar logs were etched and stained...nuh-uh. Frozen, she turned to Jessica. "Jessica Hamilton, I could shoot you."

"Gotcha," Jessica commented with a quick turn of her head, sending dishwater blonde hair spiraling with the movement.

"Aim for the head, Sam," Bethany said. "She doesn't have a heart."

Jessica laughed. "Bite me."

Only Samantha wasn't laughing. "Have you guys ever experienced *déjà vu*?" Saying the words made her spine tingle.

In unison, they turned to stare at her.

"Sam, honey, you feeling okay?" Jessica put a hand to her forehead, doing a fake temperature check. "The palm reader from last night didn't put anything in your breakfast burrito, did she? Ya know, I was thinking that was a strange meal choice for a Kansas resident to chef up."

Samantha took a deep breath. "That's just it—I let

her read my palms."

They gasped in unison. "You did what?"

"Why? Don't you watch Dateline?" Bethany blurted out.

Samantha put the truck into park. "I don't know. You two had gone to bed, and we just got to talking. One thing led to another, and curiosity...won out." It was odd, the connection she had felt to Fern. Being a nurse, it was normal for her to bond with her elders. However, this was different. She felt like her soul had been laid bare.

Jessica asked. "So, what did she say?"

Samantha cleared her throat, again. She had not slept well. She'd spent most of her night pondering Fern's questions. "She asked me if I swam." She paused to glance at her two friends. "If I lived by a river, and if I was a twin."

"I knew it! It's all made up," Jessica finalized.

"And then, she told me to stop looking so hard for a man," added Samantha. "She said, 'He'll show up when you aren't looking.'"

Never before had Samantha known her friends to be so quiet. It was worse than a morning hangover without Ibuprofen.

"Oh, that's just too weird," Bethany faked a shudder. "That sounds an awful lot like 'If you build it, they will come'."

"Yeah, well, you're not a baseball field, Sam, so I wouldn't take any of it to heart," Jessica advised. "Besides, looking for a man is the last thing you are doing. You run mach speed away from them."

Jessica was referring to Samantha's past three dates. Not one of them had been her type.

Her friend was right. She was not a believer in palm reading and figured Fern had guessed as much, one reason she hadn't pushed the subject last night. She'd simply told Samantha what the deep lines in her hands indicated. Still, seeing the Twin Rivers Ranch entrance made her think twice.

"I promise," Jessica soothed. "I booked this ranch over six months ago. The name is just a coincidence. Perhaps she heard one of us mention it." As soon as the words left her mouth, Jessica halted, her mouth agape.

"B-but I didn't say anything, and you guys didn't know until..."

Exactly.

Samantha shook her head, sloughing off the cold chills. She was on vacation. A vacation she very much needed. Nothing was going to spoil this summer or her time with her friends. She wasn't going to think or talk about anything that wasn't fun. That meant no talking about her parents, or their fruitless attempts to marry her off to the next rich politician's son, no worries about job opportunities, and no palm readers. Zip. Nada. None.

She put the truck into drive and headed through the Twin Rivers entrance.

The lodge and cabins were still out of sight, but Samantha was awestruck by the picturesquely snow-tipped mountains looming in the distance. The tall peaks were surrounded by a vast display of lodgepole pines and aspens that seemed to flow like waves beneath the mountain tops. The view was intensely serene and exactly what she had hoped to see after driving nearly two thousand miles.

Continuing down the dirt path at a slow pace, she followed the twists, turns, and bends in the road lined with wooden split-rail fencing. She found herself noticing every authentic detail, anticipating what was beyond the next hillside, and bit her lip as a multiplex of emotions rippled through her, the apprehension she'd felt moments before wiped clean by the prospect of escape. "No more electricity, guys. It's *au natural* from here on."

The comment earned a wretched sigh from Bethany. "And just how am I supposed to live without my straightening iron for a whole week? Because curly hair is not in style."

"You could always do a Britney and shave your head," Samantha answered.

They laughed.

"Unless it runs on batteries, I don't know. And don't even think of swiping the batteries from my vibrator," Jessica added.

"Well, it doesn't," stated Bethany. "But, oh, well, I'll just try to keep a hat on and think about all the damage I'll be saving my hair from the constant drying, spraying, teasing...my God, we'll look like shit the entire time!"

Chuckling, Samantha remarked, "That's kind of the idea."

Bethany snickered. "Lord knows the cows don't care. They haven't had a bath in years."

One thing was for sure, her friends could always make her laugh. "It'll be kinda like our last week of grad school, when the snow storm hit," said Samantha, remembering the relief of not caring what she looked like for an entire week amongst endless, drudging final examinations.

"And even then I had my vibrator."

Samantha laughed as she guided the truck down a seemingly endless road. "Well, by all means, please remind us when your birthday gets here, so Beth and I can buy you a new and improved model—I'm sure yours is about worn out."

Bethany spoke from the backseat. "Yeah, we wouldn't want you to go without."

"Easy for you to say, Beth. You're the one sitting in the back seat wearing the princess-cut Harry Winston on your left hand," said Jessica.

"And so I should be, after six years of dating!"

"You and Brad are perfect for each other," Samantha stated. "You both have brown hair and brown eyes, you live two streets away from one another, and you met on the teeter-totter. It doesn't get more perfect than that."

"Ah, thanks, Sam. You aren't doing too bad yourself. Let's see," said Bethany, using her fingers to count. "A lawyer, a doctor, and a..."

"Third generation banker," Jessica finished for her.

Bethany continued with her point. "All in one week. Not too shabby."

Samantha pulled her sunglasses down the bridge of her nose. "Not too shabby? They all fretted over me like I was a piece of antiquated china. I mean, God forbid they do or say something out of line and lose the opportunity to marry into a buttload of money." Turning to Jessica for moral support, she said, "You would've hated it, trust me."

Jessica frowned. "I know, Sam. I remember the double date we went on with the senator's son. You were miserable. And tried so hard to hide it."

Samantha rolled her eyes and sighed. She was so thankful for this chance to get away.

Around the next bend, Samantha got her first view of the Twin Rivers Ranch.

Nestled in the heart of an enormous mountainside, the ranch resembled a small town. Overlooking the valley and smaller buildings below, the Twin Rivers lodge was constructed of logs and stones. Several hundred feet away were buildings and cabins, all mimicking the lodge but on a much smaller scale, each with its own distinct personality.

As the girls passed the buildings and cabins they read signs in western motifs, signs spelled with antlers and horseshoes saying Barn-Mart, Liquor, and Spa.

"Barn-Mart?" asked Bethany from the backseat. "Think that's western for Wal-Mart?" she said, her eyes open wide with hope. "Does that mean they'll have *Bridal* magazine on the shelves?"

Samantha and Jessica exchanged doubtful glances.

"Um, judging by the size of it—no," answered Jessica.

"Probably just basic survival items like toilet paper and soap. And, if we're lucky, tampons." Grinning, Samantha winked at her friend.

"Oh, come on, Sam, you can't call tampons a survival item. They didn't even have them in the old days," Jessica retorted.

Beau whinnied from the trailer. "Well, it's good to know Beau approves of the place," Samantha said.

She could see Dolly in the rearview mirror, her front paws on the door rests as she attempted to get a better view. Even the dog was excited.

A few miles back, Jessica had used her cell phone to call the ranch and let the proprietor know they would soon be arriving. Mary had instructed them to park at the barn, where they could unload the horse and someone would be available to help them with their luggage.

Samantha pulled up to what she presumed was the barn, located a short distance away from the other buildings at what Samantha was beginning to feel was the edge of "town." The barn bore a striking resemblance to the other buildings but had a more traditionally western rustic appeal, built out of more weathered wood that had undoubtedly stood the test of time.

As she parked the truck and trailer she could see that beyond the barn the land widened into a beautiful rolling pasture overlooking yet another valley full of aspens and pines. When she thought she had seen it all, there, close by in the bend of the mountain, perched high atop the ridge, was the most adorable structure she could ever have possibly conjured up in her vivid imagination.

It didn't look as much like a cabin as it did a cottage. The roof was thatched with reed and straw, like in medieval times, and adorned with a small moon-shaped dormer window that hinted at a warm and cozy loft. At the opposite end, a chimney top was visible. Dutch doors on the front of the structure added simplicity and character, beckoning the viewer to come inside. Stone steps led to an antique metal picket fence placed decoratively across the front yard.

"Wow." As the girls stepped out of the dually, Samantha pointed towards the cottage and asked Jessica, "Is that part of the ranch? I thought you said we were staying in a cabin."

Jessica shrugged her shoulders. "I don't know, Sam. I don't remember seeing that in the brochure, though."

"Which brochure, the fake one?" She tilted her head.

"No, smartass. The real one."

Bethany's footsteps came from around the side of the truck before she appeared with a bag in each hand and let them drop to the ground with a thud. "Thank God we're here." She put her hands on her hips, taking a satisfied look around. "Because if I had to spend another day listening to you two sing *On the Road Again* along with Willie Nelson, I was going to opt to ride with Beau in the trailer."

Samantha looked at Jess and grinned. Guilty.

"Well," asked Jessica, "what do you think? Is it what you expected?"

Samantha looked at Bethany. Her beaming smile mirrored her approval.

"Any place would look good after spending two days in the backseat of a bouncy dually," said Bethany, pretending to be aloof. "No offense to your truck, Sam."

Samantha glared at her in mock ire. Grabbing

several bags out of the truck, she placed them on the ground near the front of the vehicle. "The place is beautiful, Jess. Of course we haven't seen the rest of it, but so far it's perfect. You couldn't have picked a better vacation spot. Really."

"And you, Beth?" Jessica asked, poking her head around the side of the truck. "Beth?"

"Yeah, I heard you," Bethany responded, her eyes fixed on something that captured her attention. "Sure the place is beautiful, but what I'm looking at now also falls into the beautiful category."

Samantha and Jessica asked in unison, "What?" They turned, following Bethany's line of sight to a pair of buttocks adorned with snug-fitting jeans, a brown leather Wrangler logo on the right back pocket. The male specimen, center of their attention, had just dismounted and was tying his horse to the post outside the building marked Bunkhouse.

"Is it just me," Bethany remarked with a satisfied smile, "or is that not one of the best-looking pairs of Wrangler jeans you've ever seen? Dear God, you guys might have to fan me."

"Oh, no," replied Jessica tersely. She put her palm up in a gesture to stop Bethany's next comment. "You're an engaged female. I'm not. And since Sam's not looking, he's all mine."

Laughing at both of them, Samantha shook her head. "Enough gawking at the hired help. There's bound to be plenty of time for that." Letting Dolly jump out of the truck, she motioned to her friends. "Come on, let's go introduce ourselves."

****

All Dalton MacLaine wanted was a good meal, a hot bath, and a week's worth of quality shuteye. Three days of driving cattle and mending fences with only a quick dip in the creek for cleanliness and beef jerky for food was enough to make him take back a year's worth of complaining about a few lumps in the bunkhouse featherbeds.

Constructed of massive native logs, stone arches, and cedar shingles, the ten-thousand-square-foot lodge was an impressive sight to his tired eyes. He got the shivers every time he saw it nestled among the pines in the heart of the mountainside. He was proud of this eighty-thousand-acre dude ranch located not far from Daniel, Montana. The ranch had been homesteaded over a hundred years ago and had remained in the MacLaine family ever since.

The ranch had begun welcoming guests for weekend getaways long before Dalton could remember. Weekends quickly turned into weeks, the guests complaining two days were a mere tease. Guests just couldn't seem to get enough of the place.

The ranch boasted five guest cabins, each tucked away in its own secluded location. Guests were offered a vast number of outdoor activities, including trail riding, fishing, hunting, swimming, canoeing, tennis, hiking and—Dalton's least favorite activity at the moment— cattle driving.

He could see that most of the new guests had arrived and were making their way to the lodge for what Aunt Mary liked to call "the meet and greet hour" scheduled prior to dinner. Knowing he would most likely miss both occasions, he decided to stop by the bunkhouse and let the rest of the wranglers know his plans to head into town for more antibiotic. The hot bath would have to wait. The injured filly they'd found in the yearling pasture was a priority.

He opened the door to the bunkhouse to find all five wranglers newly bathed and shaved, seated at the table playing a hand of cards. The aroma of soap and aftershave wafted across the room, reminding him of his need for a shower.

Old Jasper eyed his condition. "Heck, Dalton, we didn't know what happened to you. Thought perhaps that blonde woman of yours sexually assaulted you on horseback." He smirked as the rest of the table laughed along.

Dalton ignored the comment with a bland smile, thinking he would have traded places with any one of them, simply to be clean and to finally have a chance to sit and relax. "Piss off, Old Jasp." He crossed the room to his nightstand and grabbed the keys to his truck, seeing, for the second time this week, a note in recognizable cursive penmanship, asking "Busy tonight?" Unusual for him, he took time to crumple the letter, then tossed the crinkled ball across the room and bonked the old man square on the head. One of the wranglers snatched the sphere off the floor and yipped "woo-hoo" after reading the wrinkled message.

Leaving the room, Dalton paused next to Old Jasper's chair and leaned down close to whisper in his ear. "Tell you what, for an old man, you sure do smell awfully pretty," he teased.

Old Jasper grinned.

"So where you headed, Dalton?" asked Young Jasper, Old Jasper's son. He pushed his chair back, the legs scraping the hardwood floor as he stood and dug into his front pocket for his cigarettes. Tilting his head down, he lit a slender roll. "Not into town, I hope. I hear we have some good-looking guests this week."

"Oh, really?" Dalton's brows raised. "And I suppose the source of this information is no doubt my younger brother." He shook his head and folded his arms across his chest. "If Clay ever decides to start scouting cows like he scouts females, we can all expect to spend a lot less time on the drives."

The roomful of men snickered.

"The filly won't make it if she doesn't get more medicine. Tell Aunt Mary not to expect me for dinner. Give her my apologies for not meeting the guests."

"Will do, Dalton. And I'll be sure and help keep those good-looking guests entertained," Young Jasper added, with a satisfied grin.

****

The walk from the barn to the lodge allowed the girls a closer look at the layout of the ranch and the Elkhorn Valley in which it was located. The valley was spacious enough for the ranch, the buildings well protected, cradled between the Beartooth and Pryor mountain ranges.

A narrow dirt road led the way through the heart of the ranch and took them past several of the guest cabins they'd seen as they drove in. All were imitative of the lodge yet uniquely designed, set back a discreet distance from the main road to allow privacy.

The girls were quick to locate several of the stores a

short distance away from the guest cabins. The Barn-Mart and the Spa were located across the road from the Bar and another building called Billiards. Adjacent to Billiards was a large, two-story cabin with an etched wooden sign above the door that said Bunkhouse. All the buildings had wooden porches and sidewalks linking them together. Hitching posts were located in front of every establishment.

Samantha felt as though she had just walked onto the set of *Little House on the Prairie* and was indeed Laura Ingalls herself, minus only her lunch pail and long skirt.

The lodge was located farther up the mountainside but remained in clear view of the small town over which it presided. Pines and aspens accented the stone path leading the way to the lodge.

"Look, you guys." Bethany pointed up the hill. "There's a chapel."

Set back off the beaten path on the slope of the mountainside was a very small but charming wooden church. Stone steps led down to a small iron gate in front of the building. A pair of stained glass doors adorned the front of the structure, with colorful windows on the sides. The chapel was complete with a wooden steeple and bronze cross. Samantha smiled when she noticed the bronze bell inside the steeple. She could imagine hearing the chimes and seeing the guests meeting there for a small Sunday morning sermon. It was evident that much time and care had been spent on the structure.

"You know, Jess, you were really holding out on us by not telling us all about this place," said Samantha.

"Yeah, I know. But I knew you two would fall in love with it once you were here." Jessica had a contented smile on her face. "And Bethany, I couldn't help but think of you when I saw the church in the brochure, you being the engaged one and all. You never know, you might just want to bring Brad back here to get hitched."

"Well, it's cute enough, that's for sure. But I think it's more fitting for you or Sam to get married in. I'll keep my high and mighty, rich and costly, downtown two-story Lexington cathedral—if you don't care."

"Hey, guys, since we're on the subject, and as close to

a holy site as we've been since our parents forced us to Sunday school—I have a confession." Samantha desperately needed to get this off her chest. "Um, you know the inheritance money from my grandma?"

Duh-like, her friends looked at each other.

"Of course we do. As does everyone else, back home." Jessica was so good at pointing out the truth. She rehashed the hearsay. "You get it the day you marry."

Samantha's silence in response to this announcement had Bethany worried, the whites of her eyes blooming. "Sam, what did you do with the money?"

Jessica was fast to answer. "Nothing. It's not hers yet." But her eyes snapped to Samantha's for an explanation.

"Grandma changed the trust before she died. It's been mine since I turned twenty-one."

"Damn," Jessica drawled. "We've been hanging with a millionaire." Samantha laughed at her friend's blasé attitude. Neither one of these two friends could care less about her money. They were witness to its associated drama.

"I donated it to charity." There. She'd finally told someone. She waited for a reaction.

"Good for you," Bethany praised. "Now you can find a man who's into you and not your greenery."

And from Jessica, "Which charity? I'll remind myself not to send them anything—for the rest of my life."

Samantha laughed. Typical Jessica. "I was fair. I divided it up amongst a bunch of them."

"You did good, Sam," Jessica told her. "When your parents kill you, I'll be sure and wear a really hot dress to your funeral."

Just then they heard something approaching from behind them and turned to see a golf cart headed their direction. The driver was a fairly tall man, his head tucked under the canopy of the golf cart. Salt-and-pepper gray hair peeked from under his dust-coated cowboy hat, matching the thick mustache that bristled his upper lip. Samantha guessed him to be in his forties. The knees of his faded blue jeans were covered with mud, but the warm welcome in his smile made Samantha feel at ease.

"Hello there, ladies." The man stopped the cart and

climbed out, wiping his hands on his shirt as he approached them. "Welcome to the Twin Rivers Ranch. I'm John MacLaine. Feel free to call me John. I believe I spoke with Jessica on the phone when I took the reservation?"

"You did," answered Jessica. "That would be me," she said as she shook hands.

"It's good to finally meet all of you." He stepped back a polite distance. "Please excuse the filthy jeans and attire." He dusted the rim of his hat with the handkerchief that had been looped around his neck. "The wranglers just got back from a cattle drive, and we've been trying to get all the calves sorted into pens for tomorrow's castrations."

Samantha caught Jessica's anxious smile and noticed Bethany was smiling but with a modest amount of uncertainty. "Don't worry, Beth." Samantha reached out to pull her close for a squeeze of encouragement. "John wouldn't have you do anything that would cause you to get hurt, I'm sure."

John was quick to respond. "Samantha's absolutely correct, Bethany. We very much want our guests to enjoy their vacation. Our guests are free to do as much or as little as they like on the ranch. Jessica explained on the phone that she and Samantha were the ones interested in working for a discounted fare. And please don't feel left out, because most of the guests this week are what we call pure vacationers, meaning they are not doing any chores or labor during their stay. That's one of the reasons why we are so proud of our ranch—we can be flexible to both types of vacationers. We accommodate the guests who want the down-and-dirty working ranch experience and also the guests who want to spend their time lounging by the pool and going to the spa."

Samantha was thankful for John's explanation of the ranch. She felt Bethany's tense shoulders relax and saw a true smile return to her face.

Exhaling a deep breath, Bethany laid her palm on her chest and replied to the sky, "Lord, thank you." Lowering her gaze, she turned to John. "Okay, now we've got to talk hot stones."

Any and all tension that had been in the air quickly

and quietly dissipated. Samantha was sure about one thing: she very much liked Twin Rivers.

Chapter Two

John escorted the girls and their luggage via the ranch golf cart to the lodge, taking them back over the ranch's main road, where the terrain was much easier than the footpath for the motored vehicle.

As he drove, he explained that the rest of the guests had already arrived and dinner would be ready within the hour, if that suited them. He mentioned that Mary, his wife, whom they would be meeting shortly, held a meet-and-greet for all the guests in the lodge's entrance, or "the elaborate mudroom," as he called it.

"You girls will like the food, I think." He turned his head to speak over the back of the seat. "Mary does the majority of the cooking herself and is most proud of her meet-and-greet appetizers." He smiled under his cowboy hat.

Jessica, hearing the word "food," couldn't help but ask, "So what's for dinner?"

"As far as dinner goes, I'm not sure, but for appetizers Mary has her traditional pork chop-and-steak skewers, coconut shrimp, gorgonzola apricots, and water chestnuts wrapped in bacon and brushed with her secret honey-bourbon glaze."

"Bourbon? Did you say bourbon, John?" asked Samantha from the back of the golf cart. "Because I just so happen to have brought along the best bottle of apple pie liquor you've ever tasted, and I'm sure it will go quite nicely with Mary's bourbon water chestnuts." Excited, she wiggled half out of her seat.

Lifting his hat off his head and resettling it, John conceded, "Yes, ma'am. I imagine we can get that liquor of yours drank, Miss Matthews—without any problems."

"Please, call me Sam."

"Sam it is, then. And, Bethany," he said as he looked her way, "Jessica told us you're a vegetarian, so Mary has kept that in mind, as well. I heard her say she fixed you some special vegetable skewers and parmesan-stuffed mushrooms." He winked.

"Sounds like my kind of food," replied Bethany. "And to think I was afraid I wouldn't fit in, being the city slicker."

John smiled and shook his head in response. "You'll fit in just fine. We've had, oh, I don't know how many guests in all these years." He paused to mentally calculate. "And not a one felt like they didn't fit in. Maybe for a few minutes, but after that they felt like part of the family."

"How many guests do you typically have for the week?" asked Jessica from the back of the golf cart.

"It varies from week to week, but usually we have around a dozen or so, between ten and fifteen. We try not to book over twenty. We feel the guests don't get the one-on-one treatment and hospitality they deserve if we start taking on too many at one time."

"And how many guests for this week?" Samantha asked.

"Fifteen, I believe."

Samantha was glad Jessica had thoroughly researched and found the Twin Rivers Ranch. It was an exciting place. She was already in love with the layout and couldn't wait to ride Beau and take in the scenic views from horseback.

The smell of the ranch was a combined scent of cows, horses, and hay, with a background of clean fresh mountain air, tinged with evergreen—an aroma that Samantha could not get enough of. The outdoor redolence was comparable to her family's Kentucky farm, yet different. She secretly hoped that, when it came time to leave, the odd but consoling fragrance would linger upon her clothes and remain a memory.

John circled the perimeter of clustered buildings, then drove back to the main road which led through the ranch's small town. Dolly ran alongside the golf cart, getting some much-needed exercise, her tongue lolling out.

The sun was beginning to set beyond the mountains to the west, casting the sky and clouds into brilliant hues of orange and yellow, and Samantha turned to find

Jessica also looking at the sunset. They looked at each other, both knowing no palm reader in the world could spoil this.

"Samantha, will your horse be okay until after dinner?" John asked as they neared the front entrance to the lodge. "If you want, I can drop Jessica and Bethany off at the lodge, and take you back down so you can unload him—it's up to you."

Samantha paused in thought, trying to decide what was best to do. She knew the answer, of course: Beau. However anxious she was to see the lodge and meet the other guests, he came first. "I'd better get Beau settled before dark. I'm sure he's just as tired and hungry as we are and probably anxious to see where in the world I've taken him."

"Well, John, now you have met the real Samantha. She always puts her horse and dog first," Jessica said.

John pulled the golf cart up to the front of the lodge. As he put the brakes on and stepped out from under the cart's awning, he remarked, "The Indians used to have a saying for that. I think it was 'He who feeds horse and beast first has them by the soul.'"

****

Mary MacLaine was waiting for them at the top of the massive stone steps of the lodge, an appetizer tray in hand and a warm and welcoming smile on her cheerful, rosy-cheeked face. She wore a red apron, the name Twin Rivers Ranch embroidered on the front. Above her left breast her name was spelled in western motif next to a small sketch of the ranch's brand. The brand looked much like the pound key found on a telephone but with a slight curve to the lines, indicative of two sets of winding twin rivers. A delicious smell of home-cooked food radiated from the rustic front door she propped open.

"Welcome, girls. Please, come in and join everyone for some appetizers." She held out the tray of food for them to take a sample.

Once they had each taken a toothpick of food, she led them from the porch and into John's "elaborate mudroom." Samantha thought John's description of the room had indeed been quite adequate.

The room was vast, with tall walls and a vaulted

ceiling. The outside walls were built of layered masonry rock while the interior walls were constructed of hand-hewn logs. In the center of the room a large weathered wagon wheel functioned as a table, with an elegant moose antler chandelier hung above. The concrete-and-rock floor was patterned with iron horseshoes so that it looked as though a horse had just been led across it. Sconces filled with candles were located around the room.

Mary introduced the girls to the other guests in the room and to several of the wranglers who were present. The last wrangler she introduced as her youngest nephew, Clay. Samantha felt Jessica's elbow nudge her. He appeared to be close to their age, well over six feet in height, and exceptionally easy on the eyes, with his dusty blonde hair and a striking pair of dimples. He was no doubt Jessica's description of the perfect Adam. Samantha could only imagine what Jessica and Bethany would later say about him. The two of them would most likely be spending the rest of their evening, and possibly week, discussing who would make the better Eve.

"Clay will show you to your cabin and help you with your luggage after dinner," Mary said.

John informed Mary that Samantha would need to return to the barn before dinner so she could unload her horse and get him fed before dark. He also pointed out Dolly, Samantha's dog, sitting at the front door.

"Sounds fine, dear," Mary said to her husband as she eyed his mud-stained jeans and somewhat-less-than-tidy appearance, "but you need to take a shower before dinner. I'll get Minus to help Samantha with her horse and dog while you get cleaned up." Before she left the room she announced with a smile, "Please, everyone, eat, drink, and make yourselves comfortable."

Samantha turned at a light tap on her arm and looked down to see a small boy. She guessed his age at about six. "Ma'am, can I please pet your dog?"

She could tell by his quickly downcast eyes and slouched shoulders that he had used most of his courage in asking the question. She stooped down to his level and looked him in the eye with a smile. "Why, of course you can. May I ask your name?"

"Luke." He answered shyly, catching her eye for a

brief moment.

Samantha glanced past the little boy and saw his parents watching, even as they visited with the rest of the guests. She looked at them and smiled. His mother returned the greeting and nodded permission.

Samantha saw he wore a western button-down shirt and jeans with a pair of snakeskin boots. Knowing Dolly could sometimes be leery of strangers, she unknotted the bandana she wore in her hair. "Her name is Dolly, and she absolutely loves bandanas. Can I tie my bandana around your neck like the cowboys do?" Samantha glanced up for an example at the wrangler Mary had introduced as her nephew, and Clay, listening to the conversation, winked at the little boy.

"Dolly will smell my scent on it and know you're very special." The child's responding smile was bashful but laced with enthusiasm. Samantha wreathed the bandana about the little boy's neck and walked him to the entrance of the lodge, where she had instructed Dolly to wait.

****

A brisk Montana breeze feathered Samantha's skin. Her hair, now loose and flowing about her shoulders, glided with the rhythmical sashay of the yellow pine rocker. From the lodge's front porch, she observed Dolly and Luke's playful game of fetch tennis. Had she not been attired in riding jeans and boots, she would have joined the newfound friends.

"There you are."

At the sound of her hostess' husky but feminine voice, Samantha turned to greet Mary, then nodded towards the grassy lawn and winked. "We've been getting acquainted."

"I see that." Mary took a seat next to her. "Wonderful, because Luke hasn't spoken a word since he's been here." Snatches of Luke's laughter filled the air. "I've got Minus getting a stall ready for your horse. He'll have it ready by the time we walk to the barn."

"Minus?"

"That's what we call him. He's half Indian and he doesn't say much. The wranglers call him Minus because he only speaks in proverbs."

Samantha was eager to meet him. She'd never met a

Native American before and, apart from that, this guy sounded interesting.

"One minute he's not saying a word, the next he'll recite a proverb that's completely appropriate for the moment at hand. He's a handy guy to have around, excellent with horses, teaches us all a lot of useful things—small things that make life easier. Just doesn't say much."

Their conversation went from more about the ranch to questions of life in general.

"Are you married or engaged?" Mary asked. "I don't see a ring."

A smile and a laugh escaped Samantha. "Neither." She shrugged and gave a small sigh, pushing the wooden boards with her feet to keep the rocker in a steady rhythm. "And I can't really explain why." She tipped her head back to look up at the evening sky, as if the answer should somehow be written out in bold starry letters. "I date plenty. Just can't seem to find anyone. If you ask my friends, they'd tell you I'm single because I'm entirely too picky, but I disagree. I simply haven't found him yet, is all. I think, perhaps, I need to stop looking."

"Well, I have no doubt in my mind that you'll find the right one. You never know, he might just be around the corner."

Samantha saw Mary eyeball her watch. "Are more guests arriving?"

"No, I'm expecting Dalton home soon."

"Dalton?" Something about the name intrigued her.

"He's my oldest nephew, Clay's older brother by four years. He brought an injured filly in from the cattle drive today. He gave her a small dose of antibiotic but doesn't think she'll make it through the night without more. We're all out, so he went into town to get some Banamine and penicillin."

Samantha sprang up from her chair. "Banamine? I have a full vial with me. I wouldn't take Beau anywhere, especially not to a remote place like this—no offense—without an antibiotic and any medicines he might need."

"Wow, you come prepared."

Samantha turned, already halfway down the steps of the lodge. "That's because I'm a nurse. And happy to help." She felt so free here. A sudden rush of peace consumed her. She gestured to Mary. "Shall we?"

****

The lanterns they carried provided a lit pathway to the horse barn. Mary explained to her that the ranch had several kerosene lanterns available but that most of the lanterns were battery-powered as a safety precaution.

Each cabin was provided with several lanterns and flashlights, as well as stocked with batteries. She further explained that, while the cabins had no electricity, water and modern plumbing were indeed available.

"Some of our guests try living rustic, but others just don't like it. For those guests, we have several lavish suites available in the lodge." Mary held her lantern up and motioned towards the edge of the woods. "I'll show you the shortcut. It'll save you some time making trips to and from the barn."

The path through the woods was downhill and wide enough for two to walk comfortably side by side. Mary explained that the path was actually part of a five-mile hiking trail that circled around the heart of the ranch. "So don't worry about getting lost. Simply look to your left or right and you'll see the ranch."

Mary led the way out of the woods. The path continued along the side of the barn. As they walked, she described the layout of the ranch. "The horse barn sits at the end of town—or so we call it. Obviously it's not a town, but so many of our guests call it a town that we go along with the title. The barn looks old and rustic simply because it is," Mary quipped. "But it's as strong as steel, and there's not another like it."

Mary turned and faced the road that led through the ranch. She signaled with her hands and held her lantern out for Samantha to see in the darkness. "Next to the horse barn is the chicken-and-dairy barn. Past that is the bunkhouse where the wranglers board, and then a little farther down is the bar—because every ranch needs one— and the last building is Billiards, which is a gaming hall." Pointing across the street, she indicated the spa and Barn-Mart.

"How does all this work without electricity?" Samantha asked, puzzled, knowing only a technological world.

"Believe it or not, it works quite well," Mary answered. "For example, the bar has large built-in coolers to keep the ice and drinks cold, the spa has a wood burner and a fireplace to warm creams and salves, and the gaming hall has a pool table, bowling lanes, darts, and other games that don't require electricity." They turned back and walked towards the barn. "We've found that most of the guests like the fact that the ranch is rustic. They know if they need a touch of modern life they simply have to walk up the hill to the lodge—it cuts down their need to panic. In turn, they relax and enjoy themselves."

"So, it's the best of both worlds."

Mary shrugged, her smile modest. "We like to think so."

Light from the moon shone brightly upon the barn as Samantha led Beau inside the tall, massive oak doors which framed the entrance. She noticed regular doors were set into the large oak entrance portals for secondary access in time of bad weather.

The combined smell of horses and sawdust filled her senses, making her feel at home, and she inhaled deeply, breathing in the familiar scent. Lanterns hung on cedar poles glowed throughout the barn and continued to provide lighting along the dirt aisle which wrapped around the center pen of the barn. Horse stalls formed a semicircle at the opposite end while wooden bleachers completed the ring at the end of the building where they stood.

"Good, it looks like Minus has your stall ready," Mary said.

Samantha could see an open stall, already filled with what some guests might think looked like oatmeal but which of course was fresh, sweet-smelling oak sawdust.

Mary headed in the direction of the stall. Behind her Samantha led Beau, eager to have him in a safe stall. This would be his new home for the next week.

They stopped short of the stall entrance as a man Samantha assumed was Minus stepped out. He held a pitchfork in one hand and was dusting sawdust shavings off his shirt with his free hand.

"Minus, I'd like you to meet Samantha, one of our

guests staying with us from Kentucky." Turning, she said to Samantha, "And this is Minus, one of our best wranglers. He's been with us for quite some time now. He doesn't say much, of course, but he'll be glad to show you the ins and outs of things here on the ranch."

"Nice to meet you, Minus. Thanks for getting the stall ready." Samantha smiled at the Indian with the long black hair and the darkest brown eyes Samantha had ever seen. He nodded gracefully in response, then propped his pitchfork against the wall with a gentle swiftness and stood waiting in quiet confidence, his hands clasped behind his back. He was of average height and weight, but Samantha could sense his lean strength by his fluid movements.

"I'll get Beau settled in his stall and then we can get to work on the sick filly," Samantha suggested.

"Sounds great," Mary said.

While Samantha busied herself with Beau, Mary explained to Minus, "Samantha's a nurse. She's offered to let us have some of her medicines to help the filly make it through the night until Dalton returns with more."

Samantha gave Beau one last pet on the hindquarter and closed the stall door behind her. As they left to find the filly's stall, she turned and gave Beau one last look. She'd come back later to check on him. The horse raised his head from his pile of hay and nickered softly to her.

"He who has love in his breast has ever the spurs at his flanks."

The comment gained Samantha's attention, and she looked at Minus with interest. In the three strides they walked and the five seconds they shared, she and Minus found a chord of understanding and a little bit of something else Samantha couldn't quite put her finger on.

The filly was housed several doors down from Beau, "In case she should be contagious," Mary explained. "But I think you'll agree she's not that kind of sick."

They stopped and peered into the stall.

On the floor, in a bed of oak shavings, the dark, dapple-grey filly lay on her side, her sweaty coat glistening in the lantern light. Samantha took this as a good sign. Sweat, her grandfather had taught her, was a natural first line of defense against infection.

The filly's tail swished back and forth. Another good sign. Pain meant she was alive. If not for the visible fever and tail movements, Samantha could have easily presumed her dead.

As Minus opened the wooden stall door for Samantha, the click of the latch echoed within the wooden walls.

The filly didn't offer to stand, only continued to swish her black stubbed tail. Her breathing labored, her sides rose and fell with each breath.

Samantha walked softly into the stall and quietly placed her medical box close to the filly's head, where the young horse could see it. The filly attempted to raise her head. "It's okay. I'm here to help," Samantha soothed. She knelt in the sawdust and continued to speak in calm, audible whispers while gently stroking the animal's head and neck.

Samantha turned to find Mary and Minus watching her. Minus stood just inside the stall door with a halter and lead rope on his shoulder, ready to lend assistance. "She's awfully sick," Samantha said.

The filly's left front leg was deeply lacerated and swollen. Two puncture wounds were present on both sides of the laceration. "How'd this happen?"

"We don't know," sighed Mary. "On a ranch this big, it's hard to say."

"She's going to need stitches." Someone had doused the leg with betadine solution, the orange stain visible in the horse's hairy coat. Good thinking on Dalton's part. Samantha found it odd, but she was somehow intimidated by this man named Dalton. She had yet to meet him, but she could feel his compelling presence all around her. She wondered what he looked like. *Don't, Sam. Remember what Fern said: stop looking.*

"This is Dalton's filly?" Well, she needed to know whose horse she was preparing to mend. "Would he want me to sew her up?" asked Samantha. She looked from Mary to Minus.

Samantha, the nurse, thought of what was best for the horse. She was not about to let herself be dismayed by a male figure she hadn't met. Not today or any other day, and especially not when she'd decided to completely stop looking for a man in her life. "Well, it's just too bad, if he gets upset. Because I...I just can't leave her like this," she said, searching in her medical box for a vial of Ace. "It would be against...policy."

"And whose policy would that be?" Mary teased.

"Mine." She held the syringe out in front of her and flicked the last bit of air out of the nineteen-gauge needle. She doubted even an Indian would try to stop her with a needle that large in her hand.

"Well, then, if I'm not needed here I'll get back to my other guests." Mary turned and spoke to Minus. "If you or Samantha need anything..." Her words trailed off and she hurried out of the barn.

With the incision cleaned and numb, Samantha opted to close the wound with several inside sutures before she started with the outside ballpark stitch her grandfather had taught her. She'd found this method worked best on young horses who still had a tendency to frolic and play in the pasture.

Samantha was thankful she had spent so much time with her grandfather in the barn. Together they'd spent endless hours discussing and demonstrating practical horse knowledge. It was a far cry better than the piano lessons her mother had pushed her to take. From mending wounds to doctoring sick horses, checking pregnant mares to tacking on loose horseshoes, she had learned through hands-on experience with her grandfather. That, combined with her four years of nursing school, gave her a sure confidence as she tended to the filly.

She realized this was her first work done on the ranch. Having never met Dalton, she wanted his first impression of her to be one of competence. She was, after all, working on his horse. That alone was intimidating. Certainly Dalton must have done his fair share of mending wounds.

With her last stitch in place, Samantha wrapped the wound in cotton and applied vet wrap around the leg to secure the dressing. Minus continued to hold the lantern while she medicated the filly, injecting her with a dose of Banamine for pain and inflammation as well as penicillin for infection.

"That should take care of her," sighed Samantha. She rose and stood looking down at the horse. The filly's respirations had slowed, becoming more even, and she wasn't sweating as profusely. She seemed to have settled. Satisfied, Samantha nodded and checked one last time that the royal blue vet wrap around the filly's front leg was secure. Surely Dalton would approve, even if he turned out to be a complete ass.

Chapter Three

Minus led Samantha to the dining room, where the guests were taking their seats around a large planked picnic table. A buffalo head mounted on the wall opposite an enormous stone hearth accented the room, while flickering light from the candles placed evenly down the center of the table was reflected in the darkened windows of the back wall.

The kitchen door swung open.

Mary, her smile wide and bright, stepped out balancing a platter of delicious-smelling steaks. Behind her followed a boy carrying a tray of salad and bread.

"Oh, good. You two were able to make dinner on time." Mary adjusted the serving dish. "Follow me, Samantha, and I'll show you to your seat." She spoke over her shoulder. "The girls have been filling us in about your drive here."

Mary led Samantha to a seat across from Bethany and Jessica, next to Clay. Minus took his seat opposite Clay. Samantha saw the two men exchange an unspoken look as the conversation continued.

"So that was the only wrong turn we took. Which ended up okay because we saw some amazing views of the Bighorn Mountains," Jessica was saying.

"That is, when we weren't too scared to look. Sam had the truck in low gear and the brake pedal plastered to the floor," divulged Bethany.

Oh, no. Her buddies were exposing her tendency for bad directions. Loudmouths. The table looked to her for a response. She shrugged and tee-heed. "Pass the turnips?"

Next to her, Clay roared with laughter. Then, settling down, he asked her, "So what made you want to haul a horse all the way from Kentucky?"

Samantha's brows flew up in amazement, and she took a moment to think. It had never occurred to her to leave her horse behind. Or her dog, for that matter. That was her answer, plain and simple. "I never thought to leave home without them."

Bethany interjected, "See, that's Sam for ya. She won't leave home without her animals, and I won't leave home without my American Express."

Across the table, Jessica nodded. "Yeah, that'd be like me leaving without my Wal-Mart card." Samantha gave her a quick smile. Having grown up on the poor side of Lexington, Jessica never forgot her roots, and Sam admired her for that.

She also noticed that her friend had caught Clay's attention with the remark, but then he turned back to Sam, his dimples accenting his white smile. "Mary tells us you make quite the nurse, Samantha. She said Dalton's filly should be up and bucking in no time."

Samantha looked up at Mary, to find her taking a seat next to John at the end of the table. Mary winked at her as she passed the bread basket around.

"Well..." Samantha paused. "I hope so. The filly was in worse shape than I expected," she confessed. "I can see now why Dalton was determined to get her some medicine."

"Samantha's good at that," Bethany remarked from across the table. "You can always count on her to show up with a needle in hand, asking if anyone needs anything."

The guests laughed.

Clay took a piece of the Texas-style toast and passed the basket her way. "Well, that's good. Just keep those needles of yours pointed away from me, Samantha, and we'll get along just fine." He flashed a quick grin. "I'll be more than happy to let you use that brother of mine for a dartboard."

"That brother of yours," she said, putting emphasis on the words he used to designate Dalton, "might just want to see me as the dartboard if his filly doesn't make it through the night."

"Nah," entered John into the conversation as he buttered his toast. "Dalton'll just see to it that your horse bucks you off by the end of the day tomorrow, is all."

Samantha laughed. She wasn't expecting that frank an answer. She covered her mouth to cough, fearing she might choke on the sip of water she'd just taken. Her friends sat across from her, grinning.

From farther down the table one of the guests spoke up. Samantha recognized him as Luke's father.

"Do you remember the time Dalton got unseated in the creek?" His question was more to the wranglers than to the other guests at the table, and from it Samantha assumed this wasn't his first stay at the ranch. He finished chewing the bite he'd taken right after bringing up the subject, and then, with a smile, he continued. "That was the funniest thing. Dalton didn't see it coming. One minute he was letting his horse drink, carrying on a conversation, and the next he was butt-up in the creek."

Clay nodded, grinning. "Oh, I remember that, all right. And I dare say Dalton remembers it, too."

"What caused the horse to spook?" asked Samantha. She had this picture of Dalton painted in her head—tall like his brother, dark-skinned, with the coordination of an athlete. Trying to picture him face down in a creek was near hilarious.

Clay laughed. "A frog." He took a bite of steak.

"A frog?"

Luke's mother joined the conversation. "Yes, that was it! I remember now. A bullfrog jumped out of the creek and the horse bucked."

Samantha saw Luke with a shy grin on his face, listening to their informal discussion.

"Didn't Dalton change the horse's name after that?" Mary asked the table.

Samantha and her friends exchanged glances. They weren't expecting to have such a lively and deliciously gossipy dinner conversation.

"Yeah," answered one of the wranglers at the end of the table. Samantha identified him as Young Jasper from Mary's earlier introductions in the mudroom. "The horse's name used to be Buddy. Now it's Buck." His dry tone indicated he didn't find the story amusing.

Meanwhile, Samantha threw her head back, laughing. Dalton MacLaine whetted her curiosity. She had to admit she was eager to meet him. She wondered if he would live up to the fabricated image she had of him in her head. Was he the tall Wrangler-wearing stranger they'd seen striding into the bunkhouse? If so, his backside lived up to her expectations. How exactly could a pair of eyes not focus on those firmly shaped buttocks? But, of course, she had been looking.

At that moment Fern's euphonious voice sounded in her head, repeating the words—*Stop looking...when you aren't watching*. Perhaps it had been the look in Fern's eye, her expression so absolute and all-knowing. How a complete stranger could read her thoughts so well she didn't know and didn't care to know. It was eerie.

****

After dinner several of the guests meandered into the great room, the room the lodge had been centered around. Mica shades and rawhide details filled the room with western flair. An inviting reading loft lined with bookcases and shelves hovered, with its massive cedar banister, over the tan leather sofas and plump cushions below. Here the guests were free to put their feet up and chat or watch their favorite show on the large flat-screen television. The room created a feeling of old-time comfort while at the same time providing modern conveniences.

The river-rock fireplace with its dual hearths continued into the room and gave a warm glow. A plush bearskin rug stretched before the fire on the hardwood floor. In the corner an extravagant cedar bar provided a place where the guests could order drinks or make their own special blend of liquors.

Seeing the bar, Samantha went to retrieve her bottle of apple pie liquor from her luggage. She returned to the room holding the bottle by the neck and supporting the heavy end of the bottle in her open palm.

"Thata girl, Sam," Jessica proclaimed from her seat at the bar. "Break out the liquor."

"This is the drink I was telling you about." Samantha waggled the bottle at John as she proceeded to the bar, where she found a display of various shot glasses. Selecting two of the traditional thick glasses, she poured in the dark amber liquid until each was half full, then handed one to Mary and one to John. Mary smelled hers before taking a swallow. "Smells just like a slice of apple pie."

"I know," Samantha agreed. "And it tastes even better."

Samantha poured her friends each a shot and crossed the room to hand them their glasses. Jessica gulped her drink in one swig. Bethany managed the same in two swallows.

"Must be good stuff—that or you Kentuckians are in the habit of drinking awfully fast." Clay chuckled, his spurs jingling as he turned to his aunt. "Well, how is it?"

"Amazing. Tastes just like homemade apple pie." She stepped to the counter and placed her empty glass in the stainless steel sink while Clay declined a drink from Samantha's special bottle and opted for a beer instead. Samantha settled next to Jessica on one of the rawhide-backed bar stools that smelled of oil and leather and creaked as she crossed her booted legs. She sipped the sweet liquid, feeling relaxed.

From his seat on the leather couch, John remarked, "I notice Sam is just sipping her drink, whereas Jessica and Bethany devoured theirs."

All eyes turned to Samantha for an explanation. "I can't handle my liquor like they can," she replied, nodding to her two friends. And indeed she couldn't. Already she could feel her ears burning after only a few sips.

"Don't let her innocent look fool ya," Jessica said. She nudged Samantha with her elbow. "I've seen her bong a beer like no man should."

Samantha's guilty smile gave her away.

The brawling ring of the telephone came from the hallway, and Mary went to answer it, her footsteps echoing on the wooden floors.

"That'll be Dalton," said John. He looked to Clay, who shrugged his shoulders with raised brows.

Samantha could see concern on John's face. He seemed worried about Dalton and his absence this evening. "You girls will have to excuse Dalton when he arrives tonight. He had a long day in the saddle, with this sick filly complicating the drive. I don't think he even got to see the bathhouse before he left to go after the medicine."

Samantha looked from Bethany to Jessica. Good. Neither one of them had noticed the flush of heat she'd felt come to her cheeks upon hearing Dalton's name in association with the bathhouse. Why? She asked herself.

Why does the mention of this man fluster me? I don't even know him. She could picture him now, or the image she had of him so far—dark, tanned, muscular, with steam rising all around him, water drops on his solid chest as he reaches for his terrycloth towel... *Stop it, Sam!* She hoped it was just the liquor causing her thoughts to stray, making her feel so abnormally warm.

Several of the guests had already retired to their cabins for the evening, saying they wanted to get a good night's rest in preparation for their first day of activity. Samantha was beginning to feel tired herself, not to mention overheated due to the liquor. Perhaps the bathhouse was a good idea. Perhaps a cold bath was an even better idea. Surely that would awaken her and remove steamy thoughts of Dalton.

Mary returned to the room, her smile subdued. "That was Dalton on the phone. He found the medicine, but it will be a little while before he gets home. Clay, will you show the girls to their cabin? John and I will see to the other guests."

"Sure. I'll be more than happy to escort three inebriated females to their cabin." He set his empty beer bottle on the bar and winked.

Mary and John bid the girls good night. "We'll see you in the morning. Breakfast is at seven. And the lodge is always open, should any of you need anything," Mary added before the girls retreated down the front steps.

With Clay as their escort, Samantha and her friends walked the winding path of pines and aspens to their cabin. The dirt path, flattened by many years of use, was not far from the lodge or the main road of the ranch yet secluded by an abundance of aspen groves and lodgepole pines.

The night air was crisp and mildly cool. Samantha felt the breeze upon her face, and her hair tossed lightly in the gentle breeze. She remained tepid, the liquor filling her with mull and relaxation.

Ahead in the distance a flicker of golden light shone through the tree branches, a light that bobbed with her footsteps. She quickened her pace with Dolly's eager pull on the leash.

The golden light was revealed as a lantern hung on a

wooden hook outside the front door of their cabin. The darkness kept hidden the details of the cabin at the same time the moon brought to light the two-story structure. Dormer windows graced the second story with a soft glow. Rocking chairs were at home on the front porch, their shadows lining the hand-hewn, chinked-log siding. The familiar smell of wood smoke from the fireplace prompted Samantha to smile with pleasure.

Clay opened the cabin door, allowing the girls to enter as he held the screen door open with his backside. "Now, if you like to hear the howls of coyotes, then I suggest you sleep with the door open and the screen pulled. Otherwise, I highly suggest you close the front door."

"Do they ever decide to come down the mountainside and pop in for a social call?" Bethany was worrying again.

"Only if they think the view is worth admiring," spoofed Clay.

Samantha saw him glance teasingly at Bethany and then wink at Jessica.

"I'm just going to point a few things out to you," he said walking through the cabin, lighting various lanterns. "Bath water can be warmed on the log stove or over the fire in the fireplace, whichever you prefer. Candles and matches are in nearly every cabinet." He walked into the kitchen and opened a deep drawer. "This here works as a cooler, should you want to keep your Kentucky liquor cold." He took a sneaking look at Samantha.

Samantha grinned back at him.

"So, what if there's an emergency and we need fast help?" asked Jessica.

Clay folded his muscular arms across his chest with a smile, considering her question. His answer was absolute. "Just walk outside and scream."

Jessica turned to look at her friends in jest. "Which one of us screams the loudest?"

The two friends simultaneously pointed at Bethany.

"Gee, thanks."

"No, seriously, scream or yell if anything should happen. This cabin is the closest one to the main road. And the closest to the bathhouse, which is probably why my aunt gave you this cabin," Clay said matter-of-factly.

"I'm sure she thought you girls would never make it to dinner on time with just one bathroom."

"And where's the bathhouse?" Samantha was anxious to take a relaxing bath and permanently remove her thoughts of Dalton, even if it meant deliberately dumping the first bucket of cold water on top of her head.

"If you're headed that way, I'll show you."

"Great. I'll go get my things." She walked out of the kitchen, stealing a look at Jessica, whose expression telegraphed an urgent need to talk—no doubt regarding Clay—before she departed for the bathhouse.

Samantha spoke from the foyer of the cabin where they had left their luggage, her question intentional for Jessica's sake, but also because she honestly did not know where she was going to sleep, "Is it okay if I take the loft?" She smiled, waiting to hear Jessica's attentive reply, knowing her friend would be quick to answer.

"Sure," replied Jessica promptly. "I'll help you carry your things."

"Clay, I'll be right back," hollered Samantha from the next room. She handed Jessica her heavy duffle bag of blue jeans, for appearance's sake. Jessica lugged the heavy bag and followed her upstairs.

Samantha ascended the steep, wide steps to the loft, feeling as though she were in a pint-sized turret. The wood was dark with a clean, earthy fragrance. A peculiar kind of stained wood lined the walls from top to bottom. The turret-like space was lit by a small lantern hung on a horseshoe hook. Samantha thought she saw what looked like an escape door built into the side of the wall. She quickly dismissed the thought, thinking instead of how she should monitor her future consumptions of alcohol.

At the top of the steps both of them dropped her luggage with a clunk and took a deep breath. "Shoo. I think you really did need help carrying your bags," exhaled Jessica.

"No doubt." Samantha huffed from the physical exertion. "I think my cardiac output just went into overtime." She sauntered over to the queen-size feather bed and plopped down on it. She lay back, catching her breath. She could feel the softness of the linens under her shoulder blades where her halter top left her skin exposed. She couldn't wait to slide between the crisp sheets.

"So?" whispered Jessica. "Isn't he gorgeous?"

Samantha turned on her side, propping herself on one elbow. "Oh, he's gorgeous, all right. And just your type—fun, outgoing, with a wicked sense of humor."

"I know," Jessica said, giggling under her breath.

"How old is he?" She remembered Mary saying Clay was several years younger than his brother, but she hadn't mentioned ages. She was so curious about Dalton.

"Twenty-four."

Which would make Dalton a yummy twenty-seven.

Jessica was ecstatic. Samantha had never seen her in such a frenzy before, especially over a guy. Her friend was usually the cool, calm, and collected type. "Well, you've got a week to spend with him—that is, if he's available." She forced herself off the comfortable bed in search of her toiletry bag. Finding her satchel, she knelt next to it, retrieving her soap and bathing products.

"And that, my friend, is where you come into play. Perhaps you could nose around, nonchalantly of course, on your way to the bathhouse and find out for me."

"Oh, I imagine I still have enough liquor in my bloodstream to ask that question. Now, just how nonchalantly, I don't know…"

Jessica reprimanded her with a shove from her booted foot.

Samantha fell flat on her derrière.

"Okay, so maybe it won't be so nonchalant," commented Jessica with a snort.

****

The lodge lights had been dimmed by the time Dalton arrived back at the ranch several hours later than he'd hoped. He would have liked a long relaxing bath, a plate of his aunt's savory vittles, and a full night's rest, but that was long out of the question. The simple task of finding medicine for the filly had been anything but simple. He'd checked with several neighbors, but no one had any to spare. When he resorted to contacting the vet, he found the man was out on an emergency call similar to the filly's. Dalton backtracked to the nearby ranch the veterinarian's wife indicated, where Dr. Beard was able to supply several doses of the needed antibiotic and confirmed he would stop by soon to check on the young horse.

Dalton parked his truck at the lodge, to avoid disrupting any guests who might be sleeping in the cabins on the main road. Also not wanting to wake his aunt and uncle from their peaceful night's slumber, he quietly headed down the stone path to the bunkhouse. He figured he could always raid the bar for some peanuts, although peanuts weren't his dinnertime preference. A cold beer, on the other hand, would do.

His intentions were to take an extended and relaxing bath, preceded by a cold beer and succeeded by a cold beer. Then he would check on the filly and give her the medicine. He hoped she would endure the night. It'd be a shame if she didn't. Her breeding and conformation were top-notch. He'd hand-selected her as the best in this year's remuda. She would make an exceptional roping horse, not to mention a fine broodmare.

Clay gathered his soap and shaving cream from the bunkhouse with a catlike quietness. A chorus of snores from around the room continued in an unchanging hoarse melody as he undressed at the side of his bed and wrapped a towel around his lower waist. His Aunt Mary would object to him parading around half naked, but he figured the late hour was in his favor. Not many guests braved the night without a lantern, which instantly gave them away. Dalton had no need for a lantern. Having grown up on the ranch, he knew the layout like the back of his hand and his eyes were accustomed to the dark.

As the latch to the ridged wooden door clicked behind him, Dalton traversed the three stone steps that directed him to the pathway between Billiards and the nearest cabin, the midwife's cabin, an old homestead named after its previous owner. Through the pines, Dalton could see the faint glow of the lantern from the cabin's second story windows.

Dalton and his uncle agreed the midwife's cabin was best suited for guests who were working on the ranch, due its close proximity to the barns. He recalled John mentioning several females had signed up to trade labor for a vacation discount for the next week. This meant the girls would spend half the day as they pleased and the rest of the day working on the ranch, helping the wranglers.

Dalton found it admirable that many of the guests wanted to help with chores and have a hands-on ranch experience. The problem, however, was that many of them, although their intentions were good, were inexperienced and often enough created more work for the ranch hands. He always took ample time explaining and demonstrating the various maneuvers and techniques of working with the cattle and horses to keep extra work to a minimum. He emphasized the importance of getting the job done and tried to motivate the guests to find contentment in accomplishing a hard day's work.

Feedback from the guests had skyrocketed. Letters and responses to surveys came in declaring the ranch a "Grand Adventure" and a "Best in the West" vacation resort. More so than ever, guests began volunteering to take part in the work. Dalton often wondered if he'd created a monster. On frustrating days, he believed so; on good days, he reconsidered. Contemplating the week ahead, he was uncertain how the females would adapt to ranch life and work. Frankly, he couldn't imagine they would be worth a damn.

Dalton reached the bathhouse and the small nook in which it was nestled. The structure, once an old shed on the midwife's cabin property, was recessed into the tree line, with spruce trees and pine branches hanging low over the galvanized tin roof. Renovation plans were for the shanty to have two separate rooms, one for each sex, but the ranch's current laidback policy was "whoever's next in line." Considering how tired he felt, not to mention his rumbling stomach, he would take a bath with a toad if necessary.

****

Samantha soaked in the oversized clawfoot bathtub for what seemed like an eternity. She had heated water in the iron cauldron over the fire as Clay had instructed and, by using a large saucepan from the kitchen as a scoop, was able to warm the water in the tub to the desired temperature. She'd elected to make the bath water swelteringly hot, causing steam to rise from the washtub as the warmth collided with the coolness of the bathhouse climate, encompassing her in a cloud of moisture and wetness. Bubbles, hollow and airy, encircled her with a soft honeysuckle smell, their globes sparkling in the dim candlelight.

Tranquil and dreamy from both exhaustion and the effects of the apple pie brandy, her thoughts dwelt on Dalton. Her imagination worked in overdrive, conjuring up fictitious characteristics he might possess. Once again she pictured him to be dark and muscular, with his skin tanned golden bronze from working outdoors on the ranch. Her inebriated state discharged her typical lucid thoughts and she continued to ponder curiously about him, despite her earlier self-admonishments to the contrary.

Would he be tall? Would he be clean shaven? Or burly, with a five-o'clock shadow because he liked to sleep in late? Was that him she saw at the bunkhouse, or someone else? Would he have dimples as Clay did? Or, instead, a stubborn jaw line? And, most importantly, why was she asking herself all of this? Could it be, as Fern had predicted, that she would soon be meeting someone, perhaps Dalton, who entailed swimming, a river, a twin? *Yeah, right.*

After Samantha had washed and conditioned her hair, she rose from the water and enfolded her long heavy tresses in a towel atop her head. With an unsteady sway, she stepped out of the tub. Her toes, bare and dripping, met the cool cobblestone floor. Finding a second towel next to the washtub, she unfolded the squared bundle and placed the soft, cotton cloth in front of the fire as a makeshift rug.

Gracefully naked in front of the stone hearth, she stood to let the fire warm her and dry her skin. She noticed the logs on the fire were quickly disintegrating but the coals remained amber in color, providing sufficient heat. She applied lotion to her body, rubbing the sweet-smelling cream into her soft skin. Her tired head was spinning from the liquor and the warmth of her bath, and the amber coals seemed to move in a swirling motion as she gazed into the fire.

In a blissful and besotted state, she began to

fantasize, imagining Dalton stepping into the bathhouse through the adjoining door that connected the separate rooms. This was a real possibility, she considered momentarily, because she couldn't remember latching the door. She envisioned him behind her, walking slowly up to her as she faced the warm embers, his expression intense and fiery, his stride slow and steady, a towel around his waist oscillating with the movement of his thighs.

He would trail his index finger along the curve of her hip and upward to her breast, reaching the delicate pink orb and teasing until it hardened from his touch. His delicate caresses would cause her to shiver with delight, sending goosebumps over her flesh.

She'd take an unsteady step backward and feel her backside meet his warm, solid abdomen. He would loom over her like a giant warrior, his large and tapered hands balancing her, bracing her arms on both sides. She wouldn't dare look at him, her captor, for fear she would recognize the wistful, seductive expression in his desire-filled eyes. Instead, she would lean further into him, keeping her face turned towards the heated embers of the fire, allowing him to nuzzle and nip her neck.

She could smell the fragrance of his aftershave, the masculine scent arousing her senses. Even in her drunken state, she hoped she would remember his intoxicating aroma.

Coarse but yielding palms would skillfully splay across her breasts and abdomen, moving slowly down her torso to gently cup her buttocks. He'd emit husky, resonant moans as he kissed and suckled her neck, his breath heated and tranquilizing.

She would feel his passion growing, his hands more questing, his lustful digits lingering over the soft line of hair between her thighs. She'd gasp as his fingers slid inside her, caressing her, urging her to a place she had never been before.

Never had she allowed a man such liberties. Her instincts would warn her to stop his roaming hands, but the pleasurable sensations brought on by his arousing touches would be too much for her to deny.

Suddenly feeling somewhat sobered, Samantha opened her eyes and saw the darkened hearth and blackened coals. Good—they were no longer swimming in circles. The room was illuminated by only a small candle across the room in the window ledge. She turned her head slightly to the side, wishing she could see the illusive manly image she had concocted in her imagination, and the towel slipped from her head and tumbled to the bathhouse floor. Her long mahogany hair, darkened by wetness, spilled over her shoulders. Instinctively, she stooped to pick the towel from the floor.

In the space of that second Samantha could have sworn she was not alone. A cold influx of air drifted into the room. She turned to look at the adjoining door.

It was closed.

Had she latched that door all the way? She recalled Clay emphasizing that if the door was not latched properly, it would open if someone entered through the other side. She shook her head, half believing it would clear her thoughts. It did not.

Regardless, her Dalton hallucination was over. What she wouldn't have given for a few more minutes of imagination with him. Or perhaps what she would have given. Dear God, her grandmother was probably rolling in her grave. And hallucination or not, she needed to monitor her future consumptions of alcohol. At least she was the only witness to her inebriated state.

Samantha was, however, sure of two things. By morning, she would absolutely and positively no longer allow herself to have thoughts of Dalton. And secondly, she did indeed smell aftershave.

****

Dalton didn't meander nor stroll to the bunkhouse. His strides were long and purposeful, not to mention hell-bent on finding Clay so he could wring his younger brother's not-so-scrawny neck. Clay had devised this rendezvous. Dalton was sure of it. But who was she?

His younger brother was widely known for his pranks and antics, always engaging in tomfoolery of some sort. Since they were kids Dalton had known his brother's reputation for practical jokes and mischief. Clay used them as paybacks when Dalton's teasing provoked him, and this time, no doubt, he'd been perturbed by Dalton lassoing and hog-tying him with a pigging string on today's cattle drive.

Dalton chuckled under his breath. Even in his fury, he found the image of his brother humorous. Clay's face had turned an embarrassed shade of beet red by the time both their mounts reached the yearling pasture.

Speaking of red faces, Dalton was certain his was flushed, and not only from fury. He'd been taken aback by the desire and lust he'd felt upon seeing the woman in front of the fire. The moment was odd. He hadn't been at all attracted to that blonde when Clay had introduced them last weekend at The Silver Spur, a local tavern on the outskirts of Montana Springs. She hadn't been his type at all. In fact, she was the opposite—polished beauty with no brains, and that he could get delivered to his doorstep any day of the week, if he wanted it.

There, standing beautifully naked in front of the fire, as if she had been put on display for his eyes only, had been the most alluring and intoxicating woman he had ever seen. He had intended to pull the adjoining door shut but was held captive by her petite yet voluptuous hourglass figure. Her skin was aglow with firelight. Her full breasts cast shadows over the creamy white flesh of her slim waist. Firm, round buttocks beckoned to be groped.

He had stood motionless in the doorway, his eyes transfixed on the beauty before him as she applied lotion to her body. Her hair was wrapped in a towel, her face turned toward the hearth.

Dalton was positive he was being set up by his younger brother. He didn't doubt that Clay and the blonde were in cahoots. His brother knew he would be arriving home late after driving into town to find medicine for the filly. The note he'd tossed away in the bunkhouse had been bait.

He forced himself to turn away from the alluring scene.

As he bathed in the next room, his lust grew by the minute. His hands ached to feel her soft skin and to take satisfaction in caressing her until she moaned with pleasure.

Or at least that was how he remembered a woman responding to his touch. In the past few years, most of his desire was aimed at getting a good night's rest so he could accomplish another full day of work the following morning. By evening, women were simply an afterthought. Only on rare occasions when his aunt would host a ranch gathering, or perhaps when he went into town, did the female sex trigger his attention or entice him in any way. The notion of sexual intimacy, however sublime and hypnotic, left him feeling uninterested the following sunrise when he awoke with hollow emotions.

Dalton knew he would one day marry and awake every morning to the same set of amorous eyes. That day was simply not going to be tomorrow or anytime in the near future. The woman who would one day wear his gold band on her ring finger, the one he would pursue for marriage, would have to await his proposal. He wanted to succeed in ranching first. His hopes and aspirations of owning a ranch, like the one he and his father had once envisioned, consumed his daily life.

Quickly, he had bathed. With a towel once again swathed around his waist, he stood before the connecting door, now half ajar. Should he or shouldn't he? His mind had raced back and forth. The good angel over his right shoulder advised him to listen to his own good judgment and the words of marriage he had just considered. The dark angel, perched on his left shoulder, like a predatory hawk, reminded him of the immediate gratification waiting unclothed and equipped next door.

And with that delightful thought in mind, he had started to step into the room, opting to seduce the beautiful blonde, only to discover it was not the blonde at all but instead a tantalizing, chestnut-haired vixen with the ability to overpower his mind and body. How unbelievably close he had come to walking in on her. And she was a guest! At his family's ranch!

Chapter Four

Pale light seeped from under the closed entrance door of the bunkhouse. Dalton, driven by his temper, paused to catch his breath. He very much wanted to take his brother by surprise when he throttled him with his bare hands. Also, he had respect for the wranglers who had long ago retired for the night. Monday morning's hustle and bustle with the new guests would come all too soon.

The door hinge squeaked as Dalton peered inside, his focus aimed on the far corner of the bunkhouse, where Clay had his bunk. His brother would be awake, of course, waiting to gloat about how he'd gotten him but good. Dalton quietly guided the door to a closed position and strode across the room, mindful of his footsteps on the plank floor.

He found Clay in a deep sleep, prone, with his left cheek cushioned on the feather pillow. He faced a pine wall, a shelf of dusty hats and worn chaps in shades of black, tan, and russet. The coppery tone of the russet leather chaps brought forth the image in Dalton's mind of a waterfall of dark titian-colored curls cascading in layers of wetness down an all-too-feminine backside and derrière. Dalton thought for sure his brother had been the conspirator, but Clay's youthful, innocent expression and obvious deep slumber gave him pause. If he were responsible, he'd be awake to razz him about it.

Annoyed and with no answers, Dalton left his brother's side, an impatient scowl frozen on his features. He was exhausted and wanted only to sleep, although he would consider bartering an hour's worth of slumber for some food to lessen the hunger pains in his stomach.

Passing by his own twin featherbed, he grumbled inwardly, assuring himself that he would sleep better after he checked on the filly and gave her a dose of medicine. He exited the bunkhouse once more.

Two strides outside the door, he realized he was not

alone.

Dog.

The deep, low, canine growl was more a warning than the sound of an imminent attack. Dalton cursed to himself. First, he had encountered an untamed female and now an untamed dog. Great. Peanuts were no longer on the agenda.

Agitation pulsed through him. His thoughts toyed with the idea of the growl belonging to a coyote or some other mangy mongrel. He squinted in the dim light, pondering the likelihood of a coyote. Coyotes rarely assaulted or even charged humans. They preferred the flavor of animal flesh, except in the case of small children, and that, Dalton decided, wasn't the case at this late hour.

He continued to the barn, determined to give the filly her medicine.

The rumbling snarl persisted behind him, where the animal continued to follow.

He didn't need to feel for the switchblade in his back pocket. The compact metal piece, now rubbed to a smooth, dull shine from years of wear, was within easy reach.

Dark clouds muffled the moon's glow but a faint glimmer came from the horse barn. The throaty growl from the hound ceased as the animal scurried into the bushes surrounding the stable. The faltering light ahead of him flickered as he passed the dairy barn. He knew that flutter—the sign a lantern was about to go out.

Dalton accessed the stable from a seldom-used rear entryway. More of a window than an entrance, the Dutch door allowed him to enter unnoticed. He inhaled deeply, detecting a sweet, freshly-bathed feminine scent in the air, one newly familiar to him. His lips quirked into a gentle smile and his thoughts raced. What he wouldn't give to see her face. As he crept farther into the barn, it occurred to him most men weren't given the luxury of tasting the fare before they saw the menu.

Lantern rays glowed in a golden, dim haze with only an occasional flutter above the grey filly's ten-by-twelve pen. Dalton stood in the darkened shadows of the aisleway and observed the woman.

She was clad in only a thin white robe and flip-flops.

The lantern she had carried was placed out of reach from the young horse. Long auburn hair hung loose in wet tendrils down her back and over her shoulders as she knelt beside the animal. The thin fabric of the robe, damp and snug across her backside, was sheer in the lantern light. For a moment he relived the scene in the bathhouse and desire once again flared through him. As the flickering continued from the lantern he hoped it would remain lit.

He watched her every move, each gesture so simple yet sensual. Small, delicate hands roamed in gentle glides along the young horse's jawline and neck. She eased the filly with gentle, soothing strokes until she had worked her way down to the injured leg.

The leg was swollen to the fetlock. Dalton eyed the bandage, silently thanking whoever was responsible for doctoring the young horse. His aunt had mentioned over the phone that one of the guests had attended the filly. Could this strange and beautiful woman be the one accountable? He watched as she diligently checked the bandage with two fingers, monitoring the dressing for tightness. Impressed by her intuitive skills, his eyes followed her hands up her slender arms, past a modest display of ripe cleavage, to her face.

Delicate, arched brows and long, curved lashes accented her downcast eyes as she nursed the young horse. Her generously full pink lips compressed together in anticipation of the filly's pain as she flexed the leg, checking the joint for range of motion.

The reaction caused the young horse to spring to its feet, sending the woman scrambling to hers and stepping back closer to Dalton. Now only a thick board of cedar separated him from her. Upon standing, the filly gathered her balance and shook like a wet dog, sending specks of sawdust and timothy hay falling in the flickering golden light. Mesmerized, Dalton watched the beauty reveling in the shower of chipped wood and hay, laughing as she stretched her arms out to catch the debris.

Dalton tipped his head to hear the soft whispers she spoke to the young mare, but was unable to decipher the words, his concentration focused on her angelic, heart-shaped face. A laugh escaped her rose-colored lips again as the filly nuzzled the soft skin on her neck. Caring, maternal eyes turned in his direction, but remained there for only an instant. Reaching into her pocket she pulled out a peppermint candy and offered it to the young horse. The filly chomped the hard mint until it was gone. After a small kiss to the filly's nose, the unidentified female left the stall.

In the darkened aisle he followed her to a nearby stall. A low neigh greeted her from within the pen. Calm and casual, he propped his shoulder against a wooden corral post and anchored one ankle over the other. He recalled his uncle asking his opinion regarding a guest bringing a horse to the ranch. Dalton couldn't remember the response he'd given, but his uncle must have consented.

He watched as the scantily-clad female lifted the latch and opened the stall door. The lantern's glow revealed a dark horse's head, his black nose already in the petite palm of his owner's hand, a pink tongue licking the salt from her skin.

"Goodnight." She spoke to the horse as it continued licking. "See you in the morning."

Dalton uncrossed his booted feet and took a step forward out of the shadow of the corral post. His denim pant legs brushed against one another, rustling. He saw the horse's ears prick forward and then lay flat against his head. *Amazing*, he thought. Horses have an incredible sense of smell. The animal had known of his presence but didn't act on it until he sensed a threat to his owner.

With her clean, fresh fragrance filling the air, the nameless female moved to step out of the stall but was intercepted by her horse, his head and neck planted over her shoulder in a protective stance. "Beau?" she queried, reaching to rub his head with a soft laugh. She stopped, feeling his ears pinned, sensing his anger. She looked from her horse to the unlit aisle, her expression wary as she searched the darkness, focusing on the direction of her horse's fixed stare.

With her jaw clamped in a stubborn attitude, she jerked the collar of her flimsy robe together and crossed her arms. She turned to speak to the dark horse in low, inaudible tones.

Dalton couldn't decipher the color of her eyes, but he'd be willing to bet they were blue. Ocean blue. With a storm brewing in them. He could see her squinting toward the dark aisle, the corners of her eyes pinched as she watched the shadows, and it wasn't fear he saw in them but anger. Untrusting, are we, princess? Dalton grinned—she was cute when she was mad.

Her body language remained calm and quiet as she soothed the riled horse with gentle strokes, but the glare she cast into the shadows betrayed her outer calm. Fear, Dalton realized, was not an expression she was familiar with. He could see her inner strength in her vivid features, a cute button-nose scrunched and nostrils flaring under a forehead tense with worry.

As if on cue, Dalton heard the same throaty growl he'd heard earlier. He was unable to pinpoint from which direction it sounded, but it was close—too close.

And inside the barn.

****

The familiar and reassuring sound of Dolly's threatening growl gave Samantha instant solace. She felt the tension in Beau weaken. Keeping her eyes on the darkness, she stooped to pick up the lantern she had placed on a low hanging nail near the feedbox of the stall. The lantern flickered, the pauses of golden beams becoming shorter and weaker with every flutter. *Please, don't go out!*

She yearned to call for Dolly, needing the security of her dog's presence. She knew Dolly was near because Beau had settled, as he always did when his faithful canine companion appeared.

Samantha wished she were truly sober. She still felt the flush on her cheeks and the slight warmth in her ears from the alcohol. Given the unfamiliar environment and the unusual wounds to the filly's leg, she dreaded what her dog could be growling at. She fidgeted with Beau's mane, mindlessly coiling the long, black hair around her index finger. She'd had too much to drink and, clearly, the alcohol had gone to her head. She paused. But why was Dolly growling?

Her plan of action was to stay as calm as possible. With her free hand, she smoothed her damp hair off her face, flipping the long strands behind her back. The moistened locks of hair dropped and she felt their slap against her skin under the thin robe. Taking a deep breath, she cracked the stall door, managing to slip from under the neck of her horse. He nickered to her as she latched the wooden clasp of the door. She was thankful the lantern hadn't burnt out. The last thing she needed was her stallion running loose on a Montana ranch of eighty thousand acres. She didn't like leaving him, but she was concerned for Dolly. The last time she'd seen her dog, Dolly was looking quite cozy on the steps of the cabin, camouflaged by the marbled black and gray stone that matched the Catahoula color and markings.

Trying not to act frightened, Samantha turned to creep out of the barn. Dolly's menacing growl grew louder. Apprehensive, Samantha clenched her fist, her right palm sweaty as she gripped the metal handle of the lantern. She held the blinking light out in front of her, and scanned the dirt aisle. Ahead of her, she could see the barn doors, one side still propped open. A few more steps and she would be outside the barn under the safety of the moonlight. She quickened her pace, the soles of her flip-flops popping against the bottom of her feet.

With a poof, the lamplight faded out. Goosebumps prickled her arms and a cold chill sliced through her. Halting, she parted her lips to call Dolly's name.

Too late. A large hand covered her mouth at the same time a strong arm encircled her waist. She closed her eyes against the whirling sensation as the man whisked her into a nearby corner of the barn. She managed to elbow the stranger twice in the ribs—or what she thought were ribs but must have been the groin area, for he took a quick gasp of air. He was tall, whoever he was, and she didn't appreciate being manhandled, not one bit.

She wiggled, trying to break free of his grasp. Her yell for help was a mere whimper, smothered by the firm hand clasped over her mouth. A deep "shoo" to be quiet was the only acknowledgement she received. She wished she could respond with a smack across his face. The stranger held her tight against him, letting go just long enough to move a heavy arm over her flailing upper limbs.

The only weapon she could think of was the lantern she held. The idea of slugging him upside the head crossed her mind. But, given the height of her opponent, if she swung the lantern upward she'd only succeed in hitting herself.

She grew still, noticing something odd about the persistent snarl. The sound had changed and was coming from outside the barn. She could have sworn she'd just heard Dolly's deep, agitated rumble from inside the barn, not too far from Beau's stall. Granted she was further away now, but still, she had heard Dolly. Now she was hearing another animal—and it didn't sound pleased, nor did it sound like a growl. The snarl was higher pitched, more pronounced and... catlike.

Catlike!

The reality of the moment caught up with her. *Dear God. Please tell me I'm just hallucinating and drunk.* From Psych class, she knew hallucinations existed within the patient and were only perceived by the patient. If her assailant could hear the peculiar, angry sounds of the animal, then they weren't just figments of her imagination.

In a moment like this, it paid to be stupid.

One thing she knew: she felt safe, which was odd. Moments ago, she had felt trapped and helpless. Now she was silently thanking the large man who'd detained her. She relaxed, letting go of the grip on his upper arms. He removed his hand from her mouth, but not before he pressed a finger to her lips. She wished she was as good with body language as he. Knowing he meant no harm, she wondered if it was Clay who was holding her. She wasn't sure. Could it be Minus? No, this man was much taller.

She felt something at her feet and stiffened. It rested against her bare leg, feeling warm and hairy. It licked her toes—Dolly!

She sighed, much relieved. With her body still pressed against the tall male figure, she slid down the length of his frame, bending down to find the familiar feel of her dog. The warmth of the man's body took her back to her bathhouse fantasy and, after petting her dog, she stood and turned to look at her protector but could not see his face. She was slowly losing her patience. First the mysterious male she'd conjured up, the one who seemed so oddly real because he smelled of fresh aftershave. And now this man she couldn't see because of the darkness—wait. The same smell.

Her senses clicked. His shaving cream, hinting of evergreen, the exact aroma as earlier. Could it be? The same man? Her mind somersaulted, piecing together the coincidence. Could it be that this man had actually been watching her? Naked? What an ass!

The words rose in her throat. It was Dalton. She knew it. Her instincts told her it was. After all, she had feared earlier he would turn out to be an ass, although that was purely in her own thoughts. Too good to be true, just like the saying. The s-o-b. All her favorite blaspheming words came to mind.

Samantha felt him lean to reach for something. Seconds later, in the palm of her hand, he placed a cotton rope, the texture soft and round, a heavy snap at the distal end. Squinting, she wrapped her fingers around the threaded cord, silently wishing the braided fibers were in the form of a noose she could place around his neck.

In a muted tone, he spoke, "I need you to leash your dog. I can get you back to your cabin, but the passage is dark and complicated." His voice was deep and husky, soothing—which infuriated her all the more.

"Passage? What is this? A theme park?" She heard his movements become still, and could have sworn she felt him smile. "Just who are you?" she sassed. Instinctively, she pulled the front of her robe together, feeling as though he was somehow managing to see quite well in the pitch-black darkness of the night.

"Introductions later. Right now I need to get you to your cabin."

"So let me get this straight. I'm supposed to let some strange man lead me down a secret passageway, supposedly to my cabin, not knowing who he is?" She paused, letting him think that one through. "I'll have you know it's against my better judgment."

"Given the dire circumstances, I'd say you're quite the comic." His voice sounded from directly in front of her. His tone was dry.

With clenched teeth, Samantha did as she was told and fastened the snap to Dolly's collar. The clink of the snap sounded loudly in the deafening silence of the barn. The catlike growl returned, reminding Samantha to keep her mouth shut—for now.

He eased her forward, keeping her close by his side with a hand around her shoulder. She started to walk but stopped, mid-stride.

"Will my horse be safe?" She was dead serious.

"He's in a fully enclosed stall. He'll be fine." He inched her ahead in the darkness.

"What kind of animal growls like that?"

"Doubt you want to know."

"Is it the same animal that injured the grey filly?"

"Perhaps."

A door squeaked open.

From behind her he spoke, "I'm going to have to carry you. The path is uneven and not suited for flip-flops."

"I'm sure I can manage just..." Her words were cut off by the feel of his hands against her bottom as he lifted her into his arms. "Fine," Samantha finished, her one syllable pronunciation of the word as sharp as her grandmother's finest cutlery.

Samantha could tell she was underground. With each footfall she felt a drop in temperature along with a touch of dampness in the air.

At stride twenty-nine in the escape route, as Samantha was counting the number of steps in case she needed to resort to an undetermined plan B, she noticed the incline began to ascend. Ahead of them Dolly pulled on the rope attached to her collar, the dog's panting quickening to match the long, powerful strides of the male who carried Samantha as though she were but a weightless bag of groceries.

Boots thumping on wooden stairs announced their destination. At the top of the steps she was lowered to her feet and told to "be still." Dolly scratched at a door. A thick, dull wooden sound replaced the eerie silence of the passage.

"I need you to do me a favor before I open this door." He turned her by the shoulders to face him, though she couldn't see anything in the dark.

Hmph. "You won't tell me who you are, but I'm supposed to do you a favor?" Samantha waited to hear his response. She could almost hear him thinking. She was glad she couldn't see him, realizing she had much more nerve that way.

"Well," he said, his tone brash, "I could just leave you here in this dark, dreary tunnel for the spiders and rats." He drawled out every syllable, emphasizing the vowels. "I'm sure they'd find your flesh most appealing."

"I'm not afraid to smack you."

With a tinge of amusement in his husky voice, he commented, "Princess, you're much too short to reach me."

"Some other time, perhaps," she suggested, matching his impudent tone. Now she wished she could see him, just so her aim would be absolutely on target when she smote him straight across the face.

"Back to that favor."

His coarse yet seductive masculine tone unsettled her.

"This is a hidden passage. We use it only when necessary. Please keep it that way."

"How did you know which cabin I was staying in?"

The sound of a match being lit against a rough wall jarred her senses. Her question was forgotten as she adjusted to the reality of seeing his handsome, chiseled features before her in the gloomy light outside the hidden entrance to the midwife's cabin.

Damn, he was good-looking.

Chapter Five

Samantha awoke to birds chirping outside the loft window. Each of the long, rectangular dormer windows consisted of three small glass panes. Vented open, they allowed the cool mountain air to sweep in from the north. The rising sun was hidden from her view by a oversized evergreen whose prickly branches brushed against the sides of the cabin as they swayed with the wind.

Turning on her side, Samantha propped her head on the goose down pillows and tucked the soft cotton sheet close around her, enjoying the peaceful moment with the breeze tickling her skin.

Last night was a blur—a drunken bath, a male figment of her imagination, a strange growl, and a concealed passageway leading to a camouflaged entrance to her cabin. She wasn't sure whether she was on vacation or had, unbeknownst to her, elected to take part in a bizarre reality show.

Today she intended to discover the identity of the unfamiliar but helpful man. Her gut instinct told her it was Dalton, Mary's oldest nephew and the owner of the grey filly. His looks were similar to Clay's but more weathered and hardened compared to his brother's youthful, refined features.

Dalton. Even his name was sexy, she thought, the way the two syllables lingered in the air like the floating bubbles she'd blown as a kid, teasing as they burst in close proximity or drifted away with the wind, leaving a multicolored illusion of vibrant, seductive hues.

"Sam! Wake up. It's almost seven," Jessica wailed as she bounded up the loft's stairs two at a time. The wooden encasements thudded with the rhythm of her steps.

Samantha, now fully awake, rolled her eyes and smiled, feeling a sudden rush of excitement. She was in Montana! She leaped out of bed, surprising Jessica as she met her in the doorway, her hair tousled and a grin on her face. "It may come as a surprise, but I didn't go deaf during the night."

Grinning back at her, Jessica tilted her head to the side. "No shit, Sherlock. I can see that. I also see you survived the bathhouse."

"I did, thank you." Clad in tank top and panties, she turned to don a pair of jeans. The bathhouse was one incident she wanted to avoid discussing this early.

"And?" Jessica was waiting for Samantha to speak.

"And what?"

"Ugh." Jessica huffed. "Did you find anything out about Clay? Remember, your job was to nose around and see if he's available?"

Samantha turned, guilt-ridden. She bit her bottom lip. "I kind of forgot to ask, Jess."

"What? Ahh!" Her friend faked a slap to Sam's forehead. "How could you? I'm dying to know if he's attached or readily available—for me!"

"I...I had a lot to drink!" Which was true. "Trust me, I did well just to make it back to the cabin." She really did do well, considering the circumstances. That strange growl. And those deep, engaging eyes. And lips. Soft, inviting lips...and a mouth which promised to speak the huskiest of bedroom endearments. She recalled his goatee, trimmed neatly along his jawline, the short manicured hairs the color of dark chocolate. She imagined how it would feel to have him nip at her neck, feeling the scruffiness of his hairs against her skin...

"Sam!" Jessica jolted her back to reality. "Are you okay? Don't even tell me you're hung over. Because I've seen you with a hangover, and, no offense, but you aren't worth a hole to piss in."

"None taken. And no, I'm not hung over. I feel fine. I just need to eat something." Tottering, she stepped into her leather boots. "I'll have you know I plan on redeeming myself."

Jessica snorted. "Well, that's good. I can't imagine you being much help castrating calves like this."

"No, I mean about your wannabe boyfriend." Glancing sideways at her friend, she smiled, displaying her best flirtatious look. "By the end of the day, I'll have the scoop on Clay." Hearing the rhythm of her sentence, her eyes popped open. Lifting her shoulders, she commented, "Look, it's not even breakfast and I rhyme!"

Jessica folded her arms with a smirk. "Yeah, well, we'll just wait and see what you find out."

****

As usual first thing in the morning, Mary sat at the small, private table in the staff kitchen, drinking a fresh-brewed cup of coffee and looking out at the view of ranch and mountains. The dark oak furniture was polished smooth by years of use—it had seen several generations of MacLaines raised from sippy cups to spurs.

Taking a seat across from his aunt, Dalton ignored the steady gaze she shifted to him over the rim of the mug. He wasn't about to divulge anything. He focused his attention out the window, watching the guests make their way up the hill to the lodge for breakfast.

"So, what'd you think about the filly?"

Dalton considered her. "You mean what did I think of some stranger mending my horse's leg?" He returned to his coffee.

Mary cocked her head. "You should be grateful. She's a nurse, and she wanted to help. Plus, she's been around horses all her life."

"She?"

"Yeah, she."

Dalton chuckled. "Isn't that great, another female on the ranch with a mind of her own."

"You won't think that when you meet her. She's quite likable."

"Is that right?" He purposely sounded mischievous. He set his cup down and folded his arms, relaxing back into the seat. A sly smile branded his thoughts.

His aunt rose from the table to refill their mugs. He could see her studying him. She fetched milk from the refrigerator and returned to her high-backed wooden chair.

"And why are we smiling so brightly this morning?" she asked, her eyes squinted, coaxing him into answering.

He stared down at the coffee cup before him, shaking his head. "I'm not smiling, Aunt Mary. That's a tired frown you see. My head's just upside down, is all." He rubbed his forehead and yawned. "I believe it's called lack of sleep with too much work."

She reached for the open newspaper. "I believe it's called need of a good woman."

"Oh, is it?" he retorted.

"You just need one that doesn't wish to have you." Fanning the pages of the newspaper, she turned to the entertainment section, avoiding his look of mute annoyance. "One just as hardheaded and stubborn as you are. Who doesn't flaunt and throw herself in your direction."

He chuckled. "Wipes out the locals."

His aunt laughed. "You'll meet your match one day. And when it happens, I'm gonna grin from ear to ear, watching."

Silence took over for the next few moments, allowing them to finish their coffee.

"We have some interesting guests this week." Her brows jumped with implication.

"Back to the nurse, huh?"

"Well, she's definitely interesting. So are her friends. Her name's Samantha, by the way." She glanced up at him and continued. "She and her friend Jessica are signed up to work, so you'll no doubt get to know one another."

"Which works perfectly with this scheme you have going on inside your head," he highlighted.

Mary snapped the newspaper into submission. "Nope. Not going there." She returned to her news article, her eyes downcast. "However, the word 'grandchild' does have a nice ring to it."

Dalton turned to look out the kitchen window again. Long, flowing, mahogany hair hung down Samantha's back as she sauntered towards the lodge. She was followed by her rare-looking spotted dog. Her two friends walked next to her.

His aunt followed his gaze. "Thought you'd find her interesting."

Dalton sighed. "Can she ride?"

"Seeing as she brought her horse, I'd assume she can." She paused before adding, "A stallion."

He rose from his seat with an agitated grunt, his chair legs a dull bawl against the planked flooring. "Well, Aunt Mary, you've managed to make the start of my morning just great." Intrigued, he kept his eye on Samantha.

Turning from the window, he grabbed his straw hat and settled it on his head. He tugged at the rim, nodded to his aunt, and commented as he walked out the cookhouse door, "Don't worry, I'm sure she's every bit as temperamental as her horse."

Mary chuckled. "For her sake, I hope she is."

****

A crisp draft of mountain air, tinged of cattle and horses and a hint of rain, greeted Dalton as he stepped out the back kitchen door.

He zipped his Carhartt vest, blocking much of the chill that penetrated his long-sleeved cotton shirt. Spring mornings in the mountains at an elevation of seven thousand feet were notorious for brisk temperatures, even occasional frosts. Midday brought a warmer climate, with temperatures as high as ninety degrees in the lowlands, but the low humidity of the mountains kept the heat from becoming sweltering.

The fluctuating weather conditions of mountain living suited Dalton, bringing a new challenge to daily life. They were like a woman's mood swings—one never took for granted the tranquil moments, since ungratefulness attracted a metamorphosis. Breathing in, his outdoorsman's nose definitely sensed a change on the way, heralded by an indescribable thickening of the moisture in the air. Rain tomorrow meant serious work today. And maybe some not so significant but muddy endeavors the following day.

The crunching sound of booted heels walking on rocks mixed with the jingling of spur rowels in a one-two steady beat announced Clay's presence. He knew the cadence of his brother's stride as well as his own.

"Twerp."

Clay looked up, seeing him. "Haven't been called that in a while." He stopped, reaching the lodge.

"Yeah. Figure you're getting a little old for it."

"Did I miss coffee with Aunt Mary?" He yawned, tapping the side of his boot against the stone steps. Dust peppered the ground.

Most work mornings on the ranch began in the staff

kitchen of the lodge, sharing a pot of coffee with their aunt. Their uncle, who had never taken a liking to the brew, opted to get an early start. "You did," he answered. "How is it my ass made it on time, with minimal amounts of sleep, but, you, who were sound asleep by midnight, couldn't?"

Clay responded with a shrug and a sideways grin. "Must have been a good dream, I guess."

"Must have. I'm sure it involved you and a female, or three."

Clay nodded his head, his answer quick. "No, just one. A certain female."

With his brows raised, Dalton slid his hands into the pockets of his vest. He experienced an odd churning in his gut. A vision of dark chestnut hair, a bewitching smile, and deep sapphire eyes in the glow of a matchstick came to him.

"She's gorgeous, Dalton. Wait till you see her."

Again, the unsettling queasiness.

"She's a guest, though, and you know how Uncle John is about that. But..." Clay paused. "She's different. She's witty, spitfire, and intelligent as hell."

Mentally, Dalton braced himself, waiting to bear the final blow but still praying Samantha wasn't the female his brother spoke of. He and Clay had never fought over a woman yet, and he wasn't about to start now. But that wouldn't keep him from cursing himself for letting her get under his skin and inside his head.

"If you laugh, I swear I'll cut your tongue out and give it to Minus to sell at the flea market. She has the most beautiful set of..."

Focus on owning the ranch of your dreams, think of nothing but what it will be like one day, he reminded himself. He suddenly felt vacant inside, like he'd lost his best friend.

"Brown eyes," Clay gushed.

Dalton's mind instantly went into rewind, replaying and repeating the key word his brother had just spoken: Brown. Inundated with relief, his nausea dissipated. He exhaled.

Clay turned to look at his brother. "What? No comment from you, the older brother with the heart of ice toward females?"

"Heart of ice?" He repeated, surprised. "Those aren't your words."

"No, they're mine." Mary stated from the doorway, shutting the kitchen door behind her. Bending down, she reached for her ostrich leather boots.

Dalton and his brother exchanged quick glances. Peculiar timing.

"Ya know, I used to think the walls of this lodge were thick and you couldn't hear anything from inside." A smile tugged at the corners of her mouth.

Dalton recognized her pompous look. She had the inconvenient ability to read him like a book, only he never let her know it.

"It helps when the kitchen window is cracked about a quarter of an inch, as it is now," Dalton grumbled.

Mary's cheeks reddened, and she pointed a finger at Dalton. "You always were a smart one." Turning to Clay, she said, "And you were always after the girls."

"Well," Dalton said, taking a step toward the front of the lodge where breakfast awaited them, "It's good to know nothing has changed in ten years." Dalton slowed, giving his aunt time to catch up. Taking her left arm, he urged her forward. He winked at Clay over the top of his aunt's head. Following along, Clay assisted his aunt on the opposite side.

"Yep, Aunt Mary, some things just never do change." Clay's comment cautioned Mary, making her stop, but it was too late. Like they had always done, Dalton and Clay flipped their aunt in the air, somersault style, landing her on her feet.

Mary repaired her tousled hair and straightened her clothing. Walking into the dining room, she smiled. "Ten years ago both of you would have gotten the paddle for that."

Dalton laughed, one thought running fervent in his mind: Samantha could still be his.

****

Dr. Beard approached him, a Styrofoam coffee cup in one hand and a sausage biscuit in the other. The vet reminded him of Danny DeVito with his scrunched, round face, balding head and distinctive East Coast accent.

"Dalton. Just the man I was looking for. I need to see your filly. There've been two reports similar to yours, so I need to survey the wound for comparison."

He had always liked Dr. Beard, a focused man who was often too intelligent to hold a decent conversation about anything other than horse-related concerns. The smell of cooked sausage reached Dalton, a tempting reminder that he still hadn't eaten since yesterday's drive. Dalton quelled the urge to pluck the sausage scone from the doctor's grasp. "Sure thing, Doc." After all, the filly did rank in priority over his empty stomach.

He spied Samantha across the room over the vet's shoulder. The back pockets of her jeans danced with the movement of her upper body as she relayed a story to another guest.

"I've already had the pleasure of speaking with Samantha, your new worker." The doctor tipped his head in her direction as he hustled toward the front entrance of the lodge. "She said it took a number of stitches to sew up."

Dalton glanced to his left as he was exiting the front doors and caught her eye. His boots might as well have been concreted to the foyer floor. Starstruck, he stood watching her. She honored him with a polite, formal smile, a treasure trove hinting of infinite possibilities.

Then a random thought occurred to him. They hadn't yet been introduced—at least not officially.

The vet was waiting on him. No time now. With a sigh and a nod, he departed.

Dr. Beard's assessment of the filly validated his concerns. The wound exhibited the same characteristics as the other two injuries reported by neighboring ranchers.

"Always a cut to the legs," he described. "Only those were high-priced bulls, where this is a mere filly."

"Mere to you, Doc, but a promising prospect for me. She's one of my favorites this year. Best in the herd."

"Interesting," he said, surveying Samantha's needlework. "But you might want to keep that knowledge to yourself. It seems our animal on the loose has a taste for expensive flesh."

"Great, a biased mountain lion. Just what we need."

He watched as the vet rewrapped her leg.

"I'd say your filly is mending exceptionally well, given the deep laceration. That's probably the best stitch job I've ever seen—including my own. Tell your Uncle John to give that pretty girl a raise."

Dalton latched the door behind them. "Thanks, Doc. Hopefully we won't be seeing you again anytime soon. We'll be keeping the guests close to the lodge for the next few weeks, just in case. I'll have the wranglers bring the yearlings in from pasture today. That way the entire herd is accounted for."

"Good idea." Reaching his truck, the vet settled into the seat. The engine fired at the turn of the key. "You tell Miss Samantha she's not only pretty, but damn fine with the needle."

"Sure thing, Doc." Forward the compliment he would, when he actually met her.

Chapter Six

"So that means we need to remain close to the lodge." Dalton heard the frustrated sighs from the guests and hated that he could do nothing but apologize. He stood near the bleachers, an apologetic smile pasted on his face. He felt their disappointment as they gathered to hear John's welcome speech.

The informal discourse focused on the layout of the ranch and location of various activities throughout the property. John was always sure to mention the whereabouts of the relief cabin, or hut, as Dalton liked to think of it, since half of it was built into the side of the mountain. The retreat functioned as a pit stop for long drives, giving guests a chance to get out of the saddle and drink a thermos full of cold, fresh mountain water from the nearby stream.

The hut was well hidden, a surprise to guests even when Dalton rode them past it for a second or third time until some of them noticed the structure. Dalton scanned the group of guests, many of whose attention had wandered, as John purposely spoke in boring monotones about the location and purpose of the cabin. It would be a disappointment to them that they wouldn't experience the retreat site.

An intriguing laugh to his left caught Dalton's attention. He turned to see Samantha, her head thrown back, the soft, creamy skin of her neck exposed, laughing at something Minus had said. No telling what, of course. Dalton watched the interaction between the two. Minus rarely conversed with any of the vacationers. She must have charmed the Indian as well as she had his aunt.

"Did you get a look at Jessica?" Clay quizzed, in his brother's ear.

Dalton shushed his brother. "She's twenty feet away."

"And?" Clay persisted, his brows raised excitedly.

Dalton turned, intending to catch a glimpse of Jessica so Clay would give the subject a rest, but his eyes focused on Young Jasper as he posted the signup sheet for the yearling roundup. Dalton frowned. He thought the sheet was a bad idea, but John wanted to give the guests a chance to participate in the one and only ride available to them this week. Dalton hoped the talk of a mountain lion in the area would dissuade the guests from wanting to ride the fast-paced, grueling trip to the yearling pasture.

Turning his attention back to his brother's request, Dalton's eyes rested on Samantha and her friends. All three women were striking. Each was unique. Dalton couldn't recall when he'd last seen a blonde, a brunette, and an almost-redhead of equal beauty together. Probably on satellite.

"Yeah, she's a looker," Dalton said to his brother, under his breath so as to not be overheard. He watched as his brother's eyes lit up, hearing his opinion. "All three of them are. Makes me wonder why they chose this place for a vacation."

"You'll know once you've talked to them. They're down-to-earth—for debutantes."

"Clay," Dalton said with a laugh, laying a hand on his brother's shoulder, "That's about the smartest thing I've heard you say today."

"That's the only thing you've heard me say today. Your mind's been busy with the redhead."

"You call that red?" Dalton asked, blurting out the question. "Or chestnut?" Dammit, he had never before put so much thought into hair color.

Clay's grin became a full-fledged smirk. "Like I said, you've been busy."

The girls were standing with Minus, appearing to half-listen to John's introduction but mostly immersed in their talk with Minus, who had suddenly decided to dominate the conversation.

"Would you look at that," Dalton said. "Our Indian friend has managed to find his tongue—his English tongue, at that."

Clay laughed. "Don't know about you, but if I was him, I'd be finding more than my tongue."

Dalton literally shook his head. He had to stop thinking about her. He needed to focus. A dangerous mountain lion was in the area, and he needed to get the yearlings in from the pasture. He had guests to think about, guests who spent a hefty paycheck for a western vacation that was now restricted to close proximity of the lodge. Sighing, he glanced at the signup sheet. No guests had yet volunteered. Good. He could escape long enough to ease the rumbling in his stomach with his first meal since yesterday's beef jerky. "I'm gonna get a bite to eat. Have the wranglers ready in thirty." His eyes roamed to the sky, seeing low clouds forming in the distance. "The rain isn't far off."

"Yes sir, big brother. Will do."

"And stop being a smartass. That's my job."

****

From Minus, Samantha had heard enough tales to last her entire stay. Most of them were humorous accounts involving the notorious MacLaine brothers. For large, daunting mountain men, they sure did mess up from time to time. Samantha's favorite was still the frog that left Dalton butt up in the creek. These tidbits she decided to keep to herself, for now, and use as ammo later.

Having seen firsthand the damage done to the filly, Samantha wasn't surprised to hear the news of the mountain lion. She saw the chagrined faces of the group when John announced the day's agenda. They were going to castrate the young bull calves. One eager male guest whooped, hollering an enthusiastic, "Yee-hah."

"I can't wait to ride, Jess," Samantha said excitedly, resettling her ball cap and pulling her ponytail out through the back.

"Neither can I," her friend answered, eyeing Clay as he spoke to an overweight female guest.

"I don't mean that kind of riding, Jess."

"Yeah, I know. But you should. I've seen Dalton looking at you."

"You have not."

"Oh, yes, she has." Bethany jumped into the conversation. "But then, I've seen him sizing up everyone. Probably part of the job description."

Samantha pretended to wince. "So much for the self-esteem I was building."

"Not to worry, Sam. You wouldn't be who you are today if you knew the effect you have on men," Jessica added.

Samantha looked up at the navy-blue rain clouds. "We'll see about that when I'm drenched in rainwater and covered in mud."

At least Dalton wouldn't be witnessing her disheveled state. In his announcement, John had mentioned the two of them were staying behind to help with the castrations. This meant she could stick with trying to get him out of her head. *Try* being the key word. Seeing Dalton clearly in the lodge this morning, knowing he was the ravishing man from last night, made her woozy. She needed some considerable distance between her and Dalton MacLaine.

"Be careful, guys," Bethany said, walking towards the spa. "Think of me covered with oils as I loll in the relaxation of fire-heated stones placed diligently on my sore, aching muscles." She exaggerated her precise words and flexed her left bicep for show.

Samantha and Jessica each fixed their friend with a mock-evil stare.

And while the thought of a deep massage sounded pleasant, Samantha was yearning to ride the Montana mountainside. Even with the threat of bad weather, the mountains posed an enticing backdrop for letting Beau have some real exercise.

"You ladies joining us for the yearling roundup?" Young Jasper appeared from out of nowhere.

Jessica answered. "You betcha."

"Then I'll have you sign this sheet saying you are." He held the clipboard for them to sign.

Young Jasper reminded Samantha of a rodeo rider, his physique lean and trim and on the small side, his height only a few inches taller than Samantha's five-foot frame. As he handed her the pen, she noted his rather large, rough hands and muscular forearms. "Do you rodeo?" she asked, trying to make conversation.

"Yes, ma'am, I do," he replied, in a crisp western drawl. He raised pale blue eyes to her in surprise, seeming shy. "How did you know?"

Samantha shrugged, keeping her expression bland so as not to seem overly impressed, but at the same time interested in his choice of hobby. "You just look like you belong on the back of a bull—that, and I know rodeo is a big sport in Montana."

"Anything to do with horses and cattle is big in this part of the country."

"Well then," Jessica said with a quick nod of her head, "we've come to the right place, because we came to rope and ride our asses off."

Samantha refrained from poking her outspoken friend with an elbow. She only hoped Young Jasper didn't read anything into Jessica's crude comment. "You'll have to excuse her." She cast Jessica a shut-up-now glare. "She's just a tad bit excited about being out west. Give her some time to let the cool mountain air revive her long-lost sense."

Jasper's eyes darted back and forth between them, a grin on his face. *Time to change the subject*, she thought. "How soon do we head out?"

"Soon. Dalton wants us back before the weather gets bad." His tone changed, his words resembling a servant's, flat and borderline-resentful. He spoke Dalton's name as though it were poisonous.

The last time Samantha had seen Dalton he'd appeared deep in thought, walking toward the lodge. Momentarily she forgot Young Jasper was standing in front of her, then jarred her concentration back to the moment. "Well, I'd best be getting Beau saddled. I'm sure he's ready to get out of the stall." Young Jasper nodded and continued to pass the clipboard around.

"Let me know if you need anything, Sam," Jessica said. "I'm going to help Clay saddle the horses."

"Yeah, I bet you are." Smiling, she shook her head, bewildered and half jealous of Jessica's confidence with men. "So much for you needing my help."

"Now, now. You never know. I might still need your assistance. After all, I still don't know if he's available."

Samantha watched as Jessica made her way toward the row of unsaddled geldings.

Inside the barn, she lost no time getting Beau

prepped for the ride. Once she had him curried, his hooves picked, and his protective overreach boots on his front legs, she quickly saddled and led him to the empty center pen for a warm-up.

With a gathered lasso in her hand, she stood in the center, allowing the stallion to move freely around her. She clucked to him, coaxing him into a faster trot. And, as she had guessed, Beau needed no encouragement. Within three strides he was into a quick lope, tossing his head and whinnying as he bucked and kicked at the air, releasing built-up energy.

As he circled the ring, Samantha noticed Clay outside the open barn doors, still engaged in conversation with the heavyset female guest. He appeared to be politely encouraging her not to ride, using his fingers to count and validate the reasons why she shouldn't join the roundup. Samantha could think of several reasons herself, with the possibility of a mountain lion being close by as the foremost concern. The ride would be fast-paced and the terrain rough. The guest was terribly overweight and not at all outfitted as an experienced rider would be.

She worked her horse until he was quiet. Outside the barn, she found an empty tie spot away from the other horses and secured his lead to a post with a quick-tie knot. She checked her saddlebag and gear, making sure she had the basic necessities. Her rain slicker was in place, draped and strapped across the back of the saddle. She peeked inside the back zippered compartment of her saddle case, finding her version of the bare essentials. Water, yes. Pocket knife, yes. Moist wipes—for all occasions known to man, yes. Tampons, yes. In a side pouch of her cantle bag she found a travel set of toothbrush and paste. Good hygiene was always manageable, even out west.

With a friendly pat to Beau's hindquarter, she turned to leave her horse and bumped into Mary.

"Well, hello. I meant to run into you, but not literally."

Samantha laughed. "That's okay. I was just finishing up with Beau."

"I was trying to find you so I could introduce you to Dalton before you head out."

Eeks. She really didn't want to have to explain last night's excursions below decks—not yet, anyway. Her nerves fired at the thought of being formally introduced to Dalton. Her brain went like slung shot into Go-Go Gadget mode, but came up short for a fast excuse. She very much liked Mary and didn't wish to disappoint her, so she nodded and followed Mary towards the dairy barn where John and Minus were sorting guests into groups.

Dalton was nowhere in sight, or at least not in Samantha's line of vision. *Whew.* Her nerves calmed. Momentarily relieved, she took a few minutes to mentally unwind. She pondered, gazing out at the mountain peaks, asking herself how one insanely gorgeous cattleman could make her so uptight. She had met, and dated, plenty of good-looking men, but none made her blush dead in her tracks. An answer to her question came faster than she expected.

It was Fern's tranquil and mellifluous voice, saying, *Stop looking...when you aren't watching.*

Recovering, Samantha waited as Mary glanced around, trying to catch a glimpse of her nephew. "He went back to the lodge to get some breakfast, but he was on his way back down just a minute ago."

Samantha pretended to hear Mary but was reliving that moment by the fire with Fern. She recalled the goosebumps and the feeling of Fern seeing straight through her. Fern knew what she desired—someone to love, someone who would love her back for who she truly was. As peculiar as it sounded, Samantha was beginning to believe the older woman. Perhaps she should act uninterested in Dalton. After all, it would definitely help soothe her jitters.

Unsuccessful at locating Dalton, Mary suggested, "Let's check back at the horse barn."

Samantha followed Mary, holding her head a bit higher than before. She was not going to let the male species intimidate her, not even such a fine specimen as Dalton MacLaine. No, absolutely not. She would take Fern's handy advice and simply treat him as she would any other person.

A smile colored her face and a sense of self-accomplishment washed over her. She shoved her hands into the pockets of her jacket and continued following Mary, sidestepping the occasional pancake of cow manure. Dolly trotted next to her, pausing to sniff the dung.

As she walked by several of the guests, Samantha spotted Luke and smiled. He was decked out in what she presumed was his favorite western outfit, complete with blue ostrich-leather boots and wide brimmed black leather cowboy hat. He wore a matching blue bandana, the Twin Rivers ranch logo sewn in the corner. Samantha had seen them on display in the gift shop window and made a mental note to add another to her collection. The darn things were good for just about everything. Sometimes she even used them on Beau to dry the sweat off his face.

Samantha recognized the female guest Clay had spoken with earlier, standing next to Luke and his mother. The guest, whose nametag read *Judy*, was pointing to a horse in the pasture and explaining to Luke, "She's pooping." Samantha looked at the horse and saw a gelding just done urinating, his body still arched and tail held up for balance, making for a clear distinction in sex. Turning her head, Samantha relinquished the urge to roll her eyes. She chose instead to bite her tongue. She concluded Clay was right on target. The guest didn't need to join the grueling pace of today's roundup.

Mary, too, had heard the comment. Approaching the barn, she stopped and shrugged. She looked unsurprised. "We get all kinds here, Samantha. Some will scare you to death and others will squeeze the vinegar out of you."

Caught off guard, Samantha squelched the impulse to laugh until she was halfway down the center aisle of the barn. She burst into a laughing fit, tears clouding her eyes.

"What is so funny?" Jessica demanded, marching down the aisle.

Samantha, doubled over, couldn't quit laughing long enough to explain.

"What? Tell me!"

"Noth—ing...it's...ju—st..." was all Samantha was able to choke out in intelligible English. She slouched against the stall doors, trying to catch her breath.

Jessica looked toward the end of the barn and turned

back to Samantha. "Whatever it is, I hope it's hilarious enough to break the ice with Dalton, because he's headed this way."

Jessica's comment had Sam glancing past her, only to see him drawing near. Serious now, she whispered, "Is it just me, or does he look insanely furious?"

Dalton bore down on them so quickly Jessica didn't have time to answer. Samantha's heart hammered in her chest.

Chapter Seven

There was no way in hell Dalton was going to let her go on this ride. Even if she was an Olympic cross-country gold medalist turned horse acrobat, he would advise her to stay put. All the horseman skills she could possibly possess wouldn't help her if she came in contact with a mountain lion.

Those were his thoughts two seconds before he found her slumped on the barn floor with tear streaks lining her beautiful face. She grasped her friend's outreached hand and pulled herself into a standing position, wiping her wet cheeks, looking at him.

Dalton folded his arms across his chest and contemplated the two females before him. Samantha, simply standing before him, roped his senses. Hypnotically she lured him to a place where time seemed to stop. There was work to do. He was busy. Yet an unspoken current of irresistibility detained him. He almost forgot his words.

"In case it hasn't yet been explained, we have strict rules about our wranglers—crying," he half quipped.

Jessica snorted. "Oh, she wasn't crying—well, not really. She was just laughing so hard she was crying. So it doesn't count." A moment of awkward silence passed. "See you out there, Sam."

Dalton tipped his head to Jessica before she sauntered off. He'd have Clay inform her. Right now, he was dealing with the chestnut-haired vixen who monopolized his attention.

After an extended stare, she smiled.

"I'm glad you're smiling because, when you hear what I'm about to say, you won't be." He saw her delicate features change before him, her once-blushing smile fading to a guarded pucker and the corner of her eyes tightening into a defensive squint. He hated being the cause of it.

"Why?"

"Because."

"Because why?"

"Because I said, that's why." He grinned. He liked her more already.

She crossed her arms over her delectable chest and began to pace. After one step in each direction, she halted and angled her head. "You're messing with me."

Dalton chuckled and raised his brows, his eyes glided down her petite frame. "Well, now that might be true. I didn't realize I was being propositioned."

"Don't change the subject. What is it?"

"You won't be going on the ride."

After a moment's consideration, she shrugged. "Okay."

He hadn't expected her to give in so easily. Not this firecracker. She answered his befuddled expression.

"After all, you are the boss." She paused, and bit her bottom lip, unaware of the effect it had on him. "But I want to know w-h-y."

"It's not safe," he answered dryly.

"That's it? It's not safe?" She stood looking at him, laughing—a petite, sophisticated, delicate and gorgeous, flower-like female confronting a large, rugged mountain man. The word spitfire couldn't begin to describe her. He could see her mind churning, mentally concocting a surefire solution to her problem, which of course was him.

"Have you taken a look at my horse?" she quizzed. "He's quite capable—and a good ranch horse. He'll keep me safe."

"Nice try, princess, but no."

No?" she repeated, perking up. "No, you haven't seen him, or no, you don't agree?"

He sighed. "No to both."

"Oh, I see," she said in much too sweet a voice. She resumed pacing, mindful to swing her derrière towards him with each turn. "So, you don't think my horse can handle the ride?" She pivoted on one booted heel.

Dalton snorted. "I know he can't. He's not accustomed to the terrain—and I daresay he's never before made the acquaintance of a mountain lion." For every turn of her hip, he was sorely tempted to swat the firmly rounded backside she poised in his direction.

"Good point, although I doubt any of your horses have, either." She halted.

Her quick-witted banter needed to stop, and he knew exactly how he'd like to end it. He was quite certain he could do some of his own bewitching on Samantha.

"Samantha." He emphasized her name, taking slow strides towards her. Her eyes followed him. She stepped back. He stopped short of touching her. A hint of honeysuckle bedeviled his senses. "There's nothing you can say to convince me. I won't allow you to get hurt."

Her eyes locked on his. She swallowed hard. Her breasts rose and fell in a faster rhythm. "I just drove a few thousand miles to ride my horse out here. You'll be hurting me more by denying me the ride."

He hadn't viewed it from her perspective. Determination in her eyes made him believe this ride represented more than a physical act. His outlook was different. He felt as though he'd found something he'd been searching for his whole life. He didn't want to lose her.

He sighed. A speck of hay dirtied her shoulder. He debated whether or not he should touch her. He couldn't resist. Grazing her shoulder, he reached to flick the scrap to the ground. Her head tilted towards his hand, ready to accept his caress. Bashful, her eyes darted to the side as he skimmed the particle from her shirt. Had she desired his touch?

"Thank you," she said.

His resolve weakened. He knew how to settle this. "I don't recall getting thanked last night."

Caught off guard, she stared at him. She bit her lip again. "You're right. I didn't. Sorry. I normally have better manners than that."

"I'll look at your horse and see if he's fit—on one condition."

Her brows narrowed. Her defenses were up.

"A proper thank you."

She licked her lips and gulped.

The light was green.

Any protest she could have made was silenced by his lips in an unbridled, soft kiss. His hands moved to cradle her head. Leaning forward, he pressed his mouth more fully against hers. He stepped closer, and her arms snaked around his neck. His hands feathered the length of her body. Reaching her bottom, he cupped her to him with the freedom of an ardent lover.

She stiffened and pulled back. Skittish, she half joked. "I believe that was proper enough."

"The best gratitude I've had in a long time."

"How about taking that look at my horse?" She spoke plainly. He could see she was trying to distance herself. "And Dalton, this won't happen again."

He chuckled. "Wouldn't bet on that." Later he'd have to admit how arrogant his tone was.

"Oh, yes, I would."

The chemistry between them was undeniable. He saw through her brave act.

"All right, then, princess. I'll take you up on that. If—and I mean if—I think your horse can handle the ride, I'll let you go. But should he come up lame, I'll be receiving my reward upon your return." His tone was definitely cocky now.

"Get ready for disappointment, cowboy." She turned on her heel.

"Meeting you was a pleasure, princess." Her quick turn of the head and piercing eyes made him grin. Before she stomped away, he took note of a slight smile on her lips.

Strolling out of the barn a safe ten minutes later, Dalton spotted the brazen beauty speaking to Minus. She caught sight of him and her eyes trailed to the spot along the fence where her stallion was tied, a firm suggestion he live up to his part of the bet.

Dalton needed no help in locating her horse. The sleek stallion stood out enough on his own. The animal had a beautiful head. His expression was alert but not frightened, and his ears pricked forward, framing his head, as if he knew he had caught someone's attention. He had only a small white star on his muzzle. With a graceful, arched neck, short back and low hocks, his conformation was flawless. The horse was fit, his muscles pronounced and strong. His coloring was magnificent, a deep bay color, dark chocolate. His mane and tail were long and thick, glistening in the light.

It was obvious he was a stallion. The thick, robust jawline and the keen expression in the horse's eyes gave that away in one glance. Admiring the horse's stature, Dalton guessed he stood at a little over fifteen hands, not too short and not too tall, but it was more the way the horse held himself that caught Dalton's attention. He could tell the horse was calm but ready to hold his own should he be provoked. Dalton considered this an attribute in a horse, although most people in the horse industry would disagree with him. The last thing any horseman wanted to work with was a stallion with self-esteem.

It had been a while since he'd seen a horse of this caliber. He wondered what kind of breeding the horse was from. Damn good stock, he figured.

It took Dalton a moment to register Samantha standing at his shoulder. He was surprised to see her in such close proximity to him. Then he noticed Minus, her newfound friend, a few feet away.

She broke the silence between them. "What do you think?"

"I'd say either of two things. One, you got lucky and found you one heck of a horse. Or two," he continued as he turned to look her in the eye, "you have an incredible eye for horseflesh."

"So you can be nice."

"Only on the rarest of occasions." He spoke with the marked courtesy of a gallant gentleman, the same as earlier.

She glared at him in return, catching his dry amusement.

Minus joined the conversation—physically. Dalton could tell something was on his mind. Perhaps it was the horse. Dalton himself was curious how she came across a stallion like this, especially in Kentucky where the Quarter Horse breed was more refined, not nearly as authentic as the foundation horses out west. "So tell me, Samantha, where did you find him?"

Samantha remembered everything about the day she first laid eyes on Beau. It was as if the events of that day had passed this morning and not five years ago.

It was late autumn. Most of the trees had shed their leaves due to an abrupt cold snap a few weeks past. The wind was frigid and gusty, the kind of wind that sent you turning back inside for another cup of warm coffee.

Drummond, the barn manager, had heard there were a couple of good draft horses being put up for auction in Greenville. They had reportedly been trained to pull a carriage. He thought perhaps they might be worth looking at and hoped they could replace Dean and Deluca, the two Clydesdales who were to be retired from carriage duty, come winter.

Samantha's great-grandfather, Lawrence Matthews, had started a tradition seventy years ago—on every grandchild's birthday, and on the holidays, the family would all gather for a carriage ride through the vast hillsides of the Matthews estate. Since the prospective animals would be for use on important familial times of celebration, Samantha thought it best to ride along.

Arriving at the auction early, Samantha wandered off by herself. She hadn't been to this auction in a long while. There didn't seem to be as many horses this time. Going into winter, the last thing people wanted was another animal to feed.

The horse was easy to spot, off by himself in a round pen, away from the other horses to be sold. He looked to be a late yearling. Caked in mud and manure, it was impossible to determine his exact coloring and markings. The animal had already begun to grow a thick winter coat, but Samantha thought he looked quite thin even considering all the extra hair he had to mask his debilitated state. She was curious why a horse in such a condition would be at this auction. The Greenville auction was known for only having the best of the best.

The wind was blowing and Samantha shivered, trying to not think about the chill in the air. She wished she had opted for a fleece turtleneck instead of a cotton one. She continued to watch the horse.

Every so often the wind would blow just right and lift the yearling's thick, mud-coated forelock, allowing her a glimpse of his head. She thought she saw kind eyes. She wanted to get a better look into them. She made a clucking sound to the horse, hoping he would respond. He remained still.

She located Drummond speaking to several of the auction officials, no doubt inquiring about the two draft horses. She was anxious to ask them about the yearling.

Seeing her on her way towards them, Earl Smooter, the head auctioneer, greeted her. "Hey there, Sam. Haven't seen you in a while."

"Yeah, there's a thing called life. Keeps everyone busy."

He nodded. "I hear ya."

"What's the story on the yearling over there?" She nodded her head in the direction of the lone, feeble animal.

Earl cleared his throat. "All we know is, some guy from Dixon brought him here to sell. Said he didn't want anything to do with the horse and didn't care what amount we sold him for. He was firm about the fact that he wanted the horse gone. The man said if we couldn't sell, he wanted the horse sent to the killers for the going price. The gentleman," Earl said with a cough, "reported the horse is extremely mean and unsafe to work with. He said the only thing in his favor is he's from good stock."

"How good? He's such a mess, I can't tell anything about him."

"Son of Smart Chic Olena. Momma's out of Dry Doc."

Samantha and Drummond looked at each other, stunned. She was trying to remember the stud fee for Smart Chic Olena. The last time she'd checked, the cost was twenty-five grand, since the sire was a world champion in several events. "He can't be that mean, can he?"

Samantha started to walk in the direction of the horse's corral.

Earl spoke. "Careful, Sam. He's already injured two of my men. One of them is in the hospital as we speak."

"I know it sounds surreal," Samantha said, speaking to Dalton and Minus, along with Mary who had joined in time to hear Beau's story, "but it was just one of those indescribable moments you don't see coming. I just couldn't leave him there, not in such a pathetic state, knowing he was on his way to becoming dog food." She continued to explain what happened next...

The auctioneer officials spent half an hour trying to coax the yearling into a shoot where it could be haltered. The men first started off trying to be gentle, but frustration soon sent their tempers flaring like flames high on lighter fluid. The horse had no intention of being caught. And when he glimpsed the whip the men intended to use, the fighting was simply upgraded.

The method of madness used to catch the yearling was one of physical exhaustion. An hour later, the officials had the young horse exactly where they wanted him— enervated with exhaustion. The animal was so severely fatigued he paid no attention to the ropes the handler used to hobble his legs together. The colt could hardly hold his head up. His nostrils flared low to the ground. Steam arose from every inch of him.

Drummond had no desire to watch the spectacle any further. "Let's go. We've seen enough."

The handlers returned to work, gathering more horses. Samantha remained standing, watching the colt, needing to see his eyes. She pleaded with him. "Please, boy."

Nothing. She got no response. Drummond was calling her name, the auction was beginning. She turned and answered "okay" in her usual soft, undemanding tone. She turned back in the direction of the yearling to find him assessing her. His head was raised, one ear pricked forward and one ear cocked back waiting for another sign of danger. She realized then that the young, putrid-looking yearling was not mean, only terrified.

The colt became hers that day for the sum of one hundred dollars.

"He's beautiful, Sam," Mary confirmed. "I watched you work him in the round pen, so I was able to get a good look."

Samantha smiled from ear to ear. She was by no means a professional when it came to critiquing a horse's conformation, but she was able to hold her own when selecting the absolute good from the pathetically bad. However it wasn't just conformation that made her choose Beau over any other horse, and she needed her audience to know that, especially Dalton, since he was still looking sour at the thought of her joining the roundup.

She was determined to go on the ride—and he knew it. Hadn't she just explained to him the connection she had with Beau? She knew the horse would guide her through a war and back.

Samantha hoped Dalton wouldn't push her into initiating plan B, which, delightfully enough, was plain and simple—blackmail. He wouldn't want his dear auntie to know he had accosted one of the staff members. And although Samantha's faith in plan B was sapped by his nonchalant demeanor, she would resort if needed.

As Samantha turned her head, she caught a glimpse of someone standing too close to Beau. Definitely too close for comfort, really. Sam recognized Judy, the guest who had been talking with Clay earlier and who was now flapping her arms around in the air, holding several long leather ties in her hand, demonstrating something—what, Samantha wasn't quite sure—completely mindless of her proximity to the stallion behind her.

Beau had already positioned himself as far away as his lead would stretch. The lead rope was pulled taunt. She knew Beau's next move would be to haunch back on his hindquarters and pull back on the shank, possibly breaking free and injuring the guest in the process.

Samantha was already at the gate, having rudely left the conversation in order to prevent an accident. Her only option was to approach Beau from the opposite side of the fence and release the quick-tie knot. Arriving just before Beau jerked, Samantha unbound the rope, allowing Beau to rush backwards.

Luckily, Dalton had watched the incident and was prompt in catching Beau's rope on the other side of the fence. Relief swarmed Samantha. She definitely wouldn't have been riding had a guest been harmed.

Amazingly enough, none of the guests noticed the near-accident. Judy maintained her ceaseless chatter, oblivious to what had taken place three steps behind her. *Stupid. So stupid.*

Wasting no time, Samantha hurried to Beau's side, wanting to avoid a confrontation between her horse and Dalton. Beau detested men, and if he acted up in Dalton's vicinity she would no doubt spend the rest of her day detaching calf testicles.

Samantha saw Beau brace himself, so she placed herself, posthaste, between him and Dalton. In doing so, her breasts brushed against Dalton's rock-solid chest. She was relieved it wasn't summer. She'd hate for him to feel her hardened nipples through only one layer of clothing. Her body was suddenly becoming a traitor, responding to his every talented, seductive whim. She only meant to retrieve Beau's lead. Her goal was not to further incite the lust she saw ignited in Dalton's eyes.

He handed her the lead, whispering, "Tease."

"You wish," she mumbled back.

"Samantha, remind me to give you a free massage when you get back," Mary said, congratulating her with a sideways squeeze, "hot stones and all. Excellent save."

"Thanks. I will."

"I see you've met my charming nephew, Dalton."

"I did. And you're right. He is charming—as any horse's ass could be." She winked at Mary. Dalton raked his eyes up the length of her body, as though he was mentally undressing her, piece by piece.

Mary laughed. "That's why I like this girl. She catches on quick. Doesn't she, Minus?"

Minus smiled broadly. He stood with his hands clasped behind his back. He glanced up at the dark sky before saying, "Losing battles oftentimes helps to win the war."

Although Minus didn't look at her when he said it, Samantha felt her stomach flip-flop. There was no way she was going to lose this bet. Because if she did, she was going to be playing with fire. For Christ's sake, the man had sexual chemistry oozing from him. Every inch of his cowboy's body secreted jump-me hormones.

"That's one we'll have to figure out later," Mary said. "Unfortunately, our American minds don't translate proverbs as fast as the Indians. Come on, Minus. Let's show the guests the Montana Indian version of battering and frying cow testes."

Samantha hoped when she turned around Dalton would have cleared the smirk off his face, but that was wishful thinking. However, his words did come as a surprise.

"The vet wanted me to tell you the stitching on the

filly was 'damn fine.'"

Samantha raised her brows and smiled, feeling satisfied and pleased that her first job on the ranch had been successful. Was this his way of apologizing?

"Good. I'll have to tell my grandpa. He taught me that stitch. We used it a lot on the weanlings and yearlings."

"Don't worry, princess, I'm not going to ask for a résumé. You just showed me your problem-solving capabilities." He tipped his head towards Beau. "Enjoy the ride, but know it's against my better judgment."

Although he was mocking her, his words were spoken as a true gentleman, void of any sarcasm. Then it occurred to her. She looked up at him, studying his sculpted features.

He peered back and she almost lost her nerve.

"You only want to win the bet," she spoke.

He chuckled and she itched to slap him. She knew that if she smacked him, it wouldn't be because she was irritated, but because she was interested—and intrigued. And that she couldn't have—wouldn't have. Her nerve was back.

"Of course, Samantha." His words were seductive, heated, spoken in the sexy, bedroom tone she had imagined. No one was near and Beau blocked their view of the other guests, so no one saw his hands trail her jawline, pause at her chin, cup her face, then reach around to cup the back of her head and pull her towards him for a soft, tender kiss. He ended the caress with one last casual peck to the lips, something a couple would do after months of dating. "And the best thing is...I only have to wait until tonight."

Chapter Eight

The nerve of that man. She was positive the kiss had gone unseen, but there was always a possibility someone could have witnessed the embrace.

Truth was, she didn't know if she cared. Sitting atop Beau, with the thunder clouds rolling in, threatening the atmosphere, everything seemed dreamlike, including Dalton's kiss. She knew if the moment could be rewound and replayed, she would react the same way. She would always remember that kiss. She had been kissed before, but none measured up to Dalton's. None made her heart twist in her chest and her senses detonate. Oh, yes, she would kiss him again, and again, and...therein lay the problem.

Because she couldn't let him.

She didn't want to be that girl remembered by that summer. However, it was an alternative to being loved for her money.

She wanted something more, much more. She wanted true love, dammit.

Samantha assumed she wasn't the first female guest to win the attentions of Dalton MacLaine. He was a lusty, attractive cowboy. But she had no desire to play that role. Up ahead, she could see Clay and Jessica riding side by side, flirting, enjoying every minute. Samantha wouldn't dare allow herself such a luxury—her upbringing had never permitted it. This was why Jessica was so dear to her.

Where Samantha was the calm before the storm, Jessica was the storm. Samantha knew Jessica's advice would have her in Dalton's arms by nightfall, willingly, in a barely-there and slit-up-the-side-to-God-knows-where negligee, but that wasn't Samantha. Her background, unfortunately, was engraved into her genes. She felt safest staying rooted in her beliefs. Besides, she truly wanted the Cinderella way of life, and for her that meant putting the horse before the chariot.

Clay led the group far up the side of Pryor Mountain, where the scenic view begged to be snapped in a panoramic frame. Samantha would have done so had she not left the camera behind in her haste to be sure of making the ride. Beneath her, Beau also felt rushed, his strides lengthening with each step. Twice now Samantha had heard his back shoes overreach and clip the front. Should he throw a shoe and turn up lame, Samantha would be answering to Dalton.

"Easy, boy." She leaned down to rub his neck. She could feel the tension in him, as if he sensed the urgency. Perhaps he could smell a foul animal on the wind. She hoped not. Knowing stallions were naturally oversensitive to their environment, and more so in uncharted territories, she had remembered to apply a small amount of vapor rub inside his nostrils.

Samantha had used the cream before, when she used Beau to pony the yearling fillies at home. The vapor was a tool to keep his mind on his job, masking the smell of the mares and their heat cycles. Today, for the same reason, she had again made use of it because they would be gathering mares and fillies.

They reached the pasture entrance moments before it began to mist. The majority of the dark, menacing clouds had passed over, leaving an overcast sky that promised more precipitation on the way.

Samantha guessed they had covered at least two miles at a brisk and steady pace, a normal day's exercise for Beau. She could tell he had plenty of stamina left. The stallion simply had too much testosterone in his bloodstream to be fatigued yet.

Clay dismounted and held the barbed-wire gate open for them. "Your horse looks good, Sam. The terrain doesn't seem to be bothering him." He winked.

"Exactly what I tried to tell your brother, only he wouldn't listen."

"He can be an ass, that's for sure."

Samantha laughed. "That's putting it nicely."

Jessica entered the conversation with a snort. "Shit. He made me as nervous as a whore in church. And I don't go to church."

Clay chuckled. "I'll have to remember that, Jessica. You know we do hold sermon on Thursdays."

"Good luck getting her there." Samantha's comment earned a mock glare from Jessica and a smirk from Jasper, who Samantha had thought was too far away to hear. Judy, the overweight amateur who had almost spooked Beau, was occupied with her bright yellow rain jacket, zipping and snapping the front so she was fully covered without her view being obstructed by the hood. Samantha wondered how she had persuaded Clay to allow her on this drive but was relieved to see she had survived the ride thus far.

Clay separated the riders, selecting Jasper and Judy to take the lowlands while he and Jessica scouted the mountain side of the pasture. Arranged gates would box the yearlings as they were herded toward Samantha. "Sam, will you be okay on your own, holding the horses steady as we bring them to you?"

"I'll be fine. Dolly will help hold them."

"Dol—?" he questioned, looking around and seeing the dog appear from behind a thick bush as she heard her name. His jaw dropped. "Humph. Didn't know she was here. Well, okay, then. If anything goes wrong, send up a flare."

The flares Clay spoke of were to be used for emergency only, as John had instructed earlier. Before the group left, Dalton and John had both insisted that each rider take one, just in case something should go amiss, especially with the tempestuous skies brought on by the storm.

After the four riders had departed, Samantha stepped down from the saddle to allow Beau a break and also to give herself a chance to stretch and to don the raingear strapped behind her saddle. The fine mist had become a slow rain, the fat droplets landing in splatters on her head and face.

She led Beau by the reins farther into the pasture, eyeing a large boulder a few feet away. The boulder turned out to be a small island of corrugated rock, cliff-like, with one side nestled along a tiny creek bed. The overhang was just tall enough for her to situate Beau underneath, keeping them both dry and clear of the sporadic wind gusts. Dolly chose to remain outside, keeping watch.

Again Samantha wished she had a camera. She felt truly out west, experiencing the vast harshness of the land for what it had been in the old days. An episode of Lonesome Dove flashed in her mind, the one where Gus retreats under a similar shelter, trying to outshoot the Indians attacking with bows and arrows. Samantha shuddered, somewhat from the cold wind but mostly from her thoughts about the reality of early western life. Good thing she was born in the late nineteen hundreds, because she didn't think she would have stood a chance being left on her own in the wilderness of Montana a hundred years earlier.

She poked her head out from under the cliff, seeing no sign of horses or riders as yet. She figured they were deep into the fields.

Turning back to Beau, she tightened the girth on the saddle a notch and checked the rest of her tack. She picked up his left front hoof and found the shoe there was indeed loose, but not terribly. All the nails were in place. As long as the ride back was smooth and slow, it should last until they reached the ranch.

She found a nearby stone to perch on. The edges were rough and poked into her skin but, what the heck, she was in Montana. Feeling the wind turn cold, she pulled the collar of her jacket together, catching a scent of evergreen and aftershave.

Damn that man, intruding on a peaceful moment.

But she had to admit the smell of him was enough to make her melt. And enough to cause her to form endless conceivabilities of what could transpire between them if only she would allow it. He was everything she had outwardly wanted in a man: tall, dark, strong, and manly beyond words.

But she knew nothing about him.

And it was best that way. She was here on vacation. She'd left behind all thoughts of graduation and degrees, job opportunities, and her father's repeated schemes for her marriage. She would never marry one of his stiff-necked business associates her age, and she knew he would never approve of a man like Dalton. So she was going to enjoy her vacation and accept it for what it was: a temporary relief from reality.

Samantha perked up into a standing position, glimpsing yellow on the lower mountainside off to her left. It was Judy, attempting to calm her horse, or so it appeared by the short check she had on the reins and the intense grimace on her face. She was leaning forward, petting the horse's neck, mouthing words inaudible at a distance. Young Jasper was nowhere in sight, but Samantha remained watching, expecting him to appear and assist the guest.

Meanwhile, however, she thought it best to get back in the saddle and leave her small sanctuary. The rain drops pelted down. Shower sprays gusted with the force of the wind. Beau tucked his head, shielding his ears from the wetness. Samantha surveyed the south bluff, still unable to locate Young Jasper. Where was he? The guest's horse now pranced sideways, tossing his head, causing Judy to shift in the saddle.

She cued Beau into a fast trot. She had intended to stay put, as Clay had suggested, and wait for the herd, but horseman's instinct prompted her to lend a hand—a much-needed one, judging by the frightened look on Judy's face. As Samantha neared, she saw that the horse and rider had ridden into a depression in the terrain, where water gushed in from all four sides.

Judy gripped the saddle horn. "He's scared. Something in the bushes."

Samantha reined Beau in next to the drop-off. "It's okay. The weather probably startled him." The frightened horse settled long enough for Samantha to lean down and grasp the bridle. "I'm going to lead you out."

Once they had cleared the crevice, the gelding jolted, jarring Beau and Samantha.

"He's still scared," Judy cried. "That growling has spooked him."

"Th-, the growling?" Samantha stammered.

"Yes, that's what caused us to slide into that pit."

Samantha brushed the thought aside, both for her own sake and for the guest's. Should she show fear, then so would Judy and, next, the horses would sense their apprehension. One disaster at a time was enough. "Let's get back on high land," she suggested, clicking the horses forward. She handed the reins of the gelding back to her. "Stay close. Where'd you last see Young Jasper?"

"I don't remember seeing him at all."

Apparently good help was hard to find in Montana, too.

Samantha was thankful for Beau's calm, settled demeanor. Looking around, she spotted Jessica on the mountainside, moving several horses downward. Clay was to the right, bringing in the rest. Young Jasper was nowhere to be seen.

"Samantha, I want off. I'm scared," insisted the woman as they reached the boulder.

Samantha contemplated this. "Okay, but you are actually safer on the horse. It's storming, and if there is something out there, you won't get far on foot." A look of eye-glazing fear crossed Judy's face, letting Samantha know she should have rephrased her sentence. Open mouth, insert foot.

The gelding paced side to side in the rocky mud. "I'm getting off." Judy threw the reins on the horse's neck.

Samantha was close, but not close enough to catch the leather pieces before they plummeted to the ground. Judy was half unseated, only one foot remaining in the stirrups. "Keep a hold of him. He's going to—" Samantha squeezed her eyes shut, dreading what she was going to see when she opened them, knowing a foot caught in the saddle usually meant one thing: a broken leg. "Run!"

The leap the gelding took catapulted the woman to the ground, twisting her leg as he fled towards the gate. Samantha secured her horse before running to help. The rider was lucky she hadn't gotten dragged. That could have killed her—this only injured her.

Judy thrashed about, yelling. She cradled her left knee, her hands blotched with blood, the rain smearing them. Agonizing screams reverberated in Samantha's ears. Not sure where to begin, Samantha yanked the bandana from around her neck. "This is going to hurt some, but it'll slow the bleeding," she said, knotting the makeshift tourniquet.

The break was complete, a compound fracture with the fibula bone protruding through the skin. Samantha knew this only because she'd detested orthopedics class, had hated having to memorize all the bones of the body, inventing different ways to remember them. She associated the fibula, the smallest leg bone, to a small lie or "fib." Clever, she'd thought at the time.

"How bad is it?" groaned the guest through gritted teeth.

Samantha answered her honestly. "It's broken, but not bad. The bleeding has slowed."

"Good. Because I don't exactly see anywhere to get a blood transfusion."

Judy was meek with her statement, but the sarcasm was much appreciated. Samantha slouched on her heels. She could use a drink. And she didn't mean water. If she wanted water, all she had to do was open her mouth and catch the rainwater streaming down the bill of her ball cap. Now she knew why cowboy hats were so popular out west—they had a wide brim to taco the water. Funny she had never thought of this before, but then again, she didn't usually ride in the pouring rain.

Samantha didn't need to use her flare to announce the emergency that had taken place. The distressed shrill from the woman had said it all, loud and clear. She could see Clay galloping towards them, his raincoat flapping in the wind. Beau, who had been quiet and still, was suddenly pawing the ground, his ears pinned in agitation and his attention focused on something she couldn't see.

Young Jasper.

The wrangler emerged from the direction Beau was facing. "I heard screaming."

Beau whinnied in her direction. She heeded his animal instinct.

"She's broken her leg." Clay arrived in time to hear Samantha's assessment of the situation. Both men knelt to inspect the woman's limb.

Clay frowned. "First a mountain lion, then a storm, and now a broken leg. Christmas has come early." The angled glance Clay shot her told he'd half expected something like this to happen to the rider.

"Fibula—that's the bone she broke," Samantha interjected.

Hearing this, Clay turned to consider her. His eyes

grew big when it dawned on him. "That's right, I forgot. You're a nurse. Heck, this ain't that bad, after all."

"Speak for yourself," countered Judy.

"Yes, ma'am. I didn't mean to sound uncaring. However, it's not every day we get graced with the presence of a nurse." He stood.

"Sam," he said, offering her a hand up. "She's going to have to be flown in."

"Flown in?"

"Yeah, by helicopter."

Judy shrieked. "I can't! I'm afraid of heights."

"Didn't you fly in a plane here?" asked Samantha.

"No, I drove to this godforsaken place."

"Well, he's right. You're going to have to be flown out. Ambulances don't make very good all-terrain vehicles. Besides, the fear of the flight might cause you to forget the pain." Nursing had taught her to be gentle but frank when speaking to patients, often gaining their compliance in the process.

Clay turned Samantha by the shoulders, his expression serious. "Sam, you're the nurse. Are you comfortable staying with her?" He paused, letting her mull it over. "It'll mean staying behind. We'll need to get the herd out so the chopper doesn't scatter them. With this weather, my cell phone isn't likely to get reception until we get back to the ranch. That could be a while, so you'll need shelter until then."

Samantha looked around at the rugged open land. She saw nothing but the rock lair. She was not Gus McCrae.

He spun her around toward the south and pointed to a spot on the mountainside. "See where the rock starts to form a cliff?"

"Yes."

"Now look down until you see the slightest bit of color change in the trees."

Samantha squinted. "Okay, I see it."

"That's the thatched roof of the retreat hut. But get a good look, because it's easy to overlook, and that you don't have time for." He continued to explain. "It's midway up the mountain, but you can make it. I've watched your horse—he's surefooted enough."

"And what about her?" Sam asked, looking at Judy.

"She's going to get a manmade stretcher—MacLaine style."

The men had the apparatus ready before Samantha could fully grip the reality of the situation. Clay sacrificed his rain gear as cushion for the homemade wooden device and used spare rope from his saddlebag to loop over Beau's neck as a harness.

"Be careful, Sam," Jessica said. "And, hey, I bet you anything we can work in a free week's stay over this." She turned to wink at Clay.

"Yeah, with *à la carte* included." Samantha situated herself in the wet saddle, a squishing sound greeting her derrière, and she decided to make the journey to the hut on foot. The rain drilled down, jabbing her in the back through her slicker.

"We'll watch to make sure you get up the mountain, then we'll head out. Any longer than that, we're likely to lose the herd to the storm." Clay double-checked the stretcher. "Figure a solid four hours before the chopper arrives, and use your flares when you hear it. Dalton will come to get you."

Dalton will come to get you. Clay's words ricocheted in her mind as she led Beau up the dense, rocky mountain. Thick evergreens and tall pines worked as organic umbrellas, shielding them from the heavy rain. Beau's hooves dug deep into the mud for leverage as she navigated him on foot, relieving additional weight.

The rain was a help in locating the hut. Samantha didn't know anything about thatched roofs, but she guessed the straw had absorbed all the moisture it could, so that now a waterfall of rain rushed over the side, pelting the rocks below.

Inside, Samantha helped Judy get as comfortable as possible. She quickly dusted the rollup beds she found on the shelves, laying them out in front of the fire she intended to start as soon as she got Beau out of the storm. She made sure to elevate Judy's injured leg. A cooler full of canned beans did the job. Unfortunately, Beano was nowhere to be found. Great. She'd have flatulence when Dalton arrived. Lovely.

The hut was tiny, round in shape, with an open floor

plan. A damp muskiness filled the stale air. Samantha crossed the stone floor and opened the one and only window. As her eyes grew accustomed to the darkness she noticed a door built into the back wall, a flat access with a latch of sorts. When one heave didn't work, she tried two and pulled with all her might. The door creaked open, revealing an attached shed. Stacked bales of straw and hay lined the far wall. At least something was going right. Now Beau could get out of the weather.

"Samantha?"

Judy's subdued whimper joggled Sam's mind as she focused on the tasks she needed to perform. She hurried to her patient's side.

"I think my blood sugar is getting low. I feel warm and dizzy."

"Are you a diabetic?" Samantha asked, spilling out the question. She prayed for the answer she wanted to hear.

"Yes."

Dear God. This was the last thing they needed. Anything with sugar was not likely a high commodity in the supplies of the retreat hut. Think fast.

She searched everywhere, fumbling in the dark area she assumed was the kitchen due to the two pans and one skillet hung haphazardly above the rock alcove. Ouch. Splintered wood grazed her fingertips as she skimmed the wooden shelves of the corner cabinets. A top drawer hosted an empty lantern, and a bottom drawer revealed an endless assortment of candles and matches. She quickly lit the wick of the tallest two, propping them on protruded rocks along the walls of the hut.

"I'll be right back," she told Judy. She ran out into the rain to check her saddlebag for gum or candy. Often on long rides she would keep something in her pack to nibble on. Beau would usually end up getting his portion of the snack, eating most of the sugary treat.

Samantha found a box of lemon drops, of all things. She recalled Beau flipping his upper lip upon tasting the sour outside coating. She hoped the small yellow candies were enough to raise the woman's blood sugar. What a story this was going to make. She could only imagine the proverb Minus would have for this moment.

Hustling, Samantha dumped them into Judy's hands. "This was all I could find." The woman shoved the round pieces into her mouth. Samantha checked the injured leg. The limb felt warm. She reached for a candle to further inspect. The swelling had increased, but nothing had changed for the worse. As long as the blood sugar got under control, they should be in the clear until the helicopter arrived. And in case help arrived late, she'd coerce Judy into eating beans, explaining the protein would stabilize the blood sugar.

Samantha busied herself in the cabin, doing her best with what she had to work with. Beau was safely inside, eating hay and drinking rain water from a dented bucket. Her soaked tube socks functioned as a rope, tying off the back portion where he was stalled. She kept a close eye on him as he limped, his left hoof bruised from a stone injury and a lost horseshoe.

Nervous anxiety overcame her. The situation was scary. Judy was stable, but her blood sugar was not. On one hand she wanted Dalton to arrive to relieve her of the burden but, on the other hand, the thought of him frightened the bloody hell out of her. She didn't know how much more of his masculine persuasion she could handle without giving in. His sexuality was off the charts. With the rain coming down in sheets, there was no chance they could trek back to the ranch tonight. Surely he wouldn't expect her to live up to her bet. Not in a situation like this. Surely.

Chapter Nine

Intense distress and worry, churned by an unaccustomed feeling of helplessness, layered in Dalton's mind. He watched the weather from the lodge's front porch and scanned the land through lightning waves. The lodge had lost power just before news of Samantha and the guest had arrived along with the herd of yearlings. Clay had given him precise details of the accident, including Judy's description of the growl and how she'd insisted the daunting snarl had been more feline-like than canine.

Mary joined him on the veranda with a sigh. "The chopper should be arriving at the retreat any time now."

Dalton nodded. "If it can land in this weather."

"Let's cross our fingers it can." She sat on the edge of the rocker and folded her arms over her chest. "Dalton, I hate to point out the obvious, but Samantha doesn't even have a gun."

He shook his head, wishing he could wake up from a bad dream. He ran a nervous hand through his hair, his fingertips pausing at the base of his neck to massage the stiffness before his arm dropped to his side. "I know. I'm fully aware of that. Not to mention she doesn't know where the cellar is—even if she could lift the hatch. So they have to be cold, wet and hungry."

Disgusted, he began to pace. After two strides, he halted and turned to his aunt. "As soon as the lightning passes, I'll head out." His aunt agreed, her lips tight with worry.

Helpless was how he felt. The hobbled feeling festered inside him and, like the storm, gathered steam along the way. From out of nowhere Samantha had become a constant in his mind. He ached to hold her in his arms and have her safe with him. Samantha was different—feisty and proud. Her touch felt so right. He could see himself with her, could see her as his wife. He wanted her home.

"At least she has her dog with her—for safety and for comfort after the guest gets airlifted out." Mary sank bank into the rocker, looking out at the rain.

Dalton chuckled at her comment. "Yeah, and her horse, for that matter. Although I wouldn't have thought of that."

"That's because you're a guy. We females think differently."

"Well, if I was her, I'd be thinking safety. Then grub."

Mary scrunched her nose. "Nah, I bet she's thinking wet clothes and outhouse."

Dalton threw his head back with a brief laugh. "That'd be my last concern."

"Not if there was a mountain lion waiting to bite you in the ass," John announced as he held a single candle high from just inside the door. "The chopper attendant just called. The guest is being flown to the nearest hospital and Samantha is safely inside the retreat."

Applause, along with whoops and hollers, erupted from inside the lodge where the remaining guests had assembled. His uncle started to turn back into the lodge, but a quiet chuckle escaped him. "Oh, and Dalton, they said to tell you Samantha expects full reimbursement for the lemon drops."

Jessica's laughing roar sounded from the doorway.

Dalton's head jerked around. "Lemon drops?"

"The ones she had to give the guest for her low blood sugar."

"Well, I'll be..." he said, looking to his aunt.

"She's more like you than you realize. Always prepared," Mary said, shrugging her shoulders.

He sniffed. "She doesn't look like any Boy Scout I've ever seen."

"Nobody ever accused you of being one, either," Mary retorted. "You know you think she's fascinating, delightful, clever, exceptional, beautiful..." Her words drifted behind her as she sashayed inside.

Shrugging off his aunt's razzing, Dalton's attention swung back out to the weather. With the amount of rain shed in the past few hours, the chances of Samantha and him returning home were scarce to none. It could possibly be a day or two before they would be able to navigate the slick downhill course leading back to the ranch. And that was if Samantha's horse was sound.

Both Dalton and Clay figured Judy weighed a solid two hundred pounds. That, added to the fact that Clay had seen Sam's horse struggling uphill in the muddy conditions, told him he'd probably won the bet between them. But did he truly mean to collect?

The lodge door creaked behind him. Heavy steps halted his thoughts of Samantha.

His Uncle John.

Borrowed guilt shot through him, seeing John's face. Like statues they stood on the porch watching the storm pass.

"I gather you're fond of this gal?" When Dalton didn't answer, his uncle added, "It's not like you to fret."

"I'd go rescue any guest in this situation, but yes, I'm fretting...on this one."

"Then treat her like she's the one."

"Sir?" Of course he would.

"Son, she's out of her element on that mountain, alone and frightened." He backpedaled. "I've seen the girls flock to you in town after you've spent months on the ranch. This one's liable to react the same."

He laughed. "Don't know about that. Samantha's more likely to set a trap—for me."

"Elizabeth would've liked her."

Dalton iced, hearing his mother's name.

"Your father, too. They would've wanted me to say something—something to guide you. I don't have their knack for words, but...I know they would want you to do right by Samantha."

His uncle was right. His parents would wish to see him with Samantha. She was a perfect fit. "My intentions are honorable, John. You've got my word."

"Good. 'Cause I'd like to see her stay." John thumped him on the arm before walking off.

Dalton carefully chose which mount to use. Each wrangler was loaned four horses for the summer. This gave each horse a break and the wrangler opportunity to better his horseman's skills, since each mount was individual in its strengths and weaknesses. Dalton decided to use the stout buckskin gelding. Although still a tad green, the horse was hardy and levelheaded, with enough stamina to endure the trip. He was also a gelding. Samantha's stallion wouldn't act up as he would with a filly.

He was alone in the bunkhouse, gathering the items they would need for the next few days, when he heard footsteps on the porch. Clay and Jessica bounded into the room, their raincoats drenched, puddles forming on the wooden floor where they stepped.

Breathless, Jessica huffed, holding out a small bag. "Here's a few of Samantha's things. I'm sure she'd want them. Just the necessities—clothes and panties. Boring stuff, really, besides the condoms." She smiled slowly at him. "Kidding." He noticed she bit her lip in the same manner Samantha did. Must be a Kentucky thing.

He added the diminutive handbag to his collection.

The bunkhouse door swung open again. This time it was Mary, holding a soft cooler. She too was soaked. "Shoo, it's raining hard out there." She pushed the yellow hood of her slicker off her face. "I've got all the cold food you two could possibly need for tonight," she stated, patting the weatherproof satchel.

Dalton noticed she said "tonight" but paused before saying so. Hmm. He didn't give his aunt enough credit. He'd have to remember that.

"Looks like you're set, Dalton. Gun, food, condoms. What more could a man need?" The dimples in Clay's cheeks wiggled at the corners of his mouth.

"Yeah, and she's there waiting for you," Jessica concluded.

Raised brows from Mary demanded a further explanation. "Did I miss something?"

Dalton read more excitement than concern in his aunt's expression. And although he hated to disappoint her, he also knew she was already calculating the number of grandchildren, so he countered with, "You didn't miss anything, Mary. My smartass sibling here just thinks he has to get the last word in, is all." He hoisted the bags and headed out the door.

****

It was pure dark. Pitch blackness surrounded him.

His flashlight was doing little good in the rain. The murky light allowed him to see only the immediate step in front of the horse. He figured he had been riding at a snail's pace for two hours. The darkness wasn't the only problem. The wind gusts swathed him and the gelding with powerful blasts of rainwater, delaying their progress.

Dalton was long past cold and wet. His raingear would have held its own had the bursts of wind and rain blown from behind instead of directly at him. He was drenched from head to toe, the majority of the water showering in from the neck of his raincoat. Reining the horse, his arm felt weighted from the sodden layers of clothing. He clamped his teeth to keep them from chattering.

He focused on Samantha and the need to see that she was safe. Anything could happen on the mountain range. He had read somewhere that, back in the old days, the common cause of death for a cowboy was falling off his horse and being dragged. The second was sickness, and the third was starvation. He'd be damned if he'd let Samantha see any of those.

Something about Samantha triggered his protective side, and it wasn't just her soft, round derrière and beautiful face. It was the way she made him feel. Alive and awake. As though he'd been on cruise control and hadn't realized it. His ultimate goal of owning the ranch he and his father had dreamed of hadn't fizzled in the least—it had become more important. Samantha inspired him to succeed. He envisioned her on the ranch, tending to a weak foal one minute and tackling him in the bedroom the next, all with her feisty, unbridled spirit. He hoped the time they spent together in the retreat hut would strengthen the connection between them and bring that possibility to her attention.

Glowing eyes in the bushes ahead jerked him back to reality. He held his light aimed at the amber orbs until they disappeared in the blur of the rain. Not likely a mountain lion, probably just a harmless raccoon or possum. But he still found himself reaching down, feeling for his loaded gun.

Once he rounded the bend of Beartooth Mountain, the wind calmed but the rain continued to splatter down.

Dalton kept the horse moving at a fast walk. The cabin was just ahead, on the hillside. The stout gelding stomped his way up the steep incline.

The illuminated tawny eyes returned, stalking them as they proceeded to the cabin. Half a mile back, Dalton had caught sight of a long, sleek tail and his worries diminished. He chuckled, despite the sheets of rain pelting down on him. He should have known Samantha would be safe. Her dog was a natural-born protector and had been trailing him all along—a good dog, though funny-looking, with a camouflage-like pattern in shades of black and grey. He'd have to ask Samantha about the breed.

Amidst the rain, a small shadowy structure appeared. A dull light shone from the window. He had arrived at the retreat cabin.

****

Samantha contemplated what her next action should be. She had set a small fire using three dry logs she'd found in Beau's portion of the hut. The cooler functioned as a stool, and so she sat staring into the flames, brooding about what to do next. The girly-girl in her desperately wanted to take a bath, but she wasn't about to go there. Dalton would no doubt arrive just as she stripped down.

She'd already taken care of nature's call, so she marked that off her list.

Hunger was next. The can of beans under her butt was sounding rather appetizing, but she wasn't about to go there, either. She was not going to spend the night in a claustrophobically small hut with a distended, gaseous abdomen. Her stomach was already bloated enough, thanks to Aunt Flo arriving early this month. Samantha smiled and bit her lip. If Dalton was determined to make a move on her, she had an easy excuse.

Boots beat a heavy tattoo on the porch, throwing her into a panic. Who could it be? Nervousness overcame her. It had to be Dalton. God, how he intimidated her! Instantly, her brave thoughts had disintegrated into fine particles of apprehension.

A hesitant Samantha answered the polite knock on the door.

Dripping wet, he regarded her with a sly grin. He

removed his hat and rubbed his forehead, pretending to ponder. "What was it I said? Something about only having to wait until tonight?"

Samantha gasped. "You wouldn't dare."

"Collect on a winning bet? Oh, yeah, I would."

He entered, shrugged off his coat and tossed it into the corner as she backed into the hut. He strode towards her.

"Is your horse lame?" He crossed his muscled arms.

Samantha's legs grew weak and parts of her body liquefied, but she was able to continue her retreat backwards, though half enjoying the cat-and-mouse game. "Yes." She stopped, the heel of her boot bumping the stone wall behind her.

"Close quarters, princess. And running outside is not an option. I doubt you'll find the mountain lion very friendly this time of night."

"Thanks for the reminder." She swallowed hard and her voice faltered as she caught a quick breath, the hard beat of her heart making her breathing short and choppy. "Funny, I didn't take you as the friendly sort."

He chuckled, deep in his throat. His voice was sexy—too sexy. "No worries, princess. I won't befriend you any more than you want me to."

Arrogant cattleman. "Awfully sure of yourself, Mr. MacLaine."

He ran one finger along her jawline and tilted her chin up. "Ms. Matthews, would you like to put my abilities to the test?"

He surprised her by walking away. Stumped, she watched as he removed his wet clothing and boots. In white briefs, he crossed to the kitchen area and lifted a board in the floor, opening a hatch. He descended down the stairs with a single candle.

One by one, he tossed up items Samantha had spent several hours longing for—bed linens wrapped in plastic, bowls and cups, cooking pans and utensils. Last, he carried a see-through container with cloths and towels.

"That's been down there this whole time?"

"Ask and you shall receive," he said, in between coughs. He donned his raincoat and boots, and turned to go outside.

"Dalton?" Was he about to leave? Her sudden emptiness baffled her.

"I'll come in through the back."

Samantha turned and stepped into Beau's part of the hut, listening for the back door to slide open. Seconds later, Dalton appeared, leading a buckskin through the opening. He coughed again and shivered.

"Here, let me." She snatched the reins. She could see him wobbling. Quickly she unsaddled the gelding and threw him a flake of hay. "Let's get you inside." She reached for his arm and felt heat coming off him. "You're burning up." She guided him to the fire and spread out a bedroll.

"Actually, I'm freezing. And don't think I didn't see your horse limping around back there." He groaned as he knelt on the padded bed, holding his head.

Samantha remained silent. She watched as he collapsed on the cot. His muscular arms plunked beside him. On her knees, she felt his forehead, finding him beaded with sweat and hot to the touch. She ran to fetch a clean rag.

Rainwater was all she had close by. She placed the cold compress first to his forehead and then to the back of his neck. Feeling for a pulse, she found the rhythm tachy but regular.

"Dalton," she said, nudging him awake. She spoke loudly. "How long were you out in the storm?"

He mumbled before answering her. "Three hours. And I'm not deaf. I'm twenty-seven, not eighty-seven."

"Fine." She got back to her point, dropping her voice. "Were you cold and wet all that time?"

His right eye peeped open. "You're the nurse. What do you think?"

Okay, dumb question. She rephrased, "How long were you chilled?"

Between coughs, he answered, "I was cold until I started coming on to you."

"Serves you right." She replaced the already warm rags with cool washcloths and pulled his boots off. She squatted next to him.

"All bets aside," Dalton said, shivering, his teeth clicking as he spoke, "can you just lie next to me and keep me warm?"

The brazen cattleman had submitted; his twin was docile and sweet. She stretched out alongside him, her toes meeting his knees. Too sick to be a threat, he was no longer to be feared, and she looped his arm so it hooked about her waist, his shoulder a perfect pillow. Her heavy eyelids commanded she rest.

****

The next day, Dalton remained febrile. Samantha did her best to keep him hydrated. She left his side only to eat and wash.

As evening approached, she asked, "Is there any medicine downstairs, Dalton? If we can reduce your fever, it would help your headache."

Dalton answered her by grabbing her around the waist and sitting her on top of him. "A lot of things would help my headache—if you'd be so inclined." His eyelids fluttered opened and then closed as she settled astride him.

Strangely enough, she didn't want to move off him. "Thanks, but I'm not that kind of nurse. I deal more with wounds, and the kidneys."

"Well you're sitting on my bladder. Is that good enough?"

Dalton's vulnerable state weakened her intimidation. She laughed at his question, crossing her arms. "The two are related, but separate. Try again."

"You've never had a patient with a headache?"

"Well, sure."

"And what did you do for them?"

"I gave them Tylenol."

"I'm not talking about that kind of headache, Samantha," he said, his tone rich and husky.

His meaning shocked her. She gasped and quickly shut her mouth. She moved to stand, but his large hands restrained her, cupping her thighs. "I thought you were sick."

"I am. My head is pounding, but as long as I don't raise it, it's not too bad."

Now that she understood his play on words, she had a sharp response ready. "Well, good, because if you can't get an erection, then you can hardly collect on that winning bet of yours."

He chuckled. His mouth movements caused sweat to trickle down his cheek. "My head was not in the gutter just then, princess."

Samantha glared at him, although he didn't see because his eyelids were still closed. She took a brief moment to enjoy the view of his unclad body. Firelight glowed on his tanned skin and broad shoulders. She itched to feel the rippled muscles of his biceps and run her hands through his dark chest hair.

"If you take a picture it'll last longer," he jested.

"You conceited ass."

"I'm kidding. Why are you so touchy?"

"I'm not touchy. I'm intimidated—by the situation."

"And which situation is that? You and me stuck in a cabin? Or you astride my cock?"

"Both!" Samantha shrieked. "And I'd gladly move off your cock if only you'd let me!" She smacked at his hands. "I hate that word, by the way."

"Guys love it." He grinned. After a moment's pause, he announced, "I have a proposition for you."

"No, thanks."

"You haven't heard what it is. It could be in your favor."

"That's doubtful." Samantha put another cold compress on his forehead. Moisture glistened on his face.

"You do what I say for five minutes and I'll call off the bet."

"God, no! There's no telling what you could come up with in five minutes."

"I promise not to lay a hand on you."

That got her attention. She remained silent, considering the trap she could fall into.

Then he added, "Better yet, I promise not to look."

"And just what won't you be looking at?"

"You. Almost naked."

"Ah-ha. Now I get it."

"Offer expires tomorrow." He coughed and shivered.

"Oh, sure, when you feel better? And are free to manipulate the situation?" It was the truth, after all.

"Yes."

"Fine, then. I agree to do whatever you want for five

minutes. Almost naked." Her voice sounded full of courage she didn't have. The one edge she had on him gave her confidence. It was also the one thing she never thought she'd be happy to have—her period. Poor Dalton was in for a shock if he thought of taking this any farther than five minutes.

Dalton released her, and she stood.

"Time starts when your clothes are off," he instructed.

Keeping her front side to him, she removed her shirt, more comfortable with him stealing a frontal view should he decide to play unfair. Next went her favorite jeans. She reminded herself that panties and a bra covered as much as a swimsuit. "Okay."

"Now just sit on me like you were."

She contemplated his trickery. This seemed too easy. His briefs were still on.

"Sit, princess. You're terrified of me and it's got to stop. Besides," he laughed, "I'm cold."

After several minutes, Samantha understood his theory. Polite teasing. The jerk. Her lower body parts throbbed, wanting instinctively to grind against him. How he remained soft, she hadn't a clue.

When time was up, he rose to a sitting position. He grimaced from the headache. His lips feathered her mouth, his hands on her bottom holding her steady. With a kiss to her nose, he shifted to his side, taking her with him. In spoon position, he said, "I never peeked."

They both fell into a deep slumber.

Samantha kept cold compresses on Dalton's forehead throughout the night. By two in the morning, his fever had begun to break. When she was certain his temperature was normal, she drifted back to sleep. Encaged by his big, protective arms, she felt content for the first time in her life. She had her horse in a stall, her dog on the porch, and a rugged cattleman in her arms.

She needed nothing more.

Chapter Ten

A clamor outside awoke Samantha. It sounded like her dog. And Dalton. She jumped up from her comfortable nest by the fire, tucking the white bed sheet around her near-naked form.

She peeked outside to assess the situation. She could very well find some power struggle going on between the two dominant animals—and yes, she did put Dalton in the animal category, after witnessing the sexual reign he'd held over her last night. She closed her eyes at the thought, and a playful smile sprang to life.

The nervous feeling in her stomach returned when she opened her eyelids. She doused her smile. Dalton, garbed in boxer briefs, studied her. His eyes scaled her up and down.

So intimidating.

"Does your dog do anything besides growl and snarl? I'm curious."

He set down the buckets of water he was carrying and crossed his arms. The ripple of muscle in his forearms did little to calm her, intriguing her, instead. From the open doorway, she did her best to remain nonchalant. "Not at you, it seems."

He laughed.

Samantha stepped out to the top porch step. "Actually that's not a snarl. That's how she smiles."

Dalton's head jerked back. "Sure it is," he said dryly, not believing her.

"Really." Samantha crouched next to Dolly, who stood inches from the cabin steps. She patted her on the head and ruffled her ears. The dog's lips curled in response, sharp white teeth exposed at the gum line. "See?" The dog reached to lick her.

Dalton looked dumbfounded.

Ah-ha. She had stumped him.

"I've never seen a dog do that," he confessed.

"Me neither." Samantha rose, standing two steps above him on the porch, level with him. "I think she does it to psych people out. The growling, too."

"I think she's overprotective of her owner—that's what I think. But at least she's not growling at me this morning like she was last night."

Self-conscious, Samantha cleared her throat. "Yeah, I think that's because she smells me on you." She bit her lip.

Dalton turned to look at her. "Nice ice-breaker, Samantha. I know I sure wasn't going to say anything." He reached out and pulled her into him, hugging her with his strong arms. Then he pulled back and looked at her. "Aunt Mary raised me to be a gentleman, but..." He brushed away a strand of hair from her face. "Last night I wasn't about to abide." His intense eyes spoke the truth, something Samantha didn't find in the men she dated back home. It was as if he didn't have the time and capability for emotional deceit.

"Yeah, well, I'd say you shot that principle all to hell." She tipped her head, smiling.

The comment sparked a mischievous glare from him. It then occurred to her that she was wrapped only in a thin sheet of cotton, a vulnerable state, to say the least. She took a slow step backwards.

He watched as she retreated. His sly grin gave his features a wolfish quality. "Not this again. You know where it got you last time."

Samantha continued backwards, stepping inside the hut. There was no way she was going to kiss him. She hadn't brushed her teeth! And she wasn't about to tell him that. Her toothbrush and paste were just inside, in her saddlebag.

Dalton, hell-bent not to allow her escape, followed.

Samantha clutched the sheet between her legs. "I...I think I need some toilet paper."

"And I'll be glad to get some for you—once I know you're telling the truth." His frolicsome grin told her he was kidding.

"Dalton MacLaine, you are such a hound. I'm standing here bleeding, and all you can think with is your lower brain."

He faked a testy glare. "Very original. Been using that one since what...the seventh grade?"

"The sixth."

Thankfully, he turned away. In two seconds, Samantha had her toothbrush in her mouth, filled with toothpaste. She was still supporting her crotch when Dalton appeared from the basement. He carried a roll of toilet tissue and another bed sheet. He looked as sexy as all-get-out as he set the white bundle near her.

"Brushing your teeth, huh? You really are a debutante." He took a seat on one of the kitchen's two stools and watched her.

Samantha spit out a mouthful of suds. "You don't have to be a debutante to like having clean teeth. It happens to be a morning ritual."

"I somehow don't think spitting into an empty water bottle is part of a morning routine for a southern belle like yourself," he teased.

"Who says I'm a southern belle?" she asked. Did he know who her father was? The thought troubled her. She rinsed her mouth one last time.

"You do. Your actions. Your words. Your red-painted toenails." He stood and came toward her. Looking down at her, he tilted her chin up with his forefinger to meet his gaze then girdled her waist with large hands. "And I very much like your toes, along with your other female attributes." He kissed her long and slow on the mouth before prying open the front of the sheet, exposing her breasts. "Including, I must admit, these two critters."

Samantha laughed, enjoying the frisky description. On her tiptoes, she stretched tall, meeting his lips. She ran her fingers through his hair and tousled the dark waves.

She tore away from him. "So you did look?"

"Yes, ma'am."

A sudden snap of tree limbs outside broke their kiss. Dalton quickly covered her with the sheet, a gesture she found reassuringly protective, and within seconds had donned his pants and boots and retrieved his rifle.

"Stay here. It's probably nothing. I need to secure the area, anyway. I'll get firewood while I'm out." Before he closed the door, he added, "Do they teach debutantes how to cook over a fire?" His eyes jumped to the burning flames of the hearth.

Before Samantha could reach for something handy to throw at him, he was long gone, chortling. She turned to look at the fire. Surely she could manage to warm up... something.

Unfortunately, toaster pastries hadn't made it into the cooler. But ham and bread, along with some butter, had. Samantha found two black iron skillets downstairs. So far, so good.

An hour later, the ham was charred black and the half loaf of bread, well, it resembled a housing brick. Good thing she didn't bet on breakfast. Perhaps the meal would've been a success had she not been trying to multitask cooking with getting a bath ready.

She had found a pair of shorts and a tank top in the bags Dalton brought. Both articles of clothing were on the skimpy side, so she put on one of Dalton's oversized T-shirts. She guessed she had Jessica to thank for that one. No telling what her friend had packed for her to sleep in. Probably nothing.

The old galvanized tin horse trough she borrowed from the horse's shed, dragging it in to a place before the fire. Beau and the gelding were getting along rather nicely, she noticed. Beau still favored his front leg.

Samantha used the water Dalton had brought from the creek and was surprised to see how crystal clean it was. As she had her first night at Twin Rivers Ranch, she heated the water in a cauldron and poured it into the makeshift tub.

In a hurry, she undressed, worried Dalton would return too soon, in time to see her fully naked. The lighting in the cabin was poor, so he wouldn't be able to see much, but the man had seen enough of her already. She draped the T-shirt over the back of the trough, just in case.

She tested the temperature of the water with her toes, inching one foot in at a time, letting her skin adjust to the warmth. The water was too hot for the rest of her body, as she dipped her butt low enough to feel a burning sting. Standing, she swished her feet in the bubbles, her best attempt to cool the liquid. She prayed Dalton wouldn't enter anytime soon.

The door to the cabin bumped open the moment the thought left her head.

Damn the luck. Naked, she fumbled, reaching for the shirt, the water hot as it splashed high on her calves. It had been her goal to be completely submerged in the water when he returned, but, clearly, she was too late. In a frenzy, she searched for the neck opening, flipping the shirt over and over. Her hands, soapy and wet, were a hindrance, and she succeeded only in holding the cotton material draped in front of her torso.

She sighed and gave up. It was no use. He'd already seen her.

Dalton was polite about it as he piled the logs of wood next to the fire. Samantha saw him eyeing their burnt breakfast. He rose and studied her. She could tell he wanted to laugh.

"I see you've managed to make a bath."

She nodded, chewing her upper lip.

"And burn breakfast. All at the same time."

"Multitasking is the mother of all inventions," Samantha quoted from a magazine she'd read last week. No idea what magazine, but nonetheless she remembered the excerpt.

He took the vulnerable moment to inspect her naked form. He clearly liked what he saw. The intense bedroom eyes Samantha was becoming accustomed to looked her in the face.

"Take a picture. It'll last longer," she echoed.

He laughed. "I would, if only you'd let me." He stepped toward the tub. "I'd also join you in the bath—if you'd let me."

Samantha flirted with the option. The notion was a fantasy. His weathered cowboy look was growing on her by the hour. Her hands itched to feel the raspy hairs shadowing his firm jaw. What more could a girl ask for on a vacation than to be secluded in a cabin with a sexy, Marlboro man looming over her, wanting to share a bath? Nothing she could think of.

"'Silence speaks approval'," he said, removing his clothes. "That's a Minus quote."

"Guessed as much," she said, making small talk as

her nerves skyrocketed. She eased down into the water and then did the blondest thing she could do: looked up, with instant focus on his male package. Her eyes immediately shifted away. She decided now was a good time to slide to the end of the tub.

Dalton sank into the bubbles with a coy grin. "It's not going to reach out and bite you, Samantha. Stop cowering."

"I'm not cowering." She fanned water at him. "I'm simply—"

"Intimidated. I know." He reached in her direction and she jerked, relaxing when she saw he only meant to retrieve a washcloth and soap. "You weren't scared of me last night when you slept beside me." His words were more of a question than a statement.

"That's because I thought you were harmless—and sick."

He laughed. "I was. You fixed me."

Samantha felt her face heat with color.

"I've met a few debutantes. They didn't at all seem sheltered, like you. Quite the bitches, actually."

"I'm confused. Is that supposed to make me feel better?" Samantha retorted, angling her head. She wondered how he had met them. On the ranch? In the barn? Like he'd met her? An unfamiliar jealous streak shimmied through her.

He shifted in the tub, his legs pulling her closer to him. "It's a compliment. What I mean to say is, you're wholesome."

What did he mean by that?

"Innocent."

Huh? She cocked her head.

"Protected."

Come again?

"Chaste," he stated.

Chaste? She thought for a second. *He means...* "Virgin?" She practically squeaked the word. Not exactly the topic she would've chosen for her first bathtub conversation with a naked man she'd met only the day before yesterday.

"Yes, Samantha. You seem like quite the virgin. I wouldn't have guessed it by looking at you, but after spending five minutes touching you, I know you are."

He sounded so sure of himself. It half annoyed her and half intrigued her. "Wanna make a bet on that?"

He chuckled softly. "No."

"Good. Me neither. I just wanted to see how much advantage you'd take of a virgin." Well, she was going to have to admit it sooner or later. Might as well be sooner. She couldn't spend another night without alcohol pretending she wasn't.

"Come here, princess." He swung her around and drew her next to him, her back against his stomach. He dampened her chest and shoulders with a washcloth and kissed her forehead. "I wouldn't be sitting here with you if I thought you were a spoiled debutante who's dated half the guys in town and seen each of their dorm rooms at least five times."

But what if he knew about her family's wealth? Would he be like the rest? More than eager?

For now, he seemed to like her for who she was. A new experience for her. She felt her body relaxing against his muscled form. The sudsy water made their skin soft and slippery, so she propped her feet on his knees for leverage, mindful not to slide farther downwards between his legs.

She decided it was her turn to ask the questions. Not facing him made the conversation easier. "How long have you lived on the ranch?"

"Ever since my parents died in a car accident. Clay and I were little kids. Preschool age. John and Mary took us in." He splashed more water on them. "My turn," he said. "What do your parents do for a living?"

Samantha tensed. "Politics, of a sort. I don't really pay much attention." Moving on... "How many women have you slept with?"

"Ooh. Now that's a question—that I refuse to answer, even for you."

"That many, huh?"

"Watch it, princess, I said it won't bite. I didn't say anything about me. How did your horse get that odd scar on his front leg?"

Samantha could see Beau's leg from where she soaked. The scar was barely noticeable with his dark hair.

"Before we had vinyl fence, he got caught in a spool of barbed wire." Samantha remembered that day. "I came running as soon as they told me. He stood still long enough for me to unravel it. Here's my scar to match." She held her left arm so he could see the horizontal scar on the inside of her left bicep.

"Ouch. That hurt," he commented. "That horse is crazy about you. He's been spying on us this entire time."

"I know. I'm surprised he isn't kicking down the walls. He approves of you." *Whereas he abhors Young Jasper*, she thought. She contemplated telling Dalton about the wrangler's negligence yesterday, but decided against ratting on him. That schmuck was the last thing she wanted to discuss. She had a myriad of questions she wanted to ask Dalton.

"Have you always wanted this lifestyle?"

Without hesitation, he answered, "Absolutely. I love ranching and everything about it. Wouldn't want my life any other way." He paused before saying, "Except for having my own cattle ranch, of course."

Ah-ha. So he was the ambitious type. Score for being a man with a plan.

"Dalton?"

"What? He asked, kissing her on the head.

"I have to pee."

****

Dalton packed for the return trip to the ranch the next morning with secret melancholy. He hated to leave the hut and the peaceful quietness he'd found with Samantha. The shelter seemed to be their own small space in the world. Had sex been involved, he would've compared the past few days to a honeymoon. But that wasn't the case, and he wasn't about to gripe. Waiting would only be icing on the cake. And for Samantha, he was willing to wait.

Postponement was also what Samantha needed. Dalton could tell she needed time. Time to think, time to imagine, time to wonder. He wanted that for her. He didn't want her to regret or think of their first time together as casual. Something about her satisfied the empty abyss inside of him, and he longed for her to crave the same desire he had. For the first time in his life, the term "settling down" had a nice flow.

Oddly enough, he couldn't get Samantha to open up about her life in Kentucky. She spoke of her grandfather and the equine teachings he'd passed on to her but slammed the door when her upbringing was mentioned, shifting the conversation to a safe topic such as her horse.

Dalton had noted the similarity of her stallion's scar to the filly's wound. The location and appearance of the blemish could be a coincidence. Nearly all the ranches in Montana were outlined with barbed-wire fencing. But his gut told him otherwise. It was too suspicious for only valuable bulls to be mangled and targeted. Yet, the filly's maiming negated this assumption.

He watched Samantha now, her soft, delicate movements as she saddled her horse. She cinched the girth and situated the breast strap as seriously as an artist painting a canvas, never losing touch with her horse. Dalton sensed this was just one of the reasons her horse was so in tune to her—she always let him know where she was and what her next move would be. It was the same technique cowboys used with breaking horses; however, once the horse was broken, the rider returned to robot mode, tacking and riding one horse as they would another, taking the relationship for granted.

He continued eyeing her as he bridled the buckskin gelding.

"Good as new," she said, leading her horse around. "Whoa." She stopped and petted him on the neck.

Dalton was mostly busy inspecting the sway of her ass, remembering how perfect she felt in his hands. "Yep, looks fit to ride. That concoction I sprinkled on his feed probably helped." He waited for her surprised reaction.

"Shut up. You did not." Her words were confident, but her eyes were uncertain. "He wouldn't let you get close enough."

"It took some time, but I managed to persuade him." He neglected to tell her the persuasion had taken nearly two hours, in which he could have been snuggled up against her warm body.

"Where was I?" she asked, double-checking the horse's girth.

Dalton tied his gelding to a post. He moved to stand

behind her, sprawling his right palm out to cup her buttocks, ready to prop her petite rump into the saddle. He did so because he knew the sexual play would be ending when they returned to Twin Rivers. "Snoring by the fire," he whispered in her ear.

"Nuh-uh. I do not snore."

"You did last night." He hoisted her into the saddle.

Dolly sprang from the bushes, ready for duty.

Dalton jerked, his right hand instinctively moving for the switchblade in his back pocket. He lightly cussed. "Your dog is going to give me a heart attack at the ripe old age of twenty-seven if she doesn't stop that."

"I trained her well," Samantha boasted.

"You sure did. You and your animals are like a small army of one, you realize that?"

"Yeah, but you're spry enough to handle them," she said from atop the horse. Long, free-flowing waves of sun-kissed chestnut hair rested on her shoulders. Astute blue eyes teased him above a sensual mouth.

Dalton grinned, turning to untie his mount. "Good thing you're on your horse, or I'd show you just how spry I am." He winked before mounting.

She laughed, a conniving look crossing her face. "Hey, Dalton, what's your horse's name?"

What an out-of-the-blue question. "Buck."

She cackled hysterically.

"Why do you ask?" He couldn't help but laugh himself.

Wiping tears from her eyes, she replied, "Oh, just a rumor." Her slender shoulders quaked, her hand covering her mouth stifling the outbursts.

"Well, you know what they say about rumors..."

"No. What?"

"Only half of them are true." And that was all he was going to say. Because he wasn't about to admit he'd gotten bucked off because of a frog.

****

Splendid didn't begin to describe the ride back to the ranch. Samantha could have ridden for days next to Dalton over the cascading terrain of the Beartooth Mountains. The weather was perfection after the storm, the sun shining, the humidity nonexistent. They took the same route home that Clay and Jessica and the others had taken in the rain, in case any yearlings had strayed. Beau galloped alongside Dalton's gelding without so much as a flinch of lameness, thanks to Dalton and his vitamin-filled potion. Some sort of Indian recipe she'd have to learn, Samantha thought.

This was her fourth day in Montana and she was loving it. Only a few days left. What would come of her and Dalton after that? Nothing? She hoped not, but reality was crashing down on her. Her insides felt as if they were melting, a heated bittersweetness dissolving her usual sanity. She had a mere three days left to spend with him.

Samantha knew what she was going to do. The next few days were too priceless to pass up. She'd go with the flow. She'd listen to her heart. For the first time, ever, she'd found someone interested in her, not in financial gain. After all, Fern had said she'd discover him when she wasn't looking, and in fact she had. A man like Dalton MacLaine was the last thing she'd expected to come across.

"How did Twin Rivers get its name?" Samantha asked. It was one of her remaining bathtub questions when she'd been interrupted by the need to visit the cherrywood outhouse.

Dalton guided his horse over a fallen tree trunk, keeping a watchful eye on their path. "The ranch, believe it or not, actually sits in what used to be a full-blown river. Two smaller rivers run on each side of the mountains now."

"So, the name has nothing to do with twins in the family?" Going back to what Fern said. Checking all bases.

"Not to my knowledge. Why? You plan on manipulating the family tree?" He asked with a wink, the same wink that made her heart sputter every time he looked at her with that smug grin. If he were an ice cream, she'd order him chocolate-dipped with caramel glazing and a dash of whipped cream.

"No. Not yet, anyway."

He lurched in the saddle, looking at her. His lips formed a smile when he saw she was kidding.

It was her turn to wink.

He laughed, a deep belly laugh that sounded genuine. "What's the first thing you're going to do when we get back, princess?"

Samantha took a moment. "Honestly?"

"Honestly."

"Answer Jessica and Bethany's multiplicity of questions about what really happened in the cabin. They'll nit-pick me to death unless I tell them at least one juicy fact."

"Ah-ha."

Samantha watched his expression turn sour, disappointed almost, as if her answer spoiled the past two wonderful days spent at the retreat hut. "All I'll have to say is that my bloody period screwed it all up." Because, in truth, she couldn't share the details with her friends. The overall feelings, yes, but not the specifics, not the lounging trough bath in front of the hearth, the water blood-tinged by her menses eliciting Dalton's remark that it only made her sexier and more real than she already was. Nope, those were his and her moments. Goony moments.

His smile returned, but it was different. Better. He read her meaning.

"What else will you do, princess?"

Samantha felt her lips curve, hearing the familiar endearment. "Eat lemon drops. I feel a craving coming on." She didn't know if the chopper attendants had passed on her message. He hadn't said anything, so she assumed not.

"It just so happens..." He twisted in the saddle and fumbled deep in his saddle pack. "Someone mentioned your request." He flung her the quaint yellow box.

"Ah, thank you. You just cured a female suffering from sugar deprivation."

"Glad I could be of service." He reined his horse. "Let's double back. I thought I saw a gleam of something in the pasture."

Chapter Eleven

Back at the ranch, Dalton and Samantha were swarmed by the guests and staff. It was late afternoon, when all ranch activities were at a halt for the social hour scheduled between work and dressing for dinner. Samantha was certain she got hugged at least a hundred times, twenty by Mary alone.

"It's so good to have you guys back." Mary squeezed her by the shoulder. "We missed you."

"Yeah, it just wasn't the same without our partner in crime," Jessica's welcome was seconded by Bethany. Jessica, muddy up to the knees of her jeans, continued, "But don't think we didn't have fun without you."

"What have you been doing?"

Jessica held up a dirty ear tag. "Ear-tagging, castrating, vaccinating. You name it."

"And I," Bethany said, holding out her left hand, "just had the best manicure and pedicure this side of Churchill Downs." She wore flip-flops and a bathing suit cover-up.

Samantha could see the questions her friends had for her brewing in their eyes. As they led Beau to the barn, she heard John asking Dalton questions about the state of the hut. The wranglers grouped around them, listening, but only she saw Dalton slip the device he'd found in the pasture deep into his pocket.

The guests' excitement fizzled and they scattered to different parts of the ranch. It occurred to Samantha that, beyond Dalton, she hadn't seen much of what Twin Rivers had to offer. Perhaps she would tonight after a hot bath—this one by herself. She was only five steps away from him and already feeling a void.

In the barn, Mary quickly dismissed herself to attend to dinner.

"Isn't it a bit early for dinner?" Samantha asked. The sun was still up.

Jessica opened her mouth to speak, but Bethany cut

her off. "It's a surprise. That's all we can say."

Samantha smiled. She loved surprises. She was on a roll with them lately.

"One you need to dress up for," Jessica described. "As in your black skimpy Prada dress. Because I have my eyes on your lacy red number."

"What's the occasion? And how much time do I have to get ready?" Excitement flared—she wanted to look obscenely beautiful. Dalton had only seen her in jeans and naked, and although he probably preferred the latter, she sought to look her best.

"Well, being the guest of honor, you can arrive whenever you wish," Jessica hinted.

"Shush," Bethany interrupted. She turned to Samantha. "She is so bad with surprises."

"Yes, I know." Samantha latched Beau's stall and dropped a fresh apple in his feeder as Jessica and Bethany headed to the cabin. His nose went after it, big teeth chomped into its juicy core. She patted his head before racing off to follow her friends.

Slam. She ran straight into Dalton's hard chest as she rounded the corner. Instantly, her heart beat more rapidly.

"Missing me already?" he mused. Samantha felt her cheeks heat. She saw him glance to see if anyone was behind him. Seeing Young Jasper on the bunkhouse porch, he doused his come-hither expression.

"No, just in a hurry." She angled her head playfully with a surefire grin, lying and teasing at the same time.

He started to walk past her, his horse following behind him giving them a short second of privacy. In her ear, he breathed, "No panties." Samantha felt the tips of his reins swat her butt. She ran to catch up with her friends, only allowing herself to skip once.

"Inquisitive minds want to k-n-o-w," Jessica said as they walked in the cabin, the screen door slamming behind them.

"Okay. First things first. Isn't he gorgeous?" Samantha asked, beaming.

"They both are," Bethany answered, referring to the MacLaine brothers. "You guys had best be happy I'm unavailable."

"Oh we are," they replied in unison.

"I better get ready." Samantha thought for a second about what she'd just said. She looked to her friends. "How am I going to do that with no blow dryer?"

"Girl, it's called *el naturale*. And let me say frizzes are now back in style." Jessica took her cowboy hat off, revealing a headful of crinkled blonde hair.

Bethany stepped forward, the queen of hair solutions. "Don't worry, girls, messy updos are the thing. We'll manage." Samantha loved that about Bethany. She was a girl's best friend and a hairstylist wrapped all in one.

Samantha bathed faster than she could ever recall and sprinted back to the cabin with Dolly hard on her heels. Upstairs in the loft, she dotted on her favorite perfume and decided to follow Jessica's suggestion to wear the slinky black dress.

The garment's modest length hit her below the knees but compensated with an open back and plunging front neckline. The material was soft as she smoothed away fine wrinkles. Wedged heels and a stylish black choker accented the look. Standing in front of the mirror, Samantha arranged the spaghetti straps on her shoulders, pleased with the way it looked.

"Hair and makeup, here I come," Bethany sang, entering the room already dressed and ready. She carried two small toiletry cases. Samantha positioned herself in a chair next to the window for better lighting and closed her eyes so Bethany could apply foundation.

"You like him, don't you?" Bethany asked.

Samantha's eyelids popped open.

"Close, please," she ordered. "You don't need them to talk."

"Yes. I do."

"Yes, you need them to talk, or yes, you like him?"

Samantha breathed out her nose and mumbled with her lips closed, "Yes, I like him."

"Good. So do I."

"Me three." Jessica hollered from downstairs. Her screech rose from the wooden floors of the cabin. Samantha laughed.

"No laughing, still powdering."

"Does he have a big dick like his brother?" Jessica

shouted from below.

Samantha's eyes popped open as her jaw dropped. Bethany stood before her, gasping.

"Don't look so shocked. You know I'm a walking hormone," Jessica stated.

"How can you see us?" Samantha asked, perplexed.

"There's this nifty little hole in the floor."

Jessica was a terrible liar. "There is not."

"Okay, so there's not, but I know the look you two get." They could hear her heels walking off into another room. Bethany continued with her cosmetic artistry.

"That girl's a humdinger if I ever met one," Bethany stated. She brushed a thin layer of slate eye shadow on Samantha's upper lid.

"Uh-huh."

"Back to Dalton, I really like him for you. I mean, I can actually see you with him."

"Really?"

"Really," she said. "Open your eyes. I'm done."

Samantha hurried to the antiquated oval mirror. She smiled, seeing herself. Bethany had applied enough makeup but not too much. She still looked like herself but improved, her blue eyes standing out, her lips pouty and full. "Okay, now the hair." She returned to her seat and settled herself once again.

As Bethany worked her magic with several dozen bobby pins, Samantha's thoughts floated back to the cabin.

Their last night there Dalton had found a Scrabble game and they played for nearly five hours by the light of lanterns and firelight. Samantha was a diligent scorekeeper, determined not to let him cheat as first one and then the other of them took the lead. However, with the final round Dalton was the winner by a pathetic two-point lead, thanks to being able to tack the letter "y" onto the word "salt." *Hmph.* She'd show him "salty," if she ever had to cook for him again.

Oh, and the beans he cooked for her that evening had given her terrible gas, just as she'd feared. She couldn't remember the number of times she woke during the night to supposedly check on Beau's leg, check on Beau's water, and to "peek out" on Dolly.

Samantha had found sleeping next to Dalton was like having her own personal, giant heating pad. She kept her back spooned into his stomach to ease her backache and planted his warm hands on her belly to ease the menstrual cramping. Either he didn't notice or he didn't care, because he remained in that position until morning.

"Okay, one last pin and we are finished," Bethany said. Samantha's attention returned to the moment. She really wanted to look good. She practically bolted from the chair to the mirror.

"I love it, Beth," Samantha screamed. The look was messy and at the same time tidy. Her long tresses were knotted and twisted haphazardly into an informal bun while the front was pulled back loosely, allowing her part on the side to accent the natural waves in her mahogany hair.

Jessica entered the room five minutes after her perfume.

"Well, you sure smell good. You could be a walking advertisement for J-Lo," Bethany remarked.

"I just wanted to be sure Clay didn't have a hard time finding me amongst all the horse manure."

"Why? Is the party in the barn?" Samantha asked.

Jessica started to answer but was cut off by Bethany with a resounding thud to the floor from her spike-heeled foot. Bethany's eyes widened, warning Jessica to keep quiet.

Jessica sighed. "I can't say, Sam. They've sworn me to secrecy."

"They?" Samantha looked from Bethany to Jessica for answers.

All she got was shrugs.

"One thing I can say," Jessica said from her stance in the doorway, "is that you look smokin' hot! I mean, if I was lesbian, I'd do you. No questions asked."

Samantha choked. "Thanks. I think."

Their heeled shoes plunked down the stairs to the kitchen. Samantha suggested a round of apple shots before leaving. They toasted to their vacation, to Montana, and to never leaving.

Butterflies danced in Samantha as they stepped down the front porch and followed the trail leading from the cabin. She couldn't wait to see Dalton. She couldn't wait to dance with Dalton. She found herself not wanting to wait to do a lot of things with Dalton...

****

Dalton surveyed the small, private dining room. The French doors to the terrace were open, the fresh mountain wind wafting in. Candles, their flames pirouetting in glowing whirls, danced shadows on the wooden walls and elegant dinnerware gracing the cozy table for two. His matchmaking aunt had outdone herself. But he didn't care. He was too busy trying to discern if he was more excited about tonight or about the thought of Samantha spending the summer on the ranch.

John had informed him of his intentions to ask Samantha to remain on as a summer wrangler along with Jessica, who'd already accepted with a boisterous "Yes!"

"I see you got the memo about the party," Mary spoke, announcing her presence.

Dalton turned. She looked guilty beyond reason. "Yes. But I missed the part explaining the occasion."

She hooked her arm in his and led him down the hall to the kitchen. "It's quite simple, really. With the guests unable to ride and all the scary talk about mountain lions, I thought everyone could use a little pick-me-up." Then, in a whisper, "I think it's working. Haven't heard one gripe all day."

"And what about the guests who didn't bring the attire for a black-tie affair?"

"Don't worry, I've covered everything. We have quite a shindig scheduled in the barn loft. Dancing, music, food. The works."

He raised his brows in surprise. "Wow. You've been busy." He paused long enough to open a beer. "Only I heard a different version. I heard it was a welcoming home party—for Samantha and me."

"Well...it's for everyone, really. But I am awfully glad to have you back! How was it, anyway?"

"Wouldn't you like to know."

Her eager eyes told him she was dying to know.

"So is she as temperamental as her horse?" she joked.

"Yes and no. She has many sides to her, just like her horse."

"That's what I like about Samantha. You'd never get bored with her."

For once, he agreed with his aunt.

"I hear she nursed you back to health."

And then some. Beer spewed from his mouth, his thoughts in the gutter. Blotting himself with a hand towel, Dalton nodded. "She sure did."

"Do you think she'll stay on for the summer?"

Suddenly edgy, he shifted his eyes to the floor. "Think so."

"As in maybe not?"

"I think she can if she's able," he clarified. "Where is she, anyway?"

"In about five minutes she'll be in the terrace dining room, where you'll meet her and have a splendid dinner." She paused. "Thank you for bringing her back safely." Her tone was serious. "Here, give me this." She snatched his beer bottle and poured the liquor into a heavy, frosted mug then handed it to him. "No nephew of mine holds a tacky beer bottle while wearing a suit and tie."

"Thank you, and you're welcome." He kissed her on the cheek and turned to leave. "It was all my pleasure."

****

Samantha sat at a dinner table fit for a queen. Delicate china and polished silverware decorated the white linen tablecloth sprinkled with rose petals. Suddenly too nervous to sit, she moseyed to the veranda, through the double entrance doors. Looking over the balcony to the first story of the lodge's other wing, Samantha was able to see through the ballroom's long windows to where guests danced and mingled. When the door to the ballroom opened, she could hear classical music playing. Was that Minus dressed to the hilt in a white suit? He looked good, his long dark hair loose and flowing. She giggled, seeing him attempt a waltz with Bethany.

Samantha turned, but not in time to see Dalton's approach. His lips met hers, his tongue dipping inside her mouth, his large hands roaming the curves of her body through her thin dress. She closed her eyes and basked in the familiarity of his touch. He pulled away and looked at her.

"You're beautiful. Absolutely stunning. The back of this dress makes me want to take it off." He spun her for another visual.

"You don't look half bad yourself." His black suit molded against his lean body. A Marlboro man turned Chippendale. "I love the silver tie. It suits you."

"Why?" he asked, kissing her bare neck. His warm breath made her shiver.

"Because your eyes are the color of graphite." Flustered, she described her thoughts with hand gestures. "It matches your intimidating appearance. And I can't believe I just told you that." Yep, definitely nervous. She could feel her armpits perspiring.

Dalton chuckled. "Why?"

Samantha shrugged. "I don't know. Because I don't normally tell people what I'm thinking."

"So I've observed." Behind them, the door inched open and waiters entered carrying covered, delicious-smelling trays of food. "Let's eat," Dalton said, giving her his arm. Samantha figured this was his way of being formal, not letting the staff know they were so informally acquainted.

The three-course meal flew by. Samantha ate like it was a buffet low on food. Thank God beans were nowhere in sight. Her favorite was the peanut-cilantro-glazed chicken. She decided she might have to sneak into the kitchen later tonight for another round. Relaxing into the high-back chair, she considered her next comment.

"Would you say the asparagus was a bit *salt-y*?" She spoke like a complete smartass.

A deep laugh blurted from him. "Good one. No."

John and Mary entered just in time to hear them chortling.

"How was everything?" Mary asked, smiling.

Samantha returned the smile. "Perfect, thank you." She rose and straightened her dress.

"It's good to have you back, Samantha. We appreciate all you did. We hope you know that," John stated.

Samantha nodded. "No problem. It was actually kind of fun."

"Good, because I have a proposal for you."

Samantha looked from John to Dalton to Mary,

noting their untroubled expressions. Dalton and Mary excused themselves through the double doors, both of them smiling. Dalton winked.

"Please, sit," John suggested. He sat in Dalton's empty chair.

Sitting, Samantha crossed her legs and folded her hands in her lap. She'd been in the principal's office once as a child, for slapping a playground bully after he'd de-winged a butterfly. She felt the same way now.

"Jessica tells me you're quite taken with the ranch."

And your nephew. But she wasn't about to go there. "Yes, I'm loving it." *And your nephew.* Wow, did she actually think that? *Focus, girl.*

"If I said we are in need of two extra ranch hands this summer, would you be interested?"

Okay, try to control the width of your smile. "Yes," she blurted. Oh, my God, she would have two more months in Montana. With Dalton. A dream come true.

"Great. You're hired." John stood. "Tomorrow you and Jessica can fill out the paperwork."

"I need to let my parents know," she said.

"Of course. Will it be a problem?"

"Shouldn't be." After all, they didn't care too much if she worked. Only if she married—who they wanted.

"There's a phone down the hall, past the lounge." He opened the door for her.

Samantha dashed for the phone, mindless of the group of people in the lounge. She hoped her parents wouldn't mind. It was customary for them to spend their summer traveling, doing something political in nature. Her grandfather would be the one missing her. She'd have to ask the stable boys to fill in for her in the flower garden. She loved helping her grandfather tend his rare varieties of flowers.

She dialed the number on the cordless phone and waited for the butler to answer. She bit her lip anxiously.

"Matthews Estate, may I be of assistance?" Smitty mocked in an English tone.

"Hey, Smitty, it's Sam."

"Hi, Sam," he said, his voice turned normal and affectionate. "How's your vacation?"

Samantha could feel her face burning. "Wonderful."

She talked fast. "They've asked me to stay and work for the summer. Are my parents home?"

She heard him sigh.

"No, they're in Washington, at a conference. But I can forward the message to them. You know they aren't going to like this." The more he talked, his gay tone accelerated. "That Richards boy has been hounding us about you. Says he can't wait for another date."

Samantha rolled her eyes. "Not happening." Across the room, she could see Dalton and his brother talking. Clay raised his beer in a toast to her. She smiled in return. "Tell them I called and give them this number."

"Will do. Oh, and Sam, are there any hot cowboys in Montana?"

"Oh, like you wouldn't believe."

He gasped. "Wow! Okay, tootles."

"Bye." She glanced around for the bathroom. She needed to re-coop. Her thoughts were scattered somewhere between right brain and left brain, in whatever part of the mind sheltered rattled impulses.

In the bathroom, she sat on the sidesaddle prop. However old, it was still authentic. She let her legs dangle out of the stirrups.

She was flabbergasted, to say the least. The thought of spending an entire summer at Twin Rivers was amazing. Jessica and she would have the time of their lives. Of course, Bethany would go home, having Brad to get back to. *Wow*. The notion was still sinking in.

The door to the bathroom burst open. Jessica bounced in. Samantha could see Dalton in the lobby. "Now you see why they made me keep it a secret?" she squealed.

Samantha hopped off the saddle and hugged her friend. "I'm so happy I could scream."

"Scream, then."

"No, they'll think I'm a crazed lunatic."

"No, they'll think that if I scream," Jessica mused. "What'd your parents say?"

"Nothing. They weren't home."

"Good. You're in the clear."

"Jess, I'd stay even if they wouldn't let me. I love this place," she confessed.

They both tidied their hair in the mirror under deer-antler lighting. "I say we have a round of shots!" Jessica said, turning for the door.

Samantha agreed. They needed to celebrate.

The group of guests moved into the ballroom. Samantha spotted Dalton and Clay heads above everyone. Dalton was immersed in a conversation with an elderly couple.

"Sam! Here's your shot." Bethany handed her a full-sized drinking glass.

"What? I can't drink all this."

"I know, it's huge. Young Jasper made it for you. He's behind the bar. He told me to tell you congratulations."

Both girls turned to look at their bartender. He picked up his drink and saluted to them, guzzling the clear liquid. Now it was their turn.

What the heck. She'd eaten a big dinner. If she didn't drink anything else, she should be okay. With Jessica and Clay joining them, they counted, "One, two, three," before swinging their heads back and gulping.

"Wow. My ears are already burning." Samantha placed her empty glass on the table behind her. She suddenly felt like dancing. Dalton was still engaged in intense conversation, but Minus was available, hanging out by the patio doors. She caught his eye and suggested they move to the dance floor. He nodded in agreement.

"I'll see you guys later. Minus and I are going to dance."

"Where's Dalton?" Bethany asked, scanning the room.

Clay heard Bethany's question and answered. "He's talking to our neighbors. Ranching stuff."

"Sounds lengthy," was her reply as Samantha veered through the crowd to meet Minus, pleased to hear the opening chords of a familiar melody. Minus twirled and dipped her to the music and Samantha laughed throughout the song, trying to keep up with him. Several times she looked Dalton's way. Once she caught his attention and he grinned. The rest of the time he remained focused on his conversation.

Samantha ended up dancing with everyone but Dalton. She even danced a samba with Bethany, who did actually know how to dance. Samantha merely followed Bethany's motions, stomping on her friend's toes at least a dozen times.

"One more drink?" Young Jasper asked, as she and Minus sat resting at the bar.

Not a good idea. "Sure. One more."

She should have said, *Easy on the liquor*. The orange-colored drink he handed her was God-awful. If this was his version of Sex-on-the-Beach, then she didn't want to imagine what Sex-in-Handcuffs would be like. But, not wanting to offend the pint-sized wrangler, she took several sips.

When Young Jasper moved to the opposite end of the bar, Samantha leaned over and asked Minus, "If you had one proverb to tell me, what would it be?"

Surprisingly, he answered her fast. "Bad love hurts good. Good love hurts bad. Great love hurts... forever."

"Then why would anyone—"

"Great love is meant to be. No amount of time can change that."

But he didn't answer her question—or did he? She was confused. She needed some fresh air. Her head was spinning. "I'm going outside to ponder, Minus. Thank you."

It might just have been the cold mountain air, but chills crawled up her spine. Something clicked in her head. Fern had said something about the lines in her palms running deep. *Later in life*—that's what she had said. Fern had seen twins and a river later in life, and Minus had just now mentioned time. None of it made sense to her.

"I'm heading to the barn to check on the horses. Want to come?" she heard a male voice ask.

Young Jasper.

He blew a perfect donut in the air with his cigarette smoke, something only sly men in the movies did.

Beau needed to be checked on, she realized. She'd better see to him before her drink saw to her. "Sure."

Young Jasper held the lantern as they walked. Waiters and waitresses passed by with armfuls of silver trays and a cooler, cleaning up what was left from the celebrations in the loft. When they reached the barn, it was empty. Multiple lanterns still glowed near the back of the barn. Even drunk, she knew they should be collected.

She carefully retrieved two lanterns and watched her step as she neared Beau's stall. Wedge heels weren't practical in the barn. The last thing she needed was a twisted ankle to go along with her new job.

She cracked the door and peeked in on her horse. He stepped towards her and nosed her with a quiet whinny. "I don't have anything for you, buddy. I can't wear a bra with this dress." As a habit, Samantha almost always had a peppermint candy hidden in whatever brassiere she wore. The boulder holder functioned well for holding small items such as dainty sweets.

"Probably can't wear much at all with that dress, can you?" She heard Young Jasper's alleged question from behind her.

Samantha whipped the stall door closed and turned around slowly, giving her mind ample time to think of a reply—if only she were good with snappy comebacks. Which she wasn't. Why was he listening? And why would he remark even if he had heard?

Because she was drunk. Where was Dalton?

She laughed, and then shrugged. "Designers these days. The fabric just gets smaller and thinner. I'm sure your girlfriend knows how it is." Bad attempt to change the subject, but worth a try. She didn't want to appear frightened.

He took a step closer. He was inches from her. "No girlfriend. And I'd be willing to bet no panties, either."

How would he be privy to that? Even Dalton didn't know—yet. Samantha had zero tolerance for crude men. Zero. "That's none of your business," she hissed. Her eyes echoed the threat of her clenched jaw. She started to walk past him. His arm shot out, thwarting her.

"Not so fast." He spun her around and flattened her against Beau's stall. Samantha could smell the liquor on his breath. She was correct about his strength. He was puny but powerful. She slammed her palm in his chest, more offended than scared.

"Let me go or I'll scream."

"No, you won't. You'll enjoy it. Just like you did with Dalton." Again, he spoke Dalton's name with malice. He released one of her hands in order to hike her dress up, his coarse fingers creeping up her thigh. Behind her, Beau whinnied and kicked at the stall.

"You don't know what you're talking about. Now get off me!" Her seething words could have scalded ice cubes. She smacked at his hands, then his face. Almost the same height, she nailed him flat on the cheek.

Low mumbles broke the silence of the slap. Young Jasper jerked away and stomped towards the barn entrance. Samantha touched a hand to Beau through the stall door before springing to the far corner of the barn with her lantern. She didn't want anyone seeing or thinking anything untoward.

Finding the camouflaged entrance to the passageway obstructed by several barrels, Samantha squeezed past them and stepped into the dark corridor. Unsure which direction to go, she paused at the first T and took a left. She couldn't remember, but she thought they had turned that way before. Dalton had been carrying her, so her view was different.

The passageway was going uphill far too long to be the correct route. She came to a door and did her best version of a drunken karate chop. After several kicks, she tried using the door knob, which, of course, worked.

A musky straw smell tugged at her senses. The thatched cabin. The adorable structure she had seen on the mountainside when they first arrived at the ranch.

Inside, Samantha scanned the tranquil setting. A small bistro table for two sat in an antique kitchen. Past that, an enchanting fireside retreat welcomed visitors with plump cushions on a cozy sofa, part of a small parlor. Samantha fixated on the hand-hewn ladder leading upstairs. Carefully she climbed the steps to a small, attractive loft.

Samantha removed her dusty heels and flopped on the double bed, the sloped ceiling above her like a blanket, relaxing her. She decided to think happy thoughts, happy drunken thoughts of Dalton and herself and how they would spend the summer. She wouldn't tell him about Jasper and his harassment. Young Jasper had been drunk, nothing more. Come morning, everything would be better.

Chapter Twelve

Finding Samantha had been easy. Dolly had led the way, having sat for God knows how long guarding the passageway entrance. Good dog. Heeled shoes had left obvious tracks also. She had gotten lost at the T. Otherwise she would have made it to her cabin, although it didn't make sense why she would have used the hidden tunnel. That he'd intended to scold her for but had been unable to do so.

He wasn't about to reprimand a passed-out angel sprawled on the bed. He had undressed her and put her to bed. Which made this morning all the more difficult. Sitting in the church pew, just inches from her, he retraced last night, unclothing her once again in his mind.

He'd inched the spaghetti straps off her arms and scooted the silken fabric down her breast and hips, inhaling at the sight of the auburn strip of hair at the cuneiform of her legs, a perfect arrowhead mapping his ultimate destination. And, as requested, no panties to hinder the delectable view.

After kissing her from head to toe, he nestled his body next to hers, inhaling her sweet fragrance of honeysuckle in the springtime, ripe and fresh and untainted. He was falling for her and there wasn't a thing he could do about it. He was toast.

She moved now in the pew in front of him, uncrossing and re-crossing her legs, her shoulders squared, moving with the rhythmic movement of a nervous foot. He could smell her from where he sat. Her hair, the coconut soap she used, the watermelon bubblegum she was trying not to chew, her every gesture and breath teased him.

He was about to go fucking nuts.

Purposely he scratched his nose so he could smell her on his fingers. The fore and middle fingers, the two he'd had deep inside her just an hour ago, before they were awakened by church bells, held the most scent, a rich, sexy aroma. He had satisfied her with his hands, and now he wanted to do so with the rest of him. The bulge in his jeans reared, armed and ready.

"Amen," announced Dalton, along with the congregation. Amen. He needed to focus. He took his time standing as the guests and wranglers exited the chapel.

Outside the chantry, Dalton convened with several surrounding ranchers in an informal meeting about the persistent mountain lion assaults. Another attack had occurred on a ranch south of Twin Rivers.

"It happened the night before last," Rex Childs spoke. "Almost took the hind leg off my Angus bull."

Dalton asked Dr. Beard, "Was the wound similar, Doc?"

"Identical, just deeper."

"And you're sure an animal is doing this?" John asked. His question had the group looking at each other.

The veterinarian answered carefully. "I can't say that for sure, no."

"Heck, we've never had anything crooked happen in these parts. I say it's a cat," Mark Turner spoke. "What's your opinion, Dalton? You and Clay are the ones with the fancy degrees. What's your take on it?"

Turner didn't know his ass from a hole in the wall—that was his take on it. "I think we need to keep our eyes open." He paused. "And not rule out mischief at this point."

Grunts and mumbles followed his statement.

The group departed with each rancher promising to keep a keen eye out for deceptive and misleading conduct, especially those with guests and new employees. Dalton and Clay headed to the bar for the ritual of post-church beer.

"Decide against sharing the evidence?" Clay raised a brow with his question.

"What evidence? All we have is a broken recording device, washed clean of fingerprints, found next to some welded barbed wire. Nothing that couldn't have fallen out of a guest's pocket."

"What did Old Man Crouse have to say last night?" Clay was smart enough to change the topic.

Dalton grumbled. "That he's thinking." Jim Crouse

owned the property west of Twin Rivers and was retiring from ranching, wanting to move to Florida with his wife and lead the good life in his easy years. None of his kids were interested in ranching, so the place was soon to be on the market. Dalton's intentions were to buy it outright, saving himself and Crouse some money. However, the old man was being stubborn.

"Well, is he thinking with his head or his ass?" his brother asked.

"The latter. There's no way I can afford the price he shot me. I've got a loan, not a winning lottery ticket." But the old man was hankering to get away and Dalton knew it. The ranch's massage therapist, Rhonda, a large, stout lady who had been at Twin Rivers for a decade, was a good friend of Jim's wife and had spilled the beans. Come fall when the weather turned, Dalton suspected Crouse would change his mind and lower his price. Or so he hoped.

"Soon you'll have a ranch. Then all you'll need is a wife," Clay noted. He zigzagged away from Dalton, ready for a brotherly blow.

"Yep."

Clay's head twisted on his neck. "What? You've seen the light?"

"I've seen chestnut."

"So it went good on top, then, eh?"

A deep chuckle escaped Dalton. They were almost to the spa where Samantha had a massage scheduled, compliments of Mary. "As a matter of fact, it did."

"Aunt Mary is going to love hearing this. She spotted Jessica and me behind the barn and gave me an earful about indiscretion. She said that's what the empty cabins are for." Clay laughed.

"As long as it's not the thatched."

"Nah, we've been using the chapel. No one's ever there, and the Bible stand is just the right height." His hands and pelvic motion insinuated grinding.

Dalton wasn't surprised. His brother was a hound.

"Yep, already baptized the kid," Clay said. He opened the door to the saloon.

Most of the wranglers were present, clustered around the bar, each getting the one beer allowed them before work on Thursdays. John had bargained with them. If they went to church, they got a beer.

"Howdy, gentlemen," Dalton said, taking a seat. "How we feeling this morning?"

"Exactly how we look," Old Jasper responded.

They looked like hell.

Josh answered, "It's open-bar syndrome. Jasper served us well."

Dalton eyed the iPod the kid toyed with. He called him an iPod specialist because he was constantly riding Mary about using the computer to download songs, saying he couldn't sit a horse as well if he didn't have music sounding in his ears. Maybe the contraption in the field belonged to the kid and was completely harmless.

"Where is Jasper?" Dalton asked. They needed to get started branding.

Jasper's father spoke. "He'll be back soon. He went into town to get a part for his truck. Blowing smoke again."

"Wasn't he just in town for that?" Clay questioned.

Old Jasper grumbled. "Yep. Tried telling him not to buy that heap."

Dalton refrained from commenting. The wranglers knew how he felt about leaving the ranch during the week to drive an hour into town for something. John must have okayed it in his absence.

"Minus at church?" Dalton asked. It was usual for his Indian friend to attend his own form of worship while everyone else gathered at the chapel.

"No," Josh answered with a grin. "He's outside with Samantha. Talking."

Dalton stood from his bar stool and moved to peer out the window. "Hmm. All these years I thought he didn't care to talk."

The men chuckled.

"Apparently he doesn't. Least not to us," Old Jasper stated.

"Maybe it's because we don't have red hair," Clay commented.

Dalton got the hint. He darted a warning look in his brother's direction. He placed his straw hat on his head and left the saloon, but Samantha entered the spa before

Dalton could cross the road.

Minus walked to meet him. "Morning, friend," Dalton greeted. Today, he half expected his Indian friend to answer. But he didn't.

"She's pretty great, isn't she?" Dalton asked.

"Indian keep eyes open and mouth shut. Indian keep wife."

Wife was a strong word for Minus to use. Two days ago Dalton would have flinched at the implication. Now he smiled and nodded. "Yes, sir. Will do." Dalton thumped him on the shoulder. He could see Samantha in the massage room through the window, the curtain not yet pulled.

From the hall, Dalton listened as Rhonda, the masseuse, readied the room, instructing Samantha to undress and lay face down on the padded table and to cover herself with a thin sheet. The curtains were drawn and a scented candle burned in the corner. Organic sounds of nature played from a CD.

"I'll be back in a few," he heard Rhonda say.

Dalton entered the tranquil room a moment later, humming under his breath, but Samantha had no clue. He eased back the sheet, mitering the fold across her lower back and under her upper thigh. Aware of his weathered hands, he squirted on plenty of soothing oil.

He began massaging her back, remembering the way it had looked last night in the sexy black dress. His hands toyed with her butt, creeping further and further down her backside with each soothing stroke. Therapists often rubbed the gluteus. No surprise there.

Dalton worked his fingers along her spine and shoulders, kneading and pinching the toned muscle of her back. He smiled wickedly every time the tips of his fingers grazed the sides of her breast. His thumbs skimmed her nipples and he felt her go stiff, saw her toes fist protectively. Now there was a spot no good technician dared to go. He repeated the move, this time pausing on the nipple.

She sprang up like a jack-in-the-box.

"Thanks, that'll be—you!" She screeched with relief, wrapping her arms around him. "I was getting worried. I thought big Rhonda had a thing for me." She laughed softly into his ear.

He shushed her with his lips. He pulled back and brushed the hair off her face. "I had to see you." His gaze drifted to her exposed breasts. "And them." Hard, pink nipples pointed to him.

"And what about her?" Samantha asked, placing his hand between her legs. She smiled suggestively.

"I have plans for her...tonight." He saw her eyes grow big. "There's a pool party tonight. Thirty minutes into it, meet me at the tunnel entrance. Say you're tired and want to get some extra sleep."

"Won't I be seeing you today?"

He kissed her. "Of course, but not alone." He could tell she had a question.

"Does anyone know?"

He caught her meaning. "Clay does, but he won't say a word. Minus knows. He knows everything. Why?" He noted her concerned expression.

She stuttered, started to say something, and then stopped.

"What?"

"Nothing." She smiled and kissed him.

Dalton returned the kiss, full on the lips, slow and soft, just as she liked. "I better get," he grudgingly said. "I'll see you later. Enjoy the massage." He walked to the door.

"Don't worry, I will."

Her comment gave him pause. He turned to find her naked, the sheet flung to the side. His eyes soaked in the sight of her feminine curves. Propped on her side with sexy, auburn long hair disheveled and loose down her back, she let his eyes rake the hourglass curvature of her small waist. Softly tanned skin hugged petite hips. Velvety pink nipples he knew from just this morning begged his attention.

Dalton grunted and closed the door despite his much engorged counterpart.

****

"The massage was wonderful. Thank you, Mary." Samantha plopped down on one of the many loungers next to the pool. Mary stooped near the edge, testing the water for chlorine.

"You're welcome. It's the least I could do."

Samantha relaxed into the rubbery chaise. "But I have to admit, I don't know what kind of worker I'll be today. My muscles feel like mush and my brain's a fried zucchini."

Mary laughed, her smile warm and sincere.

Samantha felt at home with Mary. She reminded Samantha of the beloved grandmother she still missed every day. They both had eyes that nearly squinted shut when they laughed and a natural oozing generosity, making everyone around them feel at ease. "You're like my grandma, Mary."

"Except twenty years younger, right?" Mary winked, monitoring her water samples.

"Oh, yes, although she's passed on."

Mary frowned. "I'm sorry. How long has it been?"

"Four years. I had just started nursing school." An image of her grandmother, lying weak and frail in bed, invaded her mind. She could see the bandages on the amputated legs. The smell of gangrene burned in her nose.

"What from?"

Samantha sighed. "Complications of diabetes, bad kidneys, and a bad heart."

"Did that make nursing school easier or harder for you?"

Samantha sighed. "She made it easy for me. She was my own personal textbook. With so many things wrong, I had only to look to her for answers." She paused and shook her head. "She was so regal, my grandmother. Until they took her legs, she had kept her ill health a secret from all but the staff in the east wing." Samantha knew she had revealed more than she should. She shouldn't have mentioned the east wing, but in a way she wanted Mary to know her affluent background. She pressed on. "She used to say that being a nurse would buy me freedom." With her grandmother's passing, Samantha had understood the words.

"Freedom's a liberty that comes in different forms. Sooner or later, we all fight to get it."

Mary's sentence hung in the air before she continued. "It's odd, all this nurse talk, because John and I were just discussing the need for one. Being this far out, it would be handy to have one." Mary added chlorine tabs to the filter, then joined Samantha, taking a lounge chair next to her. "Not a full-time one, by any means, but a person with a degree, who could lend a qualified hand when a guest needs a blood pressure check or insulin coverage." Mary cocked a brow in her direction. "Interested?"

Samantha propped the back of her chaise so she could sit up. She flipped her long hair over her shoulder. "Does the position come with a jazzy nametag saying Ranch RN?" She giggled.

"It can if you want it to."

"Then sign me up."

"Sign her up for what?" Jessica asked, staggering around the corner. She swayed in her black sunglasses and hot pink bikini before taking a lolling position near the pool.

Samantha took one look at her friend and laughed. "Head hurt much?"

"I feel like death."

Mary chuckled and stood. "I have a cure for that."

"You do?" moaned Jessica. "Because I'll take it—whatever it is."

"I'll go get it." Mary headed off in the direction of the kitchen, leaving Samantha to explain the nursing position she'd just been offered.

Jessica nosed her sunglasses down her face. "Nursing job? I thought we were wranglers."

"We are. This is just an additional side duty."

"By the way, darling, where'd you go last night?" Jessica snooped. "I promised your parents I'd keep an eye on you, ya know."

Samantha exhaled. She wanted to tell Jessica about Young Jasper. She also wanted to tell Mary. But she didn't want to ruin the perfect flow of everything. "I was with a dashing cattleman named Dalton MacLaine."

"Hah! I knew it. I just knew it." She waved her hands as she spoke. "You two make the perfect couple. It's like I told Beth, there's no way the two of you could get trapped in a secluded cabin, in the middle of a rainstorm, and something not come out of it."

Samantha shushed her friend and took a seat next to

her by the pool. Wearing shorts, she kicked off her orange flip-flops and dunked her legs in the water. "That's exactly what I don't want everyone to think."

"Oh, Sam, stop worrying so much about what everyone thinks. You're not at home, for all to ostracize you." She removed her sunglasses. "You've spent your whole life doing what others wanted you to do. Now do something for yourself. Do Dalton!"

Samantha gasped, but only because that's what she intended to do. She had pondered all morning long about sleeping with him. She'd taken Jessica's advice at the party last night and teased him terribly this morning, only to find it backfired, making her want him more.

"He wants you bad. He couldn't take his eyes off you in church," her friend confided. "Does he kiss good? Clay can kiss like the devil."

"Real good," Samantha gossiped. "He gets this steamy Matt Damon look on his face—like he just can't get enough."

Jessica grunted. "Yep, definitely brothers."

"Okay, she's coming," Samantha said, seeing Mary on her way down the stone path to the flowered pool garden. "Let's shut up. I'd rather her not know our intentions to sleep with her nephews all summer long."

Jessica chuckled. "Intentions? Honey, I already have."

Chapter Thirteen

Samantha relaxed in the bathhouse after a long day of branding. She found herself feeling a tad bit lonely, hoping Dalton would pop in unexpectedly. But she knew he was busy. A group of riders had trailered their horses to him for a quick clinic on colt starting. She'd heard John say it was a last-minute decision. The riders had practically begged John for Dalton's assistance. Several of the wranglers had whispered the guests were filthy rich and lacked understanding of the word "No."

But she wasn't worried. After watching him hold down calves all day, he still had found time to cast a certain look her way.

Her job had been roping. She'd branded one calf and then decided to let the guests do the dirty work. Something about singeing hair just didn't sit well with her olfactory senses.

She roped off of Mary's older mare, to allow Beau a day of rest. The colossal palomino had the heart of a giant, dragging cows to the fire like it was play work.

She smiled as she thought of Little Luke losing his bandana in the mud. His dad had been helping him hold the iron when suddenly the calf's feet jerked and Luke had stumbled backward, losing the bandana in the fall. Samantha took hers off and intentionally flung it in the mud, to make him feel better, but then just as she dismounted to retrieve it, a cow plodded along and defecated on it.

Luke had been brave enough to put his back on, so she'd done the same, though the stink had really gotten to her. "Better cow than pig," she'd told him, but she was thankful the branding had been about over for the day.

So now she soaked, bathing off the pungent manure odor. Cow crap was the last thing she wanted to be reminded of on the night she said goodbye to her virginity. She wondered what Dalton had in store for them tonight.

Reluctantly, she pushed herself up out the water and wrapped herself in her robe, remembering she had to share the bathing suite with a dozen or so guests.

She and Dolly tramped their way back to the cabin, where the dog flopped on the front porch step while Samantha went on inside, letting the screen door slam behind her.

Seated on the couch, Jessica and Bethany turned to stare at the sound.

Samantha laughed and grinned. "I love it when it does that. I feel like I'm back at camp."

Bethany nodded. "Yeah, it does sound like that, doesn't it? I'm going to miss it when I leave."

Samantha placed her toiletry bag on the loft stairs and joined her friends. "It's not going to be the same without you, Beth. Please say you'll stay. There's no telling what kind of trouble Jess and I will get into, without you around."

"Oh, I have a feeling Dalton will look after you."

"He better," Jessica snapped. "Or he'll have me to answer to."

"When's your flight?" Samantha asked.

"Brad booked the redeye for Saturday night."

Samantha grimaced. "Only one more day."

"That's twenty-four hours of commotion left to create," Jessica joked. "So, go get your suits and let's party like its 1999." She snapped her fingers and did her mock impression of an airline attendant, guiding them to their rooms.

Bethany rolled her eyes. "Goodbye, Willy. Hello, Prince."

Samantha's footsteps drummed on the wooden stairs. She made her way to the loft but not before sneaking a peek at Jessica, who was now doing her best reenactment of a Bond girl, her hands clasped together for a makeshift gun, the corner entrance wall her shield as she stood with her back plastered against it. "Give it up," Samantha taunted. "You didn't make that audition. They said you were more suited for the role of the villain."

"Hey," Jessica snapped. "It's villainess. And don't you forget!"

Samantha giggled loudly at the top of the stairs. She couldn't help herself. Jessica really had auditioned for the fiery role of Bond girl Chantilly Lace several years ago, on a summer vacation to California. Gosh, how she loved her friends. She never knew what to expect next.

****

"Wow. That's the kind of pool your momma taught you not to pee in," Jessica exclaimed as all three of them entered the pool area and then stood shell-shocked to see the transformation that had taken place.

What once was an elaborate L-shaped pool in the middle of a forest-like garden was now a reception area fit for a celebrity. Thousands of flowers flooded the poolside in shades of deep reds and purples, while floating candles bumped and swayed on the water.

Samantha cleared her throat. "So, Jess, does that mean you peed in the pool this morning?"

"Pretty much."

"Good evening, ladies," Clay announced. He carried drinks for all three of them, the stems laced between his fingers. "How are we this evening? Not yet peeing in the pool, I presume."

Samantha and Bethany broke out laughing.

"Good for you, Clay. Jessica needs someone who can call her out."

"Shut up, Sam."

Samantha glanced around for Dalton but didn't see him. Mary wasn't visible, either. They were probably busy entertaining guests.

"Mary really knows how to decorate, doesn't she?" Samantha asked, looking around. Trees lining the garden were strung with white lights. Flowered centerpieces with the ranch logo inserted into their design decorated the tables. A game of horseshoes was taking place near the tennis courts. The smell of fresh flowers and evergreen floated in the breeze.

"Yeah, it's kind of her trademark. She loves surprising the guests. I think she went a little overboard with this one, but she feels compelled, since the mountain lion threats canceled most of the riding."

"When do the new guests arrive?" Samantha asked.

"On Sunday. Current guests will leave Saturday

morning. Gives us time to reboot."

She and Jessica would have to get all this down pat. But for now, it sounded simple enough. "Beth, let's tour the grounds." Samantha could see Clay wanted to be alone with Jessica. He was starting to get that Matt Damon look in his eye.

"Let's," Bethany responded.

Nerves surged in Samantha. She mentally stopped to consider how she looked. She wore her hair loose, in long natural waves. She'd kept her makeup simple and casual enough for a poolside affair. The pastel yellow summer suit she wore with a matching bikini underneath was the perfect complement to a backyard occasion such as this. The jacket had one front button, allowing a hint of cleavage and a snippet of abdomen to show. Everything was perfect, everything felt perfect—everything except Young Jasper, who had just arrived.

With her arm hooked in Bethany's, Samantha veered them the opposite direction.

"What the—?" Bethany started to say.

"Let's go powder our noses."

Bethany bunched her nose. "What? I've never know you to powder your…"

"Sam," Jasper said, politely tugging her free arm. "I wanted to apologize for last night. I was rude. I'm sorry."

Samantha noted Bethany's surprised glance at her as they turned to face him.

"I had way too much to drink. I mixed my own, and it just went downhill from there." His crooked-tooth smile was genuine and his words sincere. The last thing Samantha wanted was to spend her summer disliking someone.

"Apology accepted. Thank you."

"Have a nice night." He strode off toward the pool.

Whew. She felt she could breathe again. Thank God that was over with.

"What exactly was that about?" Bethany quizzed.

"Nothing, I think." Oh, she might as well explain. Bethany wasn't going to let her get by without. "He was really drunk and came on to me in the barn last night. Kind of spooked me a little." Yeah, right, a little?

Bethany looked appalled. Her jaw dropped, inches

from touching her Harry Winston couture diamond necklace. "He did what? Does Dalton know?"

"No, and I'm not about to tell him." Samantha led them toward the cake table, where the layered chocolate and vanilla slices were being served. They each collected a plate and fork and took a seat at the edge of the garden, the pool in sight. "Everything is going so great, I don't want to spoil it."

"Fine. But I think you should. Stuff like this comes back to haunt you."

"I don't know how it can. I didn't do anything wrong." She took a bite of the cake and dismissed the memory of Jasper. It was like he said. He'd been drunk, was all. Now that he had apologized and cleared the air, the summer could roll on.

"Are you gonna see Dalton tonight?" Bethany hinted, her smile returning.

Just as Bethany spoke, Sam recognized Dalton's broad back in the crowd. He was wearing a simple navy T-shirt with swim trunks. The muscles in his arms crimped when he handed Luke a plate of cake and ice cream. "Could you imagine walking down the aisle one day to marry a man like that?"

"No. But I bet you can."

Dalton studied his watch, then turned his head in their direction.

"Does that mean what I think it means?" Bethany inquired.

Samantha beamed, biting her lower lip. "Thirty minutes."

****

Samantha stood before the fire, her back turned to him, reminiscent of the first time he saw her. Only this time she was dressed and wore a beautiful smile, reflected in the picture frame on the mantel. She was nervous, he could tell. He strode toward her and wrapped his arms around her waist, the whole world falling away.

"How much have you had to drink, princess?" he asked over her shoulder.

She chuckled, holding her wine glass. "Not enough." She turned to face him.

His hands moved to cradle her heart-shaped face.

"Scratch my plans. Nothing has to happen." Deep blue eyes regarded him as she considered his words.

"It's not that." She shrugged and bit her lip. "Well, maybe a little." He watched her scan the room. "It's just that I've never had anyone do something like this for me."

He loved watching her facial expressions, changing from one moment to the next. She had the uncanny ability to keep him on his toes.

"Exactly how many flowers are in this room, anyway?" she asked, her eyes searching, looking anywhere but at him.

"Samantha."

That got her attention. He rarely used her name when they were together. "You have no reason to fear me. So stop." He bear-hugged her, picking her off the floor.

When he set her back down, she sighed, her shoulders relaxing.

"Don't worry, if we get bored, there's always Scrabble." He laughed.

"I don't think so. You might find the room to be flower-y, or coz-y."

"Now, now. Nothing fun about a sore loser, princess."

"Shut up." She shoved at his chest.

He yanked her right back into him and kissed her sweet mouth. Everything about her was sweet—her smile, her composure, her voice and movements. He loved every inch of her. She was everything to him.

He ended the kiss and looked at her, seeing the woman before him. A woman he'd dreamed about, a woman similar to his mother, genuine and caring, maternal. Whisking her off her feet, he carried her to the plump sofa and placed her comfortably on him, Indian style, with her feet behind his back.

At first, they said nothing, enjoying the moment.

"I missed you today," he told her.

She blinked. "You did?"

"Yeah." He held her hands in his. "I could see you but I couldn't touch you."

"Touch me now." She placed his palms on her breasts. He grunted. With steamy, seductive eyes, she leaned forward to kiss him.

Kissing her, he unbuttoned her jacket, savoring every

minute. He loosened the ties on her swim suit top and flung the items on the chair next to the couch. Naked breasts and hardened nipples had a dangerous effect on him. He brushed the ends of her silky hair over her shoulder and kissed the creamy mounds of flesh, trailing wet paths to the hardened, pink blossoms. "Hop up," he said, patting her bottom. He unfastened her pants and suit bottoms, letting her step out of them. To his surprise, she reached for his waistband and tugged off his trunks.

"Are you sure, princess?"

She stopped and stared at him, seeming to know what he felt inside. "Yes."

With her sitting once again in his lap, he simply looked at her, reveling in every drop of life she breathed into him. He scoured her delectable body with his eyes. "God, you're beautiful." He guided her onto her back, the weight of his body holding her small form captive beneath him. Her body was a perfect match under his, her skin soft and fresh.

His fingers skimmed her silky thigh to feel her. She was wet, sex seeping from between her legs. His fingers played inside of her, teasing her. Again he saw the artistic shaving job pointing him in the direction he desired most. A lazy smile escaped him.

She giggled, a slow, deep chuckle he loved hearing.

"You're sexy when you get that look."

"What look?"

"That come-hither, do-me look."

He silenced her with his hands and mouth, both of them serenading her, engaging her, pausing only to keep her from climax. He wanted to be inside of her when she came, an aphrodisiac to numb the pain. Settling on top of her, he returned her devilish smile. She was no longer afraid.

The feel of him easing into her was sinful. Kissing her, his mouth never left hers as his tongue guided his lower movements. He rocked with her, inching further and deeper into her tight body with each gentle thrust. It had been too long for him. Yet he forced himself to move slowly, to give her time, wanting her to relish every moment. He craved fulfillment, but he waited. She was first.

Fully embedded, he felt her squeeze him with grinding motions. Bucking, her heels dug into his back. The rhythmic movement was slick from her juices. "Dalton," she whimpered, reaching orgasm. The words drove him home and he exploded inside of her, his heart pounding in satisfaction.

With one movement, he rolled her so she was on top. He was still inside her, their bodies connected on both physical and mental levels. She collapsed on his chest with a sigh.

Some time during the night, he awakened to the sound of a vociferously rumbling stomach.

"I'm starving."

He laughed. "I heard. Don't worry, I thought of that, too." At the last moment, he'd snatched two pieces of cake before heading to the barn to meet her.

He went naked to the kitchen, rounded up the cake, two forks and the last of the wine and returned to the couch to find her in his T-shirt. The long flowing locks of reddish hair he was accustomed to seeing loose around her shoulders were ruffled and messy, like a lion's mane. He loved it.

"Here you go, Tiger."

"Hey," she snapped, "if the hair's messy, it's your doing." She grinned.

He laughed. "It's okay. I hear the eighties are coming back."

"Shut up."

They devoured their cake.

"So, tell me, what's your future dream ranch like?"

He coughed. "Well, I don't know if dream is the right adjective, but, future, yes."

"Will it be a guest ranch, like this one?" she asked. She plumped the cushions behind their backs and grabbed a blanket before nestling beside him.

"No, I think I'll let John and Mary corner the market on that. It'll be a pure cattle operation. Big. A hundred thousand acres, if I can buy it all." There, he had pretty much told her he didn't have the money. He knew Samantha wasn't poor. Everything about her reeked of money. The way she dressed, her actions, the proper dialogue and pronunciation of words she attempted to distort. But Samantha wasn't like the rich bitches who normally visited the ranch. She had depth, brains, and beauty.

"I bet it'll be fantastic." She was imagining it. He could see her creative mind working. "Just be sure to remember your old friends from back when, and know that this one wants a guest room with a king-size canopy bed, close to the kitchen, with all white linens."

"Close to the kitchen?"

"Yeah, for midnight snacks like we just had. That way I can't get lost."

He chuckled. "All right, then. I won't forget."

"Dalton?"

"What?" He'd almost fallen asleep.

"I have to pee."

Chapter Fourteen

The weeks sped by. Looking at the calendar in Mary's office, Samantha couldn't believe it had been three weeks since they had taken Bethany to the airport. It seemed like just yesterday

"Out of town?" It was the third time she had attempted to reach her parents in two weeks. "Okay. Tell them I'll try back in a few days."

"Will do," Smitty replied.

Samantha hung up the phone. She glanced down at Dolly, who was sitting at her feet. "Can't say we didn't try."

Mary rounded the corner, biting her nails.

"Hey, Mary." Samantha jerked, surprised.

"Hi, Sam. Didn't know you were in here. I thought you were riding this morning."

"Oh, I am. Beau's saddled up and ready. A few of the guests were running late, so I thought I'd try calling my parents real fast." She noted Mary's jitteriness.

Mary grinned. "How's Beau this morning?"

Samantha knew what she was getting at. The past few days he'd spent pasture breeding Mary's palomino mare. "Quite content—to say the least."

Mary chuckled. "I'll bet." She took a seat behind her desk. "I think you were right to try pasturing them together."

"Yeah. Beau's weird about breeding. He won't mount if someone's standing next to him holding the rope. Probably goes back to the abuse he went through."

"He's a terrific horse. I can't wait to see how the foal turns out."

Sorrow rippled through Samantha. The foal would be born in eleven months. Next April. She wouldn't be here. Or would she? Dalton and she were seeing each other every night, by the easy secrecy of the tunnel door. They shared her bed until after midnight, when he would return to the bunkhouse to awaken in his own bed, his earlier absence unnoticed by the wranglers.

Nothing had been said in regard to relationships, life, or love, but she could feel it growing into something. She could look into Dalton's eyes and see the same emotions.

Mary knew about the bond that had formed between them. Samantha had told her herself, wanting Mary to hear it from her versus someone else. Samantha didn't divulge much, just that she and Dalton spent time together, after hours.

Boots and spurs sounded in the hall.

Dalton.

She had taken more time than she should have with her call. Oops. He'd have to discipline her later. She smiled at the thought. He whistled for her. "I better get going. You okay?" It wasn't like Mary to appear nervous. She was usually so calm and relaxed.

"I'm fine. Get going. You're being paged."

"Okay. See you later." She spun on her heel and dashed down the hallway, Dolly trailed at her heels.

"Psst," she heard, from a darkened room just off the entryway.

"Dalton?" She slowed her pace and poked her head inside the room.

A large hand yanked her by the bandana and quickly closed the door, zapping the room black. "It's me, princess. We've got five minutes." The husky timbre of his voice sent a thrill of excitement through her veins. He picked her up and settled her on a flat surface.

"Where are we?" she asked, hushing a giggle.

"In a large coat closet. Your sexy ass is on a safe."

Large hands cupped her bottom. He kissed her, his lips urgent. "I couldn't wait until tonight. The sight of you bending over, picking your horse's hooves, nearly drove me mad."

In one sweep, he jerked her pants from her hips, freeing one leg. She spread her legs for him, already wet.

"Good girl."

She heard his belt buckle clank as his jeans hit the floor. He scooted her to him and his firm member grazed her sensitive skin, buoying at her entrance. He bared her breasts and suckled each velvety bead before sinking into her. "God, you feel good."

His rich, bedroom voice appeased her on every level. She clawed at his back, pulling him closer. She felt his body jerk as he exploded inside of her.

Samantha had learned that there was nothing better than the feel of his large, sated body holding her afterwards. She buried his head in her chest, kissing the top of it, the dense brown hair becoming so familiar. Passion blistered inside her, the heat of his heavy, sapped breathing a satisfying comfort.

He inhaled deeply, then slowly exhaled. "You have my permission to always be late."

She chuckled. "I'm sure I can use that to my advantage."

****

His aunt was beside herself. She'd caught him just as Samantha and he were exiting the lodge. Thank God she didn't go looking for him five minutes earlier. Was his shirt all the way tucked in? His eyes dipped to his waistband. He smelled Samantha all over him.

"My God, what does this mean?" Panicky, Mary harped on the phone call she'd just taken from Samantha's parents. "They're arriving today—this afternoon! They didn't mention where from, just that they're arriving by chopper and leaving the following day. They said they want to check in on her and see how she's managing on the ranch. They requested it be a surprise."

Dalton had to admit, the unexpected social call was odd, but he didn't see any reason to go gray over the announcement. "They probably just miss her."

Mary rolled her eyes. "My colon says the opposite."

Dalton chuckled. "Everything'll be fine."

"How? How do we keep it from her?"

True. With Samantha functioning as the ranch nurse, it would be difficult to accomplish. The only option would be to contrive a way for her to be away from the lodge when the helicopter flew in. Today's short ride through the valley would need to change.

He took a moment to think. With no further mountain lion attacks, it was time for the cattle to return to their summer pastures. Feeding them round bales close to the barn area was costing a fortune. Soon their winter supply of hay would be depleted and the overgrazed lots would have to be seeded, as well. In addition, the guests were eager for a long ride. They could drive the cattle to the north pasture, the one farthest from the ranch. That would buy them plenty of time.

He grasped his aunt by the shoulders. "I've got it covered. You get their room ready, and I'll see to the rest."

****

"Uh, Sam, I think you might want to come take a look at this," Jessica uttered, dragging her out of the barn to where she could see the lodge and the side parking lot. They were just done riding, tidying the barn.

"Yeah. So what? It's a helicopter. We must have some high rollers coming in for the week." She grinned at her friend. "Don't you watch the travel channel?"

"Take another look, smartass."

Samantha looked again, seeing just a large black chopper with white doors and red writing... "Holy...my parents!" She reached behind her, smoothing her tangled pony tail, knowing she looked a mess.

Dalton walked up beside her. "They wanted it to be a surprise."

This couldn't be good. Her parents didn't have time for surprises. This wasn't like them. Wait. She turned to him. "You knew and didn't tell me? Did you talk to them?"

"Whoa." He held up his palms. "Aunt Mary did all the talking. I just carried out the plan to get you away from here for a little while."

She smiled. He was keeping her calm.

He patted her on the shoulder before walking off, tossing the bridle he intended to fix over his shoulder. "Dinner at seven, you two. Not an option to be late." Winking, he turned and strolled off.

Samantha heard Jessica's deep sigh next to her. "Well, you heard him."

Like robots, they headed to their cabin.

They didn't speak until they reached the entrance, the screen door screeching shut behind them. Like beat-up flour sacks, they slumped on the couch.

"What are you thinking?" Jessica asked.

Fretting, Samantha chewed on her lower lip. She untied the dusty bandana around her neck. "That this is not a good sign." She thought for a moment. "Surely they don't mean to drag me home. They can't. I have Beau and the rig with me."

Jessica snapped. "They can't drag you anywhere. You're a grown adult."

Samantha contemplated Jessica's simple diagnosis. "You're right. You're exactly right."

"You need to just tell them, Sam. You can't keep doing this to yourself. If you don't stand up to them, you are going to be headed down the aisle faster than you can think—and it's not going to be with Dalton."

Dalton. Hearing his name gave her goosebumps. She wasn't about to lose what they had started. She loved him. She would stay. And risk everything.

****

Smoothing the silken fabric of her lavender summer dress, Samantha gave herself a pep talk before entering the lodge. She tried to focus on how utterly happy she was on the ranch. She loved Dalton, and she loved this place. Even her horse and dog had taken to Twin Rivers. Ranch life suited her. If she could centralize her thoughts on all the little things that added up to such a spectacular big picture, she'd be fine. Deep breath.

"Samantha, dear," her mother greeted, hurrying to them.

She and Jessica hadn't so much as shut the door.

"Hello, Mother. I've been trying to call you." They hugged—a gentle hug like you would give your grandma for fear you might break her.

"And Miss Hamilton," she said to Jessica. "How are you this evening?"

"I'm fine, Mrs. Matthews. We've been having a blast. And you?"

Her mother led them down the hall to the dining room, three pairs of heeled shoes echoing on the wooden floors. "I'm great. I've been assisting Winston with his hectic schedule."

Hectic, for sure. Politics for them was like oxygen to the average person, but this Samantha knew. In a way, she'd come to appreciate her father's fierce, complicated lifestyle. He was going after something he truly believed in: a campaign for governor.

The dining room was beginning to fill. Several guests were already seated.

Her father, as he stood before the fireplace speaking to John, looked the complete politician in his gray pants and rich-looking tie, his dark gray hair complementing his relaxed yet professional attire. Samantha was glad to see he looked rested and unstressed.

"Jessica, where's the restroom?" Samantha's mother asked.

"This way. I'll show you."

"Ah, Samantha, there you are." Her father set his drink on the mantel and came to meet her, taking her hands in his as he reached her. "My darling. We so wanted to surprise you."

"You did. I'm shocked." Samantha noticed the decorations. Bells of Ireland and miniature calla lilies graced the table, along with new candles. Heaping bowls of fresh fruit garnished the dining furniture at both ends.

Samantha grazed the room and corridor for Dalton, not seeing him.

"Where did you fly in from?"

"California. Before that, Oregon," her father answered. He looked at her and smiled, tipping her chin. "Your freckles are back."

Samantha's fingertips flew to the bridge of her nose. She'd gotten a little careless lately, leaving her ball cap behind in the barn on her trips to and from the lodge. No one but Dalton had noticed.

John joined them briefly. "We're quite proud to have Samantha. She's been working as both a wrangler and a nurse. Excuse me," he said, leaving to lend a hand with the trays of food being brought to the table.

Eeks. Two jobs. Her father wouldn't be overly happy with the fact that she was working even one.

Samantha saw Dalton enter the room with his brother. She wanted to hop into his arms and disappear. She introduced them. "Father, this is Dalton MacLaine, John and Mary's eldest nephew." *The man I've been sleeping with for a month now.*

"Good to meet you, Dalton. I've heard you're an exceptional hand with a horse."

Dalton looked astonished, and Samantha felt the

same. She hadn't seen that one coming.

"Why, thank you."

"You did a clinic for some friends of ours recently—the Brownings. They couldn't say enough good things about you."

Oh, no! Her father had checked up on her.

Dalton paused. "Oh, yes. They have the big hunter-jumper with an attitude."

"Had. Yes."

Samantha watched Dalton smile. He was breathtaking in his casual dress shirt, the short sleeves showing off his tanned, muscular arms.

So far, so good. Maybe this was just a pop-in hello visit, although it hardly seemed coincidental that one of their family friends would have a horse in dire need of training from the same ranch where she was working.

"Whiskey?" Dalton asked. Her father's drink was empty.

"On the rocks, thank you." Her father turned to her. "Seems like a nice man."

"He is. The whole family is."

Dinner was announced and everyone ate to the accompaniment of idle chitchat. Dalton sat across from her, two seats over. If he was nervous, he didn't show it.

Next to her, Jessica was fuming. She toyed with every vegetable on her plate and stabbed at the baked quail, killing it one more time before she splish-splashed the delicate meat in gravy.

Samantha eyed her, asking what was wrong. Jessica's eyes pounced in her mother's direction.

Something was amiss.

Dessert of warm peach cobbler and homemade ice cream was the last course before after-dinner drinks were announced, to be served at the living room bar. Mary suggested the terrace dining room as a quiet place for Samantha and her parents to talk.

"That would be lovely," Samantha's mother spoke, "since we leave in the morning."

"I'll have drinks brought up to you," Mary offered.

The small dining area was the last room on the left. Samantha remembered the space well. The last time she'd walked this hall she was blindfolded, coerced by Jessica and Bethany, and told to "stay put."

A low fire danced in the grate as they entered. Samantha left the double doors open, letting the long carpeted corridor give them privacy. She sipped her half-empty daiquiri through the straw and positioned herself in front of the warm embers. The room held memories of her dinner with Dalton. He had looked delectable in his suit and tie.

"So what do you think of the place?" she asked her parents as her mother took a seat at the table, her father standing close beside, one hand on the back of the chair.

They looked at one another before answering. "It's very nice. We can see why you like it," said her mother.

But. There was a but coming. She could feel it.

"But it's time to come home, Samantha." Her mother said the words her father's eyes agreed with. You're twenty-three, Sam. It's time you start thinking about your future." Her mother shook her head. "And this ranch is not an acceptable answer."

"Why can't it be? I love it here." She turned to face the fire, her temper boiling with the flames. She hated when her parents ganged up on her, and she thoroughly despised the harebrained more-to-life speech they insisted on spoon-feeding her. If this was the only reason they'd "popped in" to see her, she certainly wished they hadn't come.

In the back of her mind, an ugly thought came forward. All the wranglers and staff now knew the wealth of her family. Great. Now she'd instantly have best friends, as well as those who wanted to see her hung by a noose.

"He's just a man, Samantha." Her mother's remark was a cold evaluation.

Samantha froze. *Oh, God.* She had left Jessica alone with her mother. Poor Jess had been forced to rat on her.

"How dare you—"

"We didn't dare do anything, Samantha," her fathered hammered. "Don't you see?" He came toward her. "We are trying to help you, guide you. We want you to have all the riches we've been blessed with and that you've become accustomed to."

"By forcing me to marry someone I don't love?" A sour

knot formed in her throat.

Her mother chuckled. "So, now you love him?"

Anger dried the tears welling up in her eyes. She turned and hissed, "Yes, I do." Defiantly, she stared at them.

Her father paced the room.

Her mother jerked up from the table. "Samantha, I won't have your grandmother's inheritance squabbled away by a nobody cow farmer. Nor will I ever see you having to pinch pennies like I once did. You will marry who we say, and that's final."

A cough sounded from her father. "We'll meet you halfway, Sam. We'll allow you to spend the summer with Dalton. Girls of your status have flings right and left. Blake won't care, as long as you're home by the end of summer."

"Blake?" Samantha blinked. She couldn't believe this.

"Blake Richards, the man you're marrying."

Blake Richards, the lieutenant governor's son. How convenient.

The discussion was over. Her mother pushed her chair back under the table and picked up their champagne glasses. They each kissed her goodnight. Her mother smoothed an erratic hair from her temple. "Don't look so defeated, Samantha. By marrying Blake, you'll grace the highest social and political circles. You won't even need your inheritance. It'll go to great use in your father's campaign."

Samantha escorted them to their room. She waited to hear the lock click before she scrambled down the hall.

Bypassing the main rooms of the lodge, she used the staff kitchen door as a retreat to the outside world, a beautiful and natural, organic world where things and people weren't forced on one another. A world where money couldn't buy love and parents wouldn't succumb to the political windfall it promised.

Salty tears burned her cheeks. She hastily removed her small-heeled sandals and raced to Beau's corner of the world. There, she found Dolly and crumpled with her in the corner of the stall. She cried and screamed. She wouldn't marry Blake Richards. She wouldn't.

Chapter Fifteen

The bar at The Silver Spur wasn't fancy. Nor was it clean. Peanut shells layered the floor in a one-inch frosting, the rough planked floor visible only in patches. Shell dust powdered his boots as he took a seat at the bar, but he didn't care. The only feeling he was aware of was deceit.

He was right to have never focused his attention on women. Also right to keep them on the backburner except in those hardened moments of need. And damn sure right in telling Clay a few months ago that he only needed a wife to procreate for the sake of his last name.

The nobody cow farmer ordered a beer and a double shot of Patron.

In a silent toast, he commended Samantha Matthews on a job well done. To the best rich bitch of them all. And a superb actress. While committed to marry one man, she possessed the ability and audacity to launch herself into a serious relationship with another one, without so much as a bat of the eye.

Serious, my ass, Dalton thought. "Flings, right and left. Girls of your status..." were the words her father had used. Yep, right out of the horse's mouth. Apparently Samantha Dear had gotten a little carried away with this fling, and so it was time for the parents to step in and call it to a halt.

Dalton considered himself fortunate to have missed the beginning of their candid conversation. If not for Mary asking him to take a fresh round of drinks to Samantha and her parents, he would've missed out on hearing about Socialite Samantha's fall from casual copulation and plunge into holy matrimony.

He left after hearing Samantha's pathetic response.

"Blake?" She had repeated, shock in her voice. As if she were asking, "Why not Richard or Tom—they were better flings last summer." Dalton shook his head. He couldn't believe he had fallen for her innocent act.

He downed the tequila. Then the beer.

"Not used to seeing you drink like that," the bartender commented.

Dalton grunted. "Second that."

The bartender chuckled, wiping his hands on a towel. "Second what? The comment or the drink?"

"Both." The waiter turned to fix the drinks.

Dalton's thoughts went into rewind.

What a conniving bitch. Never would he have thought her to be the deceitful, manipulative type. Never would he have imagined her leading a lifestyle so opposite of what she portrayed herself to be. And why him? Why Montana? If her family was so wealthy, could jet from one city to the next, why take the time with a common mountain man like himself?

He dipped his hand in the peanut tin before him and grabbed a handful, then began pinching each nut one at a time until the crisp shells snapped open. He let them fall to the floor. He didn't want them, only the satisfaction of having broken them.

An embittered song he knew sounded from the jukebox to his left, completely reflective of his mood. His gaze drifted across the bar. Not very full for a Friday night.

The bartender brought him his drink. Dalton knew him. His name was Lyle, a decent man, five years older than himself.

"Ya know, the last time you were in here, your brother was trying to fix you up with the blonde over there." Lyle tipped his head to the far corner booth.

Dalton twisted in the bar stool. The booths lining the wall were tall and the room was bleak. He hadn't seen her, or her sister sitting across from her, but of course he hadn't been looking, either. Too late, he turned back around. She'd seen him.

Great. Body language invitation. He cussed under his breath.

Lyle smiled, then blanked his features. Dalton didn't need to look over his shoulder to know she was sauntering his way.

"How ya been, Dalton? Haven't seen you in a while."

She slid onto the bar stool, her knees grazing the sides of his thighs. Long and platinum blonde, her straight hair curtained the deep vee of her tight shirt.

"Fine. Been working." He emptied the second shot.

"Drinking heavy tonight?"

He frowned. "Nah, just drinking." He wished she would leave. Her darkly tanned skin and pale hair contrasted badly with Samantha's fresh, natural features. He silently cursed himself for going there. Samantha was gone to him. Gone.

"I have a date tonight with Young Jasper," she volunteered.

Out of pure politeness he said, "Well, good."

"He should be here any minute. Said you guys were having an early night on the ranch." She waited for a response.

Again, out of courtesy, "He shouldn't be much longer." He kept his tone dry.

She leaned his way. "I'd much rather be having a date with you, Dalton." She licked her lips, her mouth parting as her eyes lingered on his mouth. She was practically sitting on his lap.

Door jingles announced a customer. Dalton returned his attention to his beer, taking a long swallow. The blonde popped up from the stool next to him.

"Hey, Jasp," she cooed. Dalton guessed that was her way of apologizing, since she had been caught salivating over another man.

"Dalton," Young Jasper crisply acknowledged, leading the blonde to her booth.

Dalton threw him a wave while he caught the bartender's shared expression of relief. Both men knew Young Jasper's intentions toward the blonde—an easy lay. She was cute, petite, and whispered to suck like a...whatever animal that is. Heck, he couldn't remember, but that's all she was for the night. Nothing more.

He missed Samantha already. He'd give anything to have one more day with her. To see her, to hold her, to be with her like before—alone in the thatched cabin, making love in the dark with the howls of coyotes in the background. He loved her. He wanted her back.

The liquor was burning in him now. It had taken the

edge off, plus a whole lot more. The warrior shield he'd had around his heart when he entered the bar was withered away. He knew he needed the armor back in place, but just to see her again, to feel her soft mouth on his, her hands wrapped around him, loving him.

He paid his bill and left, the jukebox tunes of an old Garth song lingering in his mind. Shameless. That's how he felt.

By the time he drove the hour back to the ranch, he was much more sober and a decision had been made. Because he didn't have the strength to stay away from Samantha, he'd play along with her scheme. He'd continue with the summer they started. He'd share her bed and her body. But that's where it would end. She wouldn't have his mind or his heart.

Just like the blonde with Young Jasper, she'd be nothing more than a piece of ass.

****

Saturday morning Samantha awoke to Dolly. Dog kisses to the mouth. Refreshing.

Despite the empty acrid feeling in her stomach, she sprang out of bed. Last night was the first night in weeks Dalton hadn't come to her, but she shrugged off the thought, blaming her parents. Any guy with a mature mind like Dalton's would shudder at the thought of getting caught sleeping with someone's daughter, especially when they'd just met.

Still, after the evening she'd had, she could have appreciated the comfort of him next to her.

She thought perhaps things had worked out for the best, though, because Dalton would have insisted she tell him what had upset her.

Descending the loft steps in jeans and a sports bra, she twisted into a tank-top.

Jessica greeted her in the kitchen, her mouth full and her hand waving the last quarter of a toaster pastry. "Running late?"

"Kind of. I slept in. No breakfast at the lodge?"

"Nope, I'm running behind, myself. You planning on saying goodbye to your parents before they chopper out?"

Her parents were the last thing Samantha wanted to discuss this morning, but she might as well get it out of the way. "No."

"Sam, that's awesome! I'm so proud of you for standing up to them." Jessica trotted around the kitchen counter to hug her at the sink.

Samantha returned the fiery hug and went back to rinsing an apple. "Well, that's just it. I didn't exactly stand up to them. They took my silence as approval." She gave a short laugh. "Hardly the case."

"But there's no way you're going to..."

Samantha cut her off. "Marry Blake Richards? No."

"Do they know about the money?"

"No."

Jessica's smirk practically glistened. "Ha," she said with a nod, her hands on her hips. "Exactly what they get." She paused, cocking her head to the side. "So when will they find out?"

Samantha shrugged. "I guess at the end of summer. When the bride doesn't show up."

"Wow."

They both grabbed juice boxes and ball caps before leaving the cabin.

Outside, the morning sun climbed over the Pryor Mountains, warming their faces. Birds tweeted in the trees. Pine needles padded their steps on the wooded trail to the barn.

"Does Dalton know any of this?"

"No," Samantha snapped. "I'd hate for him to know my parents are money-hungry, political lechers. I mean, look at John and Mary. They're terrific. They've raised Dalton in a very normal, down-to-earth way. Don't you think that's what he's going to look for in a wife?" Her question was more of a statement.

"Whoa. Are we talking marriage now?"

"Isn't this all about marriage?" Samantha rationalized.

"Yeah, I guess so."

"But I don't have plans to marry Dalton. I don't have plans for marrying anyone," she said, throwing her hands in the air. "I just want to enjoy the rest of the summer with him. The only problem is that now he knows I'm filthy rich, so I'm back to square one, except that..."

"You've never before got to start out at square one."

Samantha loved that they were good enough friends to finish each other's sentences. "Exactly. He liked me before, so hopefully nothing will change."

"I'll be shocked if Dalton changes," Jessica commented. "He's so centered and..."

"Normal."

"Yes, normal." They looked at each other and laughed, reaching the main road. "Are you riding or nursing today?" Jessica asked.

"I think Mary wants me to do some nursing stuff this morning. Then I'll help you guys check the cows in the east pasture."

"Okay. See ya."

"Hey," Samantha stopped her before she walked off. "Can you give the rest of this to Beau?" She held out what was left of her green apple. "He loves the green ones. Oh, did you by chance see Dalton last night anywhere?"

Jessica wrinkled her nose, taking the half-eaten fruit. "No, why?"

Samantha shrugged. "No reason. See you later."

Treading up the stone path to the lodge, Samantha couldn't shake the sour feeling of dread in her stomach. She hoped it was just gut instinct gone haywire. Her parents were always able to stir her insides. While she knew they meant well, it was never in her best interest. Kind of like all those piano lessons in the parlor. She would much rather have been in the barn helping the stable boys with the horses, or in the garden with her grandfather.

"Sam."

Samantha jerked, hearing her name.

It was Mary, coffee cup in hand, papers in the other.

"Good morning, dear. I was just going over this morning's RN duties for you." She smiled. "Care to join me by the pool for report?"

"Sure. I was just looking for you."

They took a seat under an umbrella table, the empty helicopter pad visible up on the hillside.

"Your parents got an early start this morning, said they were headed home for a while."

Godspeed. Samantha wished Mary knew. She wished she could get up the courage to tell her, to explain the marriage her parents were trying to force upon her. But, as always, Samantha just nodded, letting the tendrils of rage fester inside her. "Yep, they stay pretty busy. Politics."

"Ah."

Samantha went straight to studying Mary's cursive penmanship on Twin Rivers embossed paper. There were several blood pressures to take, as the ranch now offered that free, a few morning insulin shots, and blood sugars to check. The usual stuff. The last item on the list: dialysis patient, monitor fistula site. Hmm.

"The dialysis patient is something new to us, Sam. I've been told they lead very normal lives, besides having to watch their fluid intake. All we will do is take their blood pressure twice a day and monitor the site for bleeding when they get done with treatment at the clinic in town."

"Sounds accurate. I have a question, though."

"What's that?"

"Since Jess and I stay in the cabin closest to the barn, I tend to get guests and employees dropping in with minor problems like dust in the eyes, splinters, things like that. Is it okay that I've been tending to that in our cabin?"

Mary waved as if she were shooing a fly. "Why, of course, dear. I appreciate you taking the time. You know, you truly are a dear, Samantha. We've just loved having you."

"Loved? Mary, that's past tense," Samantha teased. "I'm here, and I'm not planning on going anywhere. In fact, I may not leave at all. You may have to run me off."

"Good. Glad to hear it."

Samantha sensed Mary knew something. Perhaps she and Jessica had exchanged views. Oh, well, what if they did. Mary had become a friend, and if there was anyone Samantha admired besides her grandparents, it was Mary MacLaine.

"Speaking of anywhere, I didn't see Dalton this morning." It was odd for her to have not seen him by now.

"John said he was up early. Harrowing the pens."

Not something he normally did. "I was just worried." Samantha shrugged her shoulders for the second time that morning, then stood. "Well, I better get, before they check out. How many new guests are we expecting on Sunday?"

"Ten. Two families of five, all of them adults, so it should make for an easy week." Mary organized the rest of her papers, shuffling them to her liking before rising from her chair.

Samantha sauntered off, glad to have tasks to keep her mind busy. She was not going to let her parents' brief visit dampen her summer. She just wouldn't. What would become of Dalton and her, she did not know, but she wanted to give it a chance.

She knew she loved him, but fear kept her from saying the words. Fear that her feelings wouldn't be reciprocated, fear the three little words would be too soon, and fear her family background would despoil something so perfect and pure.

She could easily see herself living the ranch lifestyle—she and Dalton would grow old on his dream ranch and she could tell Cinderella stories to their children about how they met and fought, and how she nursed him back to health and fell in love. Utmost, she would finally have a man who loved her for more than her bank balance.

Bang. The sour-stomach feeling was back, ramming her gut like a flat-fisted hand. Just when she thought she had herself convinced, the bitter notion returned. Why? Because of her parents? Or was something bad happening? She had to see Dalton. Something must be wrong. A thought clicked in her head: the growl. Could that animal have returned? Why couldn't she find Dalton? If anything happened to him... She shook away the thought.

Samantha jogged down the stone path to the outside paddocks. She peered to the right, to the left. She didn't see him or the tractor, but she heard it. Rounding the end of the barn, she exhaled at seeing him safe and sound. He was driving the tractor, using the disk to turn the ground. He raised his hand to her, saying a distant hello.

Samantha could feel the remoteness between them. She'd gotten to know him well enough in the past month to sense a change. The nod of his head had been cold, the softness formerly in his eyes lifted away, leaving only a bland, inanimate smile. Not the Dalton she knew.

"Don't mind him, Sam," Clay said, ambling out of the barn. "He's a wee bit on the grouchy side this morning. Must have slept on the wrong side of the bed."

Yeah, because he sure didn't sleep in my bed. Clay knew what she was thinking. She could read it in his eyes.

"Heard your parents take off this morning."

Samantha didn't say anything, just quirked her upper lip and nodded. Her voice was too on-edge for her to speak. Clay had just stated what her mind was thinking. Her parents. So they had had an effect on Dalton after all.

"Clay, do you think..." Samantha stopped, catching a glimpse of Young Jasper just around the dairy barn, close enough to overhear. While Jasper had been only nice to her lately, she didn't have an ounce of faith in him. She still didn't know how he had found out about her not wearing panties to that welcome home celebration.

"Do I think what?" he repeated.

Samantha appreciated the look of concern from him, but she wasn't about to speak another word. She faked a fetching smile. "Never mind," she said, waving a hand in the air. "I'll see you in a few."

Fully aware that she was grinding her teeth, Samantha proceeded to the lodge, determined to keep busy.

After a fast lunch, Samantha returned to the barn to help the wranglers check the cows in the east pasture. Most of them were mama cows with youngsters at their sides. Although there had been no more reports of mountain lion incidents, Dalton and John had insisted on increasing the amount of time spent overseeing the herd.

With Beau saddled and ready, Samantha met the group of riders outside the barn area. All the guests were gone, so only the wranglers were riding. Samantha had been on several wrangler-only rides, one each week she had been at the ranch, and they'd quickly become her favorite. She and Dalton always had fun devising plans to meet for a fast rendezvous once they reached the pasture. It was easy to do since the wranglers all divided and went different directions out there.

Samantha's temper had cooled. She was looking

forward to the ride. She wanted to get some alone time with Dalton. The last time she had talked to him was when she'd introduced him to her parents.

They maintained a brisk trot to the east grazing ground. Beau had just gotten his second wind by the time they reached the gate. The men rode in front while Samantha and Jessica stayed in the back. Lowering the blue bandana from her face, Samantha tied it around her neck. The cloth was great for keeping dust out of her mouth and nose, but useless for contacts. Her eyes watered from all the dirt.

Each rider headed in the agreed-upon direction, promising to meet back in two hours. Samantha took the front part of the field, as she had the time before, the occasion when Dalton and she had met at the shaded watering hole. Most of the mama cows congregated there with their babies.

Dalton wasn't back to his usual self, but he had thrown her a wink and a nod before they left the barn and another once they separated at the gate. That was a good sign. Maybe Clay had been right—perhaps Dalton had just been in a bad mood. Perhaps she shouldn't examine everything he did so closely just because she was insecure about her family.

Prowling for cows, Samantha realized no one at the ranch had treated her any differently since her parents' unexpected visit. Her cheeks blossomed in a smile. For once, she had found true friends.

She waited at the watering hole until she was certain he wasn't going to arrive. Trekking back to the tree where Beau was tethered, she was suddenly sideswiped by Dalton's large arm. He picked her up and carried her over his shoulder like a bag of grain into a thicket of tall evergreens. She laughed like a little kid. "I was wondering if..."

Before she could finish her words, he had the bandana from around her neck muffled into her mouth so she couldn't talk. He was at once gentle but rough as he bent her over a fallen tree. In one swift motion, he jerked her jeans down. He spread her legs apart with his and entered her. She squealed and hugged the tree, gripping the dead limbs for leverage as his large hands encircled her waist, his firm member thrusting in and out, dipping deeper, grinding in an aggressive manner.

Samantha was bothered by his briskness but nevertheless enjoyed the masculine control he had over her. With a fistful of hair, he smacked her bottom—hard, several times then jerked her feet off the ground, his hands on her hips possessive and rough. She heard her muted moan through the bandana and was thankful for the mouthpiece. It silenced her climax as he plunged into her one last time, releasing inside of her.

Seconds later, he pulled out her bandana and slid it between her legs. He hiked her pants up and spun her around. He pecked her on the lips and sent her off toward Beau with a final spank and a muttered, "See you tonight."

Chapter Sixteen

"No, that's not it," Samantha said to Jessica. "He's different. Detached like." It was Saturday night, a week after her parents' visit. They were just in from another wrangler-only ride. Dalton had taken her again in the woods, just like before.

All week long he had come to see her every night, but only long enough to have sex, leaving immediately afterwards. She didn't have the courage to tell him how much it bothered her.

Jessica was silent for a moment. "Sam," she said, inching closer to Beau as Samantha ungirthed him. "Do you think he knows? Or that he overheard?"

After considering, Sam shook her head. "No. He couldn't have. No one was there to hear."

Slumping against the wall of the barn, Jessica confessed, "He does seem a little different. More like the hard-headed guy he was when we first got here."

Samantha licked her lips with worry. She lifted the saddle off Beau and placed it on the saddle rack next to the stall. She reached for a curry in time to see Beau's ears flick backwards. "Beau," she reprimanded, before seeing Young Jasper headed down the aisleway in their direction.

"Beau sure doesn't like him," Jessica muttered.

The girls didn't speak again as Young Jasper approached.

Samantha hadn't told Jessica about that night in the barn. She knew her friend was incapable of keeping her mouth closed. Bethany was one thing, Jessica was quite another. Young Jasper had kept his distance and been nothing but pleasant, so she treated him the same.

He walked up to them. "Mary sent me to tell you there's been a mix-up with the dialysis patient this week. She's arriving today instead of tomorrow. Be here any time."

No big deal. The last dialysis patient had been a breeze. "Okay, tell her I'll be up soon."

Young Jasper left, and the girls returned to their conversation.

"I think it's time I say something." She led Beau into his stall and tossed him a flake of hay.

"Yep." Jessica said. She pushed herself away from the stall wall and joined Sam to stroll to the cabin.

After showering, Samantha slipped on a cute low-rise skirt and flowery tank top, appropriate for meeting a guest but attractive enough to get Dalton's attention—maybe. She wasn't sure, anymore. She'd once had him pegged, but now... She stepped into flip-flops before heading out.

She walked into dinner with a jaunty smile. Although she didn't feel the mood she was trying to create, she pretended anyway. Dalton didn't so much as glance her way as he strode into the dining room, John and Young Jasper following behind him.

At the table, Mary sat her directly across from Dalton. This was fine with her, because she was bound and determined to gain his attention.

During dinner, Samantha kicked off her shoes and propped her toes on his sandaled feet. She was vaguely aware she had his interest. His jaw clenched slightly. Under the table, though, Samantha knew she had him. She rubbed his hard erection with the arch of her foot.

"Oh, dear, you're bleeding," Mary said to Brenda, their dialysis patient for the week. The jolly, gray-haired lady turned and looked at her upper arm, where red blossomed through the sleeve of her blouse.

Samantha dropped her fork and rushed to her side. Grabbing a napkin, Samantha peeked under the sleeve. Sure enough, the needle site was seeping, and she placed the dinner napkin on the bleeding. "I'm done eating. I'll go get some gauze and tape. It's in my cabin."

"Do you care if I walk with you? It's getting dark, and I haven't seen the ranch," Brenda asked.

Samantha looked to Mary and John for permission. Mary had told her Brenda was in her early fifties and very healthy, still energetic and ambulatory. Samantha didn't see what it could hurt.

"Sure," Mary said. "Will someone walk with them?"

Samantha immediately looked at Dalton, but Young Jasper spoke first. "I'll be happy to."

Damn.

By the time they reached her cabin, Brenda's fistula site had clotted over. Samantha cleaned it with peroxide and placed a bandage on the wound, giving her several extra bandages in case it started again.

"I'll walk her back, Sam. Thanks." Young Jasper spoke over his shoulder, guiding Brenda out the door. Samantha held the screen so it wouldn't bang shut and startle the older woman.

Needing to pause and reflect, Samantha stopped to take a breather on the couch, toes curled underneath her. She quickly came to a decision: she was going to confront Dalton. She was going to demand an explanation about his sudden personality change. If his behavior had to do with her parents, she needed to know. She couldn't keep her doubts bottled up anymore.

Somewhat consoled, she relaxed back into the couch, nestling her head on the cool, plump leather pillows.

She must have fallen asleep.

The thudding smack of the screen door jarred her awake. "Jess?" She rubbed her eyes as she heard shuffling at the door.

Cigarette smoke.

She tore her hands from her face.

****

That was it. They were going to talk.

Dalton had been keeping a keen eye on Samantha, and he hadn't found any reason to believe she was lying. For two weeks, he had ignored her and treated her with a calculated impassiveness, only to find her tolerating his uncouthness. A spoiled, rich debutante wouldn't have endured such crudity.

Guilt filtered through him. He hadn't spent much time with her lately. Just like he'd planned, he'd used her to satisfy his needs and then discarded her like a bad hand of cards. But she meant more to him than that. She was his world. He just couldn't bring himself to admit it anymore.

There had to be more to the conversation he had

overheard with her parents—something he'd missed. Even now, his ears reverberated with Samantha's soft exclamation of the name of the man she was supposed to marry, repeating it as though she herself couldn't comprehend. He didn't focus on the name. He didn't want to hear it anymore, didn't want to think of her with anyone but himself.

He thought long and hard about her parents' view of him. For now he might be just a lowlife cow farmer, but he was ambitious. He had plans. Big plans. And he intended to see them through.

None of this made any sense. Samantha was still on the ranch. If she was supposed to be getting married, why was she still here? Last week Mary had shared Samantha's declaration of having no intention to leave anytime soon.

He didn't know what to believe.

At dinner she had jumped to help Brenda. Dalton had watched her intently, just as he had since that fateful night when her parents had visited. Samantha didn't hesitate to lend a hand—ever. In the barn, at the lodge, with her nursing, she was the first one to help out. Never did he see her flinch or consider.

Debutantes just didn't react in such ways. They didn't expend energy or get their hands dirty. They didn't work long hours, shovel manure, sweat. They flat out didn't help others. Yet volunteering was second nature for Samantha.

Dalton contemplated Jessica, her good friend. He had watched her, too, for signs of hypocrisy.

And found none.

Jessica was the same female she'd been when she first came to the ranch, still brazen and outspokenly infatuated with his younger brother.

Seated at the table, Dalton's conscience got the best of him. For weeks now he had taken her and been gruff and uncaring. He hadn't so much as whispered one sweet anything in her ear. He hadn't allowed himself to go there. He was too busy punishing her the only way he knew how. He ignored her and used her sexually until he felt a tiny bit of selfish relief. Somehow, during all this, he had morphed back into the lonely, sour man he used to be before she came along.

Sighing, he rose from the table and excused himself. He stole a peek at Jessica as he pushed his chair under the table. Her smile was faint and unsure, regarding. He saw hope in her brown eyes, he thought, but they lacked faith in him.

She knew something he didn't. He was sure of it. However, her loyalty was to Samantha.

Walking out of the room, Dalton saw Minus close his eyes and nod.

The fuckers were reading his thoughts.

****

"Young Jasper?" Samantha shrieked. She blanked her features and stood, trying not to appear horrified.

"Yeah, it's me." He eased the screen shut in Dolly's face, and closed the front door, as well. "I forgot my lighter."

Samantha's body went still. Her heartbeat sounded in her ears as the hairs on her arms reared. He hadn't left his lighter—clearly, the cigarette in his hand was lit.

Calm. Stay calm.

"Well, have a look around. I was just leaving." Her words sounded composed, but that was hardly the way she felt. She wanted to scream.

She couldn't leave via the hidden turret door because he was standing in front of the stairs. As luck would have it, there wasn't a back door. Turning on her heel, she headed for the kitchen. "I just have to get my purse." Purse, my ass. She was going for the only weapon she could think of—a collapsible hoof pick she sometimes kept in her bra. Knowing she wouldn't be using it tonight, she had left it on the countertop just inside the kitchen...

He blocked her entry with one arm, his hand smacking the doorway a mere inch from her face. With his arm shelved in front of her, Samantha turned to look at him, then spoke, her words deliberate. "Whatever you're looking for, Jasper, it's not here."

"Oh, I think it is." Fright tingled Samantha's spine. His voice was mean and crude, suggestive of the worst of imaginings. She ducked under his arm, fast enough to enter the kitchen, but not speedy enough to be out of reach. He grabbed her hair and twirled her around, yanking her body to his before slamming her into the refrigerator.

Samantha eyed the hoof pick from a distance. Way out of reach.

"You're what I want, Samantha." He groped her breasts with savage hands.

She ignored his words and pounded her hands into his chest, trying to mentally concoct a plan to rid herself of this situation. Being an obsessive-compulsive about dishes in the sink, she knew there weren't any forks or knives handy.

"I've seen you with Dalton. I've seen you screwing him."

Liar. And a terrible one at that.

"I saw you today," he continued bragging in her ear. He stopped groping her long enough to remove his shirt. His filthy hands returned to her abdomen and yanked her top up, her bra exposed. He tugged the brassiere over her breasts.

Samantha spat her reply. "Oh, yeah, and what was I doing?" Her words hateful.

"Getting fucked from behind."

Now he had her attention. She couldn't help but show it by staring dumbfounded at him. As easy as if she were a doll, he bent her arms behind her and clasped them using one hand.

"I wouldn't have thought you liked it rough." He panted, working to hold her. She squirmed under him. "Kind of takes the fun out of it for me."

"All I have to do is scream."

He shook his head. "Everyone's gone. You're all mine." Looking her up and down, he licked his lips. "And I like leftovers."

His empty threats stung her. How dare Young Jasper, the manipulative jerk that he was, spy on her and Dalton. Moments with Dalton were special. Resentment spliced through her.

"Dalton's on his way. He'll be here any minute," she threw back. It was all she could think to say. With her hands bound behind her and his sweaty body pressed to hers, she was managing to slowly snail her way around the kitchen counter. She heard Dolly's frantic scratching at the cabin door.

He laughed at her, howling almost. "No, he won't. He's gone to The Silver Spur. Made plans with the guys. Heard him myself." He twisted her arms harder as she fought to free herself. "He's done with you, ya know. Seeing a blonde."

God, please don't let that be true. She clenched her teeth, wanting to cry.

Young Jasper roared with laughter. "Are you gonna cry? Am I hurting you?"

Samantha had never seen the whites of someone's eyes so full of rage and hatred. She hadn't gotten fully scared until he lowered the zipper of his pants. Until then, the peril seemed more verbal than physical.

Young Jasper flung her around on the counter, inches from the equine tool she planned to turn into a weapon. "Get ready to cry, bitch, 'cause, unlike Dalton, I like using the rear entrance."

He flipped her skirt up, exposing her thong, ripping the linen off in a single jerk. "This'll be my first time with a debutante. I can't wait to hear how one screams."

Excited and greedy, he lessened the grip on her hands and that was all the freedom she needed to snatch the hoof pick and stab him in the hand—of all places. She'd been going for the groin, but at least she had made contact.

He dropped her upon impact, and she shot to the knife drawer. The thick metal of the makeshift weapon was lodged in his hand, much like a fork stuck in a smoked turkey. He yanked it out and tucked the tool into his pocket.

"Finders keepers." His grin was laced with malice.

Samantha angled the butcher knife like a sword, hoping, if it came down to it, she could use it like one.

"Get out, you pathetic piece of trash, or I swear you won't have a dick left to piss with."

He mustered up some civility, and bent down to retrieve his shirt. "Sure thing, Sam. See ya around."

"Like hell, you will. You won't have a job after today."

He chuckled. "Conveniently enough, I quit today. Going back to riding broncs." He wrapped his bloody hand with his shirt and opened the front door, letting Dolly charge past him as he stepped out, his pants still unzipped, without another word.

Samantha exhaled. Her hands still grasped the knife, and she crossed the kitchen and dropped the utensil into the stainless steel sink with a clang. She was scared. Terrified. And it wasn't entirely due to Jasper's physical assault.

It was Dalton.

She was afraid Young Jasper was right. It explained Dalton's coldness to her, his casualness the last few weeks, as if he didn't care at all about her. She slumped onto the kitchen floor, hugging her dog, crying.

****

Horrendous devastation washed over Dalton. He stood in the tree line by the midwife's cabin and watched Young Jasper leave. His jaw clenched at seeing a bare chest, the wrangler's shirt held in his hand and his pants unfastened, a zealous snarl on his face, mimicking the rumbling hatred blistering inside him.

Never would he have thought Samantha this devious.

He'd come to apologize and to confess his distrust in her. He wanted her to know how guilty he felt for cold-shouldering her the past few weeks. He didn't like the way he was treating her and he wanted the games to end. Havoc, mistrust, and insecurity didn't sit well with him, and it definitely wasn't going to linger between the sheets of their bed anymore.

That was what he had meant to say.

Bile rose in his throat at the same time relief shadowed his earlier intentions.

Impeccable timing, princess. At least fate was on his side, making it easy for him to walk away worry-free.

He stalked to his truck and drove. The guys were meeting in town tonight, since it was Saturday. He'd hoped to bring Samantha with him.

On the accelerator, his foot itched to pound the gas pedal, but the angry, bruised soul inside of him wouldn't allow it. Because she wasn't worth it. Wasn't worth him losing his temper, his calm, or his cool or anything else he would ever again consider allocating to someone the likes of Samantha. Like he'd said before, she was gone to him. Only this time it was...forever.

Chapter Seventeen

Where was he? The one thing Samantha desired at this moment, she couldn't find. Stressed and frightened, she'd give anything to see Dalton—so she could jump into his protective arms and have the world slip away.

She was going to tell him everything: Young Jasper, the forced marriage, the extent of her wealth, everything that was coming between them.

The issue with her parents she wanted off her conscience. She had no aspirations to marry into money. Never would she do such a thing. She would explain Young Jasper and the night in the barn. In detail, she would tell him what had happened just now in her cabin. No, she wouldn't press charges, but Young Jasper needed to leave the ranch. It wasn't safe to have him around guests and young children, and especially not around her!

Most of all, she wanted to tell him she loved him. After all, it was time he knew for sure how she felt.

But she couldn't find him.

Quickly, she had changed into a pair of jeans, discarding the panties Young Jasper had ruined. The skirt was salvageable but she'd never wear the thing again. She hurried to the bunkhouse, hoping to catch him before he left—if he was leaving, as Young Jasper had said—but no one was there. In the barn, she didn't see anyone.

Young Jasper was correct. Everyone was gone, or up the mountainside in the lodge. Her cry for help would have gone unheard.

But she didn't have to worry about him anymore. She had watched him lug his bags to his pickup truck and tear out of the parking lot. This she had carefully witnessed before stepping foot outside her cabin.

With only Dolly at her side, she retreated to Beau's stall, a comforting, safe haven since she couldn't be in Dalton's arms.

She picked up a brush and curry comb and began grooming the horse, trying to keep her mind busy. In no time Beau had his head cocked to the side, his upper lip twitching from the scratching sensations of the rubber hairbrush. She groomed him from head to hoof for an hour.

With her hands tired, she decided a trip to the lodge might do her some good.

Latching Beau's gate, she hesitated before turning around. She thought she heard humming. That meant Josh was near. The guy was infamous for wearing headphones.

Hoping he might know where Dalton was, she followed his musical sounds.

Yes, there he was, sitting on the bench outside the bunkhouse, bouncing his head to a fast beat.

She cleared her throat.

Josh's eyes snapped open. "Hey, Sam. Didn't see you."

"Must be a good song."

He held the small musical contraption so she could see the song's title lit in neon blue on the screen.

"Yeah, that's a good one." Samantha had seen the movie at least a dozen times, and so had everyone else she knew who sat the saddle. "I was trying to find Dalton. Have you seen him?" She was hoping he wouldn't read into her question. They were still trying to keep their relationship quiet—which she thought they had achieved, until asshole Young Jasper brought it to her attention.

Samantha could tell by Josh's contracted brows and weary eyes he already knew. "He's still at The Silver Spur. Or at least he was when I left." He shrugged. "You know me, I only stay long enough to eat."

Samantha smiled and nodded. "Did it look like he was close to leaving?" An urgent, frustrated knot balled in her stomach. She took a step forward, intending to hop into her truck and hunt him down.

Josh grimaced. He yanked the earplugs from his ears.

Samantha stopped.

He blinked before saying, "Sam, he's not alone." His words were final.

Her eyes stilled on his. Samantha knew she could trust him. He wasn't one to lie.

Her eyes were brimming, she could feel them filling with moisture. She looked away from Josh to the chain of mountains in the distance.

Today was definitely not her day.

She felt as though she had a colossal hole in her heart and an opening in the pit of her stomach for the decimated organ to plummet into. Turning back to Josh, she whispered, "Thank you."

Samantha cursed herself. She should have guessed it, should have felt it. All this time she had been blaming Dalton's metamorphosis on her parents, when in fact he just didn't want her anymore. *Wow*. She felt like she'd been hit by a semi. Two weeks ago he had been so in love with her—or at least that's how their time together had felt. She shook her head, feeling as though it would somehow sort out the jigsaw puzzle of questions rattling around in her mind.

She let the screen door slam shut behind Dolly.

Upstairs, she lit a candle before crashing on the bed. She kicked her shoes off and pulled the soft bed linens up close around her. *God, please let me sleep. Let me lie here and not worry.* She started to sob, but stopped because, emotionally, she didn't have it inside her right now.

Tomorrow. She'd cry tomorrow.

****

"Want to talk about it?" Mary prompted.

"No." Dalton hunched over his coffee cup.

Talking was the last thing he was up to. He was relieved today was Sunday, a non-guest day. He wasn't in the mood for polite mingling. And he couldn't blame his disposition on a hangover. Last night he hadn't felt like drinking. He'd forced himself to stay at the bar as long as he did. For two hours he had sat next to the blonde and listened to her ridiculous banter about celebrities and clothing. Women were fake, he decided. Some on the outside, like the blonde, and others on the inside, like Samantha, with Samantha's being the absolute worst of the two.

He heard his aunt sigh, across from him. "Well, what's on the agenda for today?"

Dalton thought about snapping a reply, but refrained. His aunt wasn't to blame. She didn't know about Samantha's cunning, her ability to sham and mislead with the methodical ease of a pathological liar.

"Figure I'll work a few colts. Got a stubborn one that needs some attention." Funny, he could have been talking about her. That was, if he cared. Which he didn't.

"Oh, which one?" she asked suggestively, seeming to read his mind.

Dalton mumbled, eyeing her, "Not the one you're thinking." He scooted his chair back, retrieved his hat from the table, and placed his mug in the sink. "See you at lunch. I'll be in the barn if you need me," he growled as he lumbered to the door.

The cool mountain air helped simmer his temper down. He had hoped to wake feeling better, relieved, but that wasn't the case. Bitterness had festered inside him all night long. He hoped to change that today. Samantha was no longer a concern of his. To him she was an employee and, just like the rest, he would treat her accordingly. Whether she liked his management or not was up to her. With Young Jasper returning to the rodeo circuit, she along with everyone else would have to pick up the slack. Part of him wanted to see her fail. The other half of him, the business half, wanted the ranch to operate at maximum potential, and that meant keeping her around. With her exceptional nursing and wrangler skills, she was a valued asset to Twin Rivers—for however long she stayed.

He saddled up the two-year-old Doc Bar mare without any trouble. The friction didn't come until he asked the horse to give her head. She fought against the bit and tried to rear.

He decided to do some ground work with her before getting on. Minus watched from a seat on a bucket, inside a stall where he had a hawthorn poultice soaking on a horse's leg.

Busy with the mare, Dalton didn't see Samantha enter the barn. When he'd finished working with the horse, he walked it to the end of the arena and there she sat on the bleachers in shorts and a hooded sweatshirt. A tingle of sadness crept up on him. He would no longer be the one keeping her warm. And neither would Young Jasper. No wonder the long face.

He led the mare up to the metal stands.

Right away, he noticed the bruises on her knees and shins. With her arms crossed, he also saw some marks on her wrists. She and Young Jasper must have had a good time. He didn't know she liked it that rough.

"Where were you last night?" she asked.

He considered her question. Had she heard he was with the blonde last night? On a ranch the size of this one, news traveled fast. Good. He hoped she felt miserable, but somehow he doubted she had the ability to feel true sadness. Or perhaps she was upset over Young Jasper leaving. Who knew how long they had been sleeping together behind his back.

"In town." He was going to make her work for an answer.

She swallowed and tucked her hair behind her ear. "Look, I had a long night, so I'm gonna be blunt." She paused. "Were you with a girl last night?"

Dalton sniffed and his brows shot up. "You got some real nerve asking me that."

She jerked her head back and squinted. "What?"

He couldn't believe she was going to continue with her lies. "You can give up the act, Samantha. I know."

She sprang up, then sat back down, acting distraught.

Dalton noticed she couldn't look him in the eye. She focused on the horse, her feet, anything but him. If she was going to make a career out of being a pathological liar, she needed to work on the part where the devious person looks the individual straight in the eye during the actual fabrication.

Finally she stood, put her hands on her hips and cocked her head to the side. A fat tear dribbled down her cheek.

"You know what?" Her voice cracked. He fought the urge to chuckle. How could he have fallen for this?

"I know about Jasper. I saw him leave your cabin last night." He glanced at the dirt beneath his feet, nudging the ground with the toe of his boot. He'd never fathomed their relationship would come to this. Scornfully, he added, "He didn't even have the decency to zip his pants."

Dalton watched her choke on her own tears. She was in a frenzy. Glistening tears washed down her face. She raked her hair off her forehead, streaking it with wetness. Her lips puckered prettily. For an instance he wanted to kiss them. She was more beautiful upset, her features highlighted—blue eyes brighter, cheeks more pink.

Chest heaving, she cried through a clogged throat, "You saw what you wanted to see! You—"

He cut her off. "I saw him walk out of your cabin, with no shirt on, and his dick almost hanging out. That was enough," he barked. He didn't know he was capable of being so crude with a female.

She went silent, her eyes downcast. After a few seconds, she stepped off the bleachers to stand beside him. Her eyes flew to his, and this time she looked him dead in the eye.

"Yeah, I guess that's what you would see." The only movement on her face came from the tears blistering in her eyes. She turned and walked away.

Only a few times in Dalton's life had the hairs on the back of his neck stood up. One was when he watched the movie *The Sixth Sense*. The other was just now. He didn't know what kind of Liars Anonymous class they taught to rich girls, but it must have been one hell of a course.

****

"Sam, don't. Don't leave," Jessica begged. It was after dinner on a Saturday evening. They sat perched on the top rail of the arena fence, gazing distraughtly at the sun setting over the mountains.

Samantha closed her eyes to dam the tears. Leaving was the only thing she knew to do. She had already tried everything else. She'd spent the last month trying to win Dalton MacLaine back.

Nothing had worked.

Working herself like a dog didn't faze him. Being overly nice did nothing at all. She visited with his family more and more, since she didn't spend time with him, had gotten to know Mary like a sister. John thought the world of her. But still, it got her nowhere closer to where she wanted to be, which was with him, in his arms, the way they used to be.

At first she had been fuming mad at Dalton for believing he knew what he saw that fateful day. She'd never imagined he would be one to jump to conclusions and think the worst based on one instance. But then she went to hashing it over. She would have been devastated to see what he witnessed, and given the newsflash of her wealthy parents two weeks prior, she too could view it as overload.

He hardly ever said a word to her anymore. When he did, it was forced, and only for work purposes. She'd become transparent.

"How long will you stay on?" Samantha asked. She knew Jessica loved the ranch as much as she.

Her friend sighed. "If I had it my way, I'd never leave." Her eyes scanned the ranch and the main road with its quaint buildings facing the street. "This place gets in your bones after a while."

Samantha raised her brows and nodded. She knew exactly what her friend meant. Twin Rivers was the world to her. It was as if she were born to work this ranch. From the horses to the cows to the guests, it seemed ranching was embedded in her. She didn't want to leave, but the overwhelming suffocation she felt from Dalton's disregard was strangling her heart, and she just couldn't take it anymore.

While leaving would only deepen the hurt, staying had become pure torture.

Jessica turned sharply to look at her, "Sam, what will you do when you get home? Your inheritance is gone. Your parents..."

"Will have cut me off?" She sniffed and half laughed. "Yep."

"So?"

"So, I'll have to use that nifty nursing degree and live like a pauper for a while."

"And live where?"

Samantha shrugged. She didn't have an answer.

"Sam, just go to him," Jessica begged. "Tell him what really happened."

"No." Her eyes started to blur and her throat constricted. She would not go to him and serve her heart on a platter for him to decimate—again. Her next words came out shakily. "I looked him in the eye, Jess. There was nothing there."

Huffing, Jessica conceded, "Fine, but say you'll come back and visit."

"You know I can't promise that." She jumped down from her position on the fence, and together they headed toward the cabin, their last night as bosom buds on the Twin Rivers Ranch.

"Gosh, what will I do without you? And what in hell will you do without me?" Jessica threw an arm around her.

"Ah, you'll survive." Sam hesitated. "As for me, maybe I'll write a book." She was joking, of course. English was not one of her many talents.

Jessica angled her head. "Hmm. I wonder what you could name it?"

"Shit for Luck."

"Yeah, that'd work."

****

The following morning, Samantha waited until the ranch buildings were out of sight before she broke down crying over the steering wheel. Not only did she shed an abundant amount of tears, she bawled and squalled like a damned baby.

She'd had a chance to say goodbye to Dalton, but passed on it despite Mary's insistence. She couldn't stand the thought of it, the finality of farewell—forever.

When she pulled out with her truck and trailer, he was riding his horse the opposite way. No backwards glance.

She cried. She was leaving the summer of her life behind her.

Forever would she remember the ranch and the countless hours spent in the saddle scouring the land for cattle. Her fun times with Jessica. Her exceptional times with Dalton. The moments with Mary in the kitchen as her new, wise friend attempted to teach her a few "simple dishes." Minus and his Indian sayings. And John with his theory that Dolly wanted to chew his arm off.

Samantha choked on the tears welling up inside her. She wanted it back. All of it. Every moment. She hadn't so much as closed the gate on the property, and she wanted it back.

All she had to do was turn around.

She told herself this at every mile marker. And when Dolly Parton's *Hard Candy Christmas* came on at mile 234, she almost did.

When she arrived at Fern's place in the evening, she was exhausted and mentally depleted. She was saddened more to learn the elderly psychic had become ill. Frank informed Samantha of his wife's recent bout with pneumonia, explaining that all reservations except hers had been cancelled. Fern wouldn't allow him to call off Samantha's overnight stay, but she was so weak she couldn't take any visitors. He apologized on her behalf.

Turning out of the drive next morning, Samantha saw the curtains in the upstairs corner bedroom flutter. She knew it had to be Fern.

Samantha opened the small envelope Frank had given her at farewell. He explained it was a note from Fern. The message simply read: "Great love hurts."

"Great love." The same expression Minus had used. Only he had said it "lasts forever."

Hogwash. That's what it was. All of it. *Great love—what a joke. Dalton hates me.* Samantha crumpled the note and tossed the correspondence into the back seat.

She switched the song on the radio, selecting a tune by Metallica. She knew the name of the group only because the DJ had said who it was. Cranking the volume, she drove, trying not to notice the mile markers.

Chapter Eighteen

Samantha was thankful for her grandfather. He called her small home across town every day, checking up on her, and when he just "happened" to stop by three times a week, it was supposedly because he wanted to see how the flower garden was doing.

She hung up the phone with a chuckle, glad to have at least one member of the family still speaking to her.

Five years had gone by, and while her lifestyle had done a complete one-eighty, many things had stayed the same. Beau was still her best friend. They rode nearly every day, and she bred him out several times a year so she could afford to pay all the bills. The pasture he had now wasn't as big, but the rich Kentucky grass counterweighed the undersized acreage.

She walked outside and sat on the treated lumber step of the diminutive back porch. Beau was in the pasture, his coat shiny and slick as he grazed near the catfish pond. Dolly's grave marker was behind him, on top of the hill, near a cluster of willow trees. On a visit to the vet, a tumor had been found in her stomach, apparently the reason she had stopped eating. The vet believed it was the dog's way of telling Samantha it was her time to go. They decided euthanasia was best. Samantha dug the hole herself.

Next to leaving Twin Rivers, it had been the hardest thing she'd ever done.

The Montana ranch she loved so well was never far from her mind. She'd been joking the day she told Jessica she might try to write. But as it turned out, she decided to do just that, in her spare time away from the hospital.

Missing ranch life, she chose to re-create it by putting words on paper. Some days it went better than others. Some days the remembrances only brought back painful memories of how great her relationship with Dalton had been. Other days it was simply fun to reminisce.

However, she had bills to pay. While she hoped the manuscript would turn into something fruitful, perhaps something providing monetary income in the world of publishing, the story carried little weight with editors. Editors from New York to New England had rejected Samantha's numerous book proposals. One commented, "It's not considered trash if you recycle."

A year ago, Samantha had set the manuscript aside and vowed never to write again. She needed to move on from that Montana summer she'd spent wrapped in Dalton's arms. The manuscript wasn't helping her pay her bills nor aiding her ability to overcome the memories of him. However, soon after that, she received a letter from Frank, informing Samantha of Fern's passing. Fern's body had finally given in to complications of her last bout with pneumonia. She had moved on to a better place. At the bottom of the letter, in scribbled handwriting, was a message Frank said Fern had insisted be sent to Samantha: "Finish what you started."

The lump formed in Samantha's throat that day had put new meaning to her life. Fern had known something all along. Samantha didn't knew exactly what that was, but she had no intention of ignoring Fern—this time. Besides, if she could bind the summer of her life into a novel, perhaps she could forget it and move on.

Samantha went back to the manuscript. She re-wrote and re-edited every page to improve the story and the characters, which now bounced off the pages with real-life eccentricities. The fictional tale Samantha had written, based on her glorious, fun-filled summer in Montana, finally caught the eye of several agents. One, Faith Callahan, helped her reach publication.

Back in the house, Samantha saw the message light on the phone blinking. Selecting speakerphone, she listened to the accumulated messages as she washed her hands at the kitchen sink.

The first was Jessica MacLaine, pleading for her to visit next week, insisting the godmother of her son be present for the birthing. This was something Samantha had been dreading these past eight months. She was longing to see Jessica and the baby, but she knew returning to Montana would be bittersweet.

The second was from Mary, she too requesting Samantha be there to welcome Clay's son into the world. Mary demanded she stay at Twin Rivers, conditioning that if she didn't, Mary would boycott Samantha's novel. She giggled, listening to her demanding nags. Mary was never good at sounding mean.

Okay, so part of her did want to go.

The phone rang and she waited to see who it was. Probably just her grandpa.

Wrong. It was Faith. She was leaving a message, rattling on about reports and agendas, saying they should meet next week to talk about the *New York Times* bestseller list...where her book had just landed!

Samantha exploded with a shriek, bouncing to the phone. "What? Are you sure?"

Faith laughed. "Yes, I'm sure! *Blue Bandana*, number five. I'm looking right at it."

"Nuh-uh."

"It's true. You might want to reconsider that vacation after all."

Samantha raked her hair off her forehead. She couldn't believe this. Never did she imagine her book would go this far. She wanted to jump up and down, but instead she bit her lip, thinking how she could now afford to get Beau a real barn, instead of a one-sided lean-to.

"Sam, are you there?"

"Yes, I'm here. Just in shock, is all."

"Weren't you thinking about revisiting Montana? Perhaps this might be the best time. Now you can put it all behind you. The heartbreak will have been worth it."

Samantha didn't know if she could so easily agree, but she could see where Faith was going. She cleared her throat. "I might. Jessica will need me." Samantha had long ago found a good friend in Faith and had told her of Jessica and Clay's prospering relationship culminating in marriage the Christmas after Samantha left.

Gently, Faith asked, "Will you have to see him? Is there a chance you'll run into him?"

Samantha took a breath. "Mary tells me he has a place of his own, that the chances are slim." She hoped to God that was true.

Because running into Dalton was the last thing she needed.

****

Dalton slammed the book on the kitchen table in front of his aunt. His face singed with remorse. "Is this true?" he roared. "Is it?"

Mary swallowed and spoke calmly over the table. "Yes."

"How long have you known?"

"Since the day she left. Or perhaps I should say, since the day you left her."

Dalton had guessed his aunt would return to his house this morning, no doubt wanting his opinion on Samantha's breakout novel.

"She's always loved you. No amount of money in the world would change that."

"Where?" he growled, feeling half dead yet more alive than ever. He had stayed up all night reading Samantha's words and had just finished this morning. "Where is she? Is she here? It'd be like you to pull that off."

He watched tears leak from his aunt's eyes. "No." Her voice was no more than a whisper. "She's not here. No amount of magic in the world could pull that off. The small amount of pride you left her with, she's determined to keep."

He stared at the novel. "Did she really tell her parents she loved me?"

"Yes."

The only sound in the room came from Mary sniffing. The staff, scared off at his entrance, had made themselves scarce and found something, anything, to do elsewhere.

"And then some. But perhaps that's something you should ask her." She reached deep inside her pocket and handed him a crumpled self-stick note. "Her address."

With his stomach in knots, he raced up the carved cedar steps of his handcrafted cabin and marched past the monstrous, king-sized bed he was so fond of, its wooden canopy bed made of solid oak. When he woke up yesterday morning he hadn't thought his day would begin with a blow like this, but then he never imagined Samantha's book would read as it had, either.

Now he knew why Mary had forced the novel upon

him.
Samantha. Samantha Matthews. A name he thought he would never mutter or whisper again. Her words brought back so many emotions. Memories and feelings he thought he'd buried so deep inside they could never be recovered.

Dalton remembered well that summer they'd spent in the mountains. He didn't need published words to remind him of their time together. What he did need, however, was a swift kick in the ass for not believing in her five years ago.

It made sense to him now. Everything did. It's why she'd stayed on at the ranch, even after he verbally abused her for cheating on him. It's why she never said goodbye. She couldn't. She loved him too much. It's why Jessica held him in such contempt after Samantha left.

Damn women and their non-communication! All of this, the past five years, could have been spent with her if only she had opened up and told him about her parents and the forced match they'd threatened. His aunt and Jessica had known all this time!

He snatched a suitcase from the apartment-sized closet. He swore to himself, cussing as he rammed clothes into it.

If he caught a flight today, he could be with her by tonight, explaining and apologizing.

Packing a toothbrush and soap, realization dawned on him. He still loved her. He wasn't a frantic person. He didn't do frantic things. As a matter of fact, he was the most level headed s-o-b he knew, yet now he was going out of his mind! He had to see her, had to tell her he loved her, was in love with her, that he would never, ever let her walk away from him—again.

****

Once again parked in front of the barn at Twin Rivers, Samantha stepped out of the truck she'd borrowed from her grandfather, acting with more assurance than she felt. Reserved, she folded her arms across her chest and glanced around, seeing the ranch accented in brilliant fall hues of orange, amber, and olive green.

Pumpkins and corn, every size and color, lined the window boxes of the quaint buildings facing the main road. Large pumpkins with faces sat plopped on steps. At every angle Samantha saw eccentric smiles, menaces, and one-toothed gaps focusing on her. They seemed to mock the way she felt. She didn't know if she should feel sad, scared, or just plain stupid for returning.

Everything else was the same—the dusty main road, the shotgun buildings and porches, the jagged mountains framing the valley, the awe-inspiring lodge situated high on the hillside. The evergreen smell she loved so much was now tinged with a dash of fallen leaves.

And, just that fast, it hit her in the stomach. She knew how she felt.

Regretful.

Like gunfire, the notion exploded into her. Five years of suppressed pressure, accumulated against her will no matter how she had tried to fight it, had just released itself in the form of ugly regret. Her veins were pulsing and her head aching from the force of it. Dear God, what was she thinking? She wasn't ready for this. She wasn't ready to be back here.

She practically swaggered to the rear of the horse trailer. Her mind told her she needed to snap out of it. Get Beau out of the horse trailer, her psyche was telling her. Focus. He might be watching.

With knees like jelly, she backed Beau out of the trailer and led him to his old stall. Clean shavings and a flake of hay were in place. A fresh bucket of water hung in the corner.

Samantha had dabbled with the thought of not bringing her horse. She didn't want to relive that summer, those blissful weeks she'd spent riding next to Dalton, racing along the mountain, the wind in her hair, laughing as Beau galloped effortlessly past the trusty steed Dalton had promised the stallion would lose to this time. Mary, however, had insisted she haul him the distance, saying the four-year-old son she'd gotten out of Beau and her palomino mare was marvelous and she'd go to any extreme to have another.

Samantha had agreed. She needed the money, but she was quick to explain she wouldn't be able to stay long. She used work as an excuse. Also, she now had a house to look after. Thelma Francis, the energetic, feisty older woman from across the street would look after her home for a time. Samantha had given her a key so she could bring the mail in and water the plants. Thelma Francis was long retired and overly spry for her age. Several times Samantha had caught a wayward glance between her and her grandfather as he instructed the outspoken and contrary woman on what to hoe and what not to over water. Samantha guessed it was an excuse on her grandfather's part that he "might have to check on" Thelma, too, while she was gone.

With Beau settled, she grabbed her luggage and headed for the lodge. Two steps away from the truck, her arms loaded down with bags and her head held high for appearance, she saw a familiar face that made her eyes water and her jaw tremble.

Minus.

Delighted to see her friend, Samantha dropped her bags and ran to him, throwing her arms around him. She hugged him tight, not at all caring how childish it might look. In return, he embraced her like one would soothe an upset youngster. As it always was with her and him, she felt instant solace. He'd always had that effect on her. He was better than any anti-anxiety med on the market.

She gathered herself and stepped back, flicking at the tears that tumbled down her cheeks. She smiled at him, feeling relieved.

They retrieved her bags and Minus put an arm around her shoulder as they turned for the lodge. "Rivers overflow for reasons not to be ignored."

Samantha sniffed, knowing his words were accurate.

Seeing Mary and John again was like coming home, a feeling of being safe and wanted.

She had arrived on a Friday, expecting to dine with the ranch's guests, but found there to be none. Thinking ahead of her long-awaited grandchild, Mary had blocked off the entire week and allowed the wranglers a vacation as well. Minus had chosen to stay, and so for dinner the four of them dined in the cozy employee kitchen.

As was customary, Samantha updated herself by reading letters posted on the message board. She read Luke's cards and noted his improved penmanship over the years. He hadn't missed a summer on the ranch. School pictures showed he was taller, his little-boy features a faint remembrance in her Montana summer. Lost time made her heart ache.

They filled Samantha in on the few changes that had taken place. No further mountain lion attacks had occurred since that summer, but in case it should, a new fence had been secured around the immediate ranch setting. It allowed visitors to ride in the safety of a wrangler at all times. With the help of binoculars, a wrangler could watch from the lodge and see if a guest was having trouble. John explained the wrangler on duty always had a firearm at his side, fully loaded and ready to aim should a wild lion or bear appear.

The four of them talked for hours, about everything imaginable. Jessica and Clay were still undecided on a name. On Monday, she would be induced if she didn't go into natural birth before then. In addition to Mary's horse, Minus and John had selected three mares they wanted bred to Beau, each with impeccable breeding. They hoped they would all take. Tomorrow night, Mary wanted to show Samantha a new ranch to the west of them. They would look at that on the way to see Jessica, since she and Clay were staying in town, close to the hospital.

They talked about everything and everyone—except Dalton.

Samantha slept well that night, awakening only three times with Dalton on her mind. Before going to bed she'd checked the parking lot for his truck or one that might be his. With five years gone by, who knew what he might be driving. She hated to admit it, but she wondered if he looked any different. The man couldn't be any better looking. Perhaps he was more muscled now. It'd be fine with her if he had gotten fat and gray. He deserved as much.

By 9:00 a.m. the next morning, Samantha and Mary were surveying the herd, having one last look at the mares. Beau had already mounted one. After lunch, they planned on breeding him to a good-natured paint with a bald face.

When they were through verifying the selection, Samantha took a ride on Beau's son. The horse was solid black, his coat rippling with muscles, and he was every bit as gentle as Beau. Mary had named him Oliver. She said the name fit him because he was dark and mysterious on the outside with a soft gentleness inside.

"I can't wait to see Jessica. I can't believe it's been five years," Samantha told Mary as they left the barn. "It seems like just yesterday we were here, roping cattle, having the time of our lives." They walked the stone path under the aspen groves to the lodge, ending the day early so they could head into town.

"Well, she still looks the same, except with a basketball belly."

Samantha shook her head and chuckled. That image she would have to see for herself.

Mary opened the back door to the lodge and Samantha entered behind her. Out of habit, her eyes settled on the inviting sofa. So many times, Jessica and she would arrive last to dinner to find the wranglers, including Dalton and Clay, sprawled out on the cushions there, waiting for their late arrival. Dalton would dart a suggestive look, teasing that he would deal with her lack of promptness later, when they were alone.

Samantha remained gazing at the couch, wishing she had it all to do over again.

"Sam?" Mary interrupted. "You okay?"

"Yes, I'm fine." She smiled. "Just an old memory." She took a deep breath. Treading the steps, she asked, "So, have you read it? You mentioned you looked for it at the bookstore."

One step ahead of her, Mary answered, "Jessica and I went and each bought a copy several weeks ago. Two days later, we'd read it. The last chapter we read together, out on the patio. You should have seen us, each so immersed we couldn't tear our eyes away."

Samantha cheesed behind her.

"I'll have you know you had both of us boohooing. We each had to grab a tissue. Actually, we ran out of tissue. Jessica didn't want to get up from the couch so she used the corner of her shirt and then later said I should have catered to the pregnant mother-to-be and brought her a fresh box." Mary reached the top step. "It was that good."

Samantha laughed, visualizing the scene just as

Mary described.

"I was glad you ended it the way you did, with a happy ending," Mary added, somewhat subdued.

Standing across from her at the entrance to their rooms, Samantha confided, "Readers don't want unhappy endings. They read to escape and to believe in the context of safety—or at least that's what the publishing world says." She chuckled. "I say emotions in reality are never safe."

Mary's smile was fragile. "We'd better get dressed, dear. We don't want to be late."

"How are we dressing? Casual?"

"Yes, that's fine. Dress comfortable. It could be a long night."

Chapter Nineteen

It was just as Dalton had imagined. The mansion Samantha lived in with her parents bore a striking resemblance to the White House, of all places. Five pillared columns framed the front, their structure massive and oversized, just like the rest of the property. Shiny, white plastic fencing in a four-rail arrangement flanked the rolling green hills on both sides of the house and barn.

Dalton drove his four-door rental car onto the bricked drive by the barn, stepped out and was immediately surrounded by three barn hands, all dressed in fancy black work pants and red suspenders. They were high-school age but definitely to be reckoned with, going by the stern looks they wore on their faces. By Dalton's guesstimate, they were the first layer of protection before the men behind the fancy front door came to greet him.

"Can we help you, sir?" the tallest one asked.

"I'm looking for Samantha Matthews. Would you know where I can find her?"

The trio appeared dumbfounded by his question.

"Sam, the daughter of—"

From around the barn, an old man popped out. His attire was identical to that of the young men. He walked with a slight limp, but was fast on his feet. "That would be my granddaughter you're speaking of. Perhaps I can be of assistance." He motioned for the boys to move on about their business.

Dalton held out his hand. "Name's Dalton MacLaine."

The old man's eyes twinkled. "Clarence Matthews. Nice to meet you. Where is it you know my granddaughter from?"

"From Montana, sir. She vacationed on our family ranch five years ago."

The man nodded, tying the pieces together. "Yes, Sam really took a liking to the place."

Hearing her spoken name gave Dalton shivers.

The white-haired gentleman guided him to a bench near a tall maple tree and they both sat.

"Sam doesn't live here anymore. Hasn't for a while now. She's got a place on the other side of town."

Dalton scratched his head. He hadn't thought of that possibility. He assumed his aunt had given him the correct address.

The old man changed the subject. "You've come an awfully far way to see her."

Not about to hesitate, Dalton answered, "It's important. I need to speak with her."

"I'll be happy to give you the directions. You just have to promise to buy a copy of her book when you get a chance."

Dalton liked the old man. "Give you my word."

Once he had the directions in his hands, Dalton drove rapidly to the opposite side of town, taking note of how the house sizes were getting smaller and smaller. He squinted at the address the old man had written down. It should be the next house over the hill. He tossed the directions onto the seat next to him, on top of his initialed briefcase.

Nah, this can't be. Samantha wouldn't live in a house this...pathetic. The red brick one-story was old, by at least a hundred years or so, the roof stained black from water damage and several of the windows cracked in places.

The yard was cared for, with flowers of all kinds planted around the house.

Dalton knocked on the front door but got no answer. The antique drapes were pulled, so he couldn't see in. He saw no signs of Samantha at this residence. He must have the wrong address.

He decided to walk around back, just to be sure. He followed the uneven, crumpling concrete drive to a shed full of hay. It had a weary lean-to on one side. Empty buckets hung on nails and manure piles showed obvious signs of it being a makeshift stall.

Looking out at the pasture, he saw a small pond. Something silver in the field sparkled in the sun just beyond it. He opened the gate, the shrill creaking nearly unbearable. So much for snooping.

Several paces into the grass, below the limbs of a

willow tree, Dalton found a metal grave marker. Not exactly the sign he was looking for, but then he didn't know what possessed him to walk out into the middle of a strange field in the first place. Desperation, he figured. He turned around and the wind picked up. Behind him, he heard the rackety spinning of the silvery marker. He hesitated before turning.

A name was embossed in large capital letters.

DOLLY.

Dalton almost dropped to his knees. He had found her. His heart catapulted as he sprinted to the house and pounded on the front door.

"Might I be of help to you, sir?" The voice was female, old and direct, and none to friendly. She cracked the door open an inch.

"I'm looking for Samantha. Have I found the right place?" he asked, catching his breath. All he could see was a thick cocoon of gray hair.

"And just who is asking?" The woman jerked the door open and stepped out onto the warped wooden porch. The crotchety old bat eyed his rental car.

"I'm an old friend of Samantha's, from out of town."

Her large beady eyes narrowed. "Oh you are, huh." Dalton was caught off guard when she traipsed to the white sedan and peeped in the windows.

After seeing all she wanted, the contrary battleaxe flounced to his side and inspected him from head to toe. She frowned. "Well, you're a bit late. Miss Samantha left town yesterday."

Dalton never knew Miss had such a wonderful ring to it. "And you are?"

I'm a neighbor. Live across the street." She nodded to the only house around. "I'm looking after things."

Yep, Dalton could see she had that task down pat. He was curious to know what her former job had been. She would have done well working for the FBI.

Dalton returned his gaze to the feisty woman. "I really need to see her. Can you tell me where she went?"

"On vacation," she snapped. "The girl needed one." She walked past him, stepped up on the porch, and spun around, eye level with him. She cleared her throat before speaking.

Never mind FBI, a drill sergeant was more likely.

"She described you to a T in that book of hers." Dalton watched her features soften while he felt his tighten, unsure of where she was going with her statement. "Yeah, I know who you are. You're the cattleman who broke her heart and left her with the pieces."

Dalton didn't so much as blink.

"Excellent job you did of shattering it, too. Might as well have pulverized it and scattered it from here to the moon." Her voice rose like an escalator.

What could he say to that? A wee bit exaggerated, but nonetheless the truth. He glanced to the ground for courage. Looking at her, he said, "That's why I'm here. I need..."

"Have you any idea the grief that girl went through for you?" the hellcat interrupted. She stepped forward.

"No," Dalton answered honestly.

"Well, I sure do. That poor woman used to bawl herself to sleep at night. I could hear her through the broken windows. In the morning I'd come over to check on her, and she'd say it was the television and that she would be sure to remember to turn it down!" She pressed on. "The only family she has left is a grandfather. Her best friends are her horse and the dog she buried two years ago."

Shaking his head with the wealth of information the old lady was heaving upon him, Dalton paused. It didn't make sense. "What do you mean, she only has a grandpa? I've met her parents."

"Then you can imagine their reaction when she refused to marry the way they wanted. And that on top of the inheritance she donated away."

Staring, Dalton's eyes jumped back and forth with his thoughts.

She clicked her teeth. "Didn't know about that either, huh, sonny?"

He closed his eyes as he came to a conclusion.

"That's right. They disowned her—cut her off! She now has this handsome house," she drove home her meaning by glancing at the ragged structure, "because her grandfather helped her get a loan." She folded her arms. "How's that for true love?"

Devastated and borderline irate, Dalton's jaw clenched. "Where is she?" he demanded.

"She's returned to Montana," she replied crisply. "So if you know what's good for ya, you'll get to headin' that way yourself, Mr. MacLaine."

The only flight Dalton could get was coach, Seat B, between a pair of avid dog lovers. The middle-aged couple had met in the lounge and persisted in talking nonstop about canine conformation and flawless pedigrees all the way from Lexington to Billings.

Dalton resorted to watching the flight channel, making his best attempt to tune them out.

When the plane landed, he waited for his one bag of luggage. It was a leather duffel bag, stuck in between two dog carriers, one pastel pink, the other baby blue.

Dalton kindly helped the lady from Seat A untangle the shoulder strap from the front wire door of the pink box.

"Oh, thank you, sir, that's nice of you." She reached inside the carrier.

Dalton barely heard her. His brain was on a mission to find Samantha as his hands worked to straighten the carrier's straps. He assumed Sam would be either with his aunt or with Jessica, most likely the latter since her friend was close to giving birth.

"I get so worried sending them on planes. Especially this one. She's so sweet and cute."

Yeah, sure she is, Dalton thought. He was almost done unraveling the half-gnawed strap when he glanced at the puppy the lady now cradled, the pink blanket coming loose as it slept in her arms. Without the blanket he could see the markings, the gray-and-black-marbled hair coat. His hands froze.

"What?" the lady asked.

Dalton answered in dead seriousness. "I need that puppy."

The animal didn't sleep for long in his arms. As soon as the lady handed her over, the small pooch began to fidget and squirm. Thankfully, Seat A lady had agreed to pitch in the leash for the outrageously-priced, highly-pedigreed pup. Dalton figured the little monster probably needed to take a whiz. He was making his way to the outside of the airport to find a small patch of grass before his green shirt resembled a lawn of any sort.

"Good dog," he told the puppy as she urinated in the grass next to the parking lot. He sat on the curb to allow her time to consider unloading from the rear hatch, because he definitely didn't want that kind of mess on his leather truck seats.

What would he say to Samantha? He watched the puppy bounce around in the grass. Perhaps the cute little bundle could be an ice-breaker.

"Dalton MacLaine. What are you up to?" He heard over his shoulder.

"Young Jasper. How ya doing?"

"Ah, I'm doing pretty well. Just getting back in town."

Dalton nodded. "Still on the circuit? I haven't seen you in years."

"Oh, yeah." He considered the pup frolicking in the grass. "What you got there? A pup?"

Chuckling, Dalton answered, "More like a small monster."

Young Jasper pulled at his ear. "Yeah, um, it looks like what's-her-name's...heck, I can't remember her name." He laughed. "Slept with her and can't remember her name. How about that?"

"How about that," he repeated, knowing exactly where Young Jasper was going with his statement. He acted like he didn't care. He stood and scooped up the animal.

"That chick I slept with that one summer—the one from Kentucky. Yeah, she was pretty good. Had awesome tits."

Walking away casually, Dalton waved. "See ya around."

Sitting in the driver's seat, Dalton felt like pounding the wheel. Everything he had done for the past three days had been centered around Samantha, and it was nothing more than a waste of time. That's right, all the memories, the good and the bad, were back in the frontal lobe of his head. The bitch had cheated on him and lied straight to his face about it—apparently one element of her story she didn't feel like adding into her compelling novel about that summer.

He remembered now that Young Jasper had been the final blow to their relationship. Seeing him walk out of her cabin that summer, half dressed, had spurred him to completely forget about her. Thank God he had witnessed it himself, otherwise he might not have believed it. He could have been the idiot fool he was just ten minutes ago—the one running back to her and begging for forgiveness with a friggin' puppy in his arms!

Dalton exited the airport and headed for his home in the mountains. He cursed himself for having put his business plans aside for Samantha. He cursed for having bought a mangy mutt he didn't know what to do with. "Dammit!" The puppy froze in the passenger seat, peeked at him, then cowered into a ball. Dalton decided he'd pawn her off on the maids.

All he wanted to do was get home and have a nice peaceful dinner and forget that Samantha Matthews ever existed.

Chapter Twenty

Samantha marveled at the exterior architecture of the cabin. Made of dry-stack moss rock and worm-kill logs, the spacious rustic cabin blended into the Montana wilderness right in front of her eyes. A driftwood horse sculpture greeted them at the massive front doors under the singular log portico.

"Mary, this place is gorgeous. I've never seen anything like it."

"I thought you might say that."

Greeted by a cordial housekeeper, Mary led the way through the dramatic entrance of the luminous foyer. Cantilevered logs supported the grand reception space, making Samantha feel like a princess in a castle.

"Dinner will be ready at seven, Mrs. MacLaine," the housekeeper stated.

Mary smiled at her. "Thank you, Gloria. I'll show Samantha around until then."

Samantha followed Mary through the open living area, past the candlelit dining space, into the elaborate atrium, complete with an indoor swimming pool. The room was built to give the feeling of being outdoors, with sparkling blue water shimmering under vaulted wooden beams.

"Tell me, Mary. Who can afford to live like this? It's amazing."

"He's in the cattle industry, and apparently he's an expert." Samantha watched her fidget with her watch.

"Are we late?"

"Oh, no. It's just my stomach. Feeling a bit sour, is all."

Samantha reached for her purse, then remembered she'd left it in the car. "I have some antacid. Should I go get it?"

Mary's brows shot to her hairline. "No, no. You stay here. I'll get it. You look around."

Samantha knew upscale living when she saw it, having lived in fine fashion for the first twenty years of her life. Never had she taken it for granted. The home she had now was at best modest but nonetheless hers. She sat at one of the café-style tables by the pool, noting the elaborate touches everywhere.

Something about this place seemed familiar to her, but she couldn't pinpoint what the familiarity was. Perhaps the residence had been featured in some magazine she'd flipped through.

"Miss," the housekeeper called out, "I'll show you into the dining room now."

She hopped up. "My friend, she went to get something. She'll be right back."

"Yes, Miss. We'll show her in." She led Samantha to her seat at a large round table. "Your host will be with you shortly."

A formal dinner setting was placed before her. For the first time ever, Samantha was relieved she knew the proper dinnerware. Above her a pounded copper lighting fixture glowed softly, and to her side a gentle fire crackled in the grate. The intricate wooden doors to the room were winged open.

A rustling of noises came from outside the room as she waited, sounding much like scurrying. Concerned voices followed.

A small puppy bounded into the room and made its way towards her.

Samantha recognized the breed instantly, surprised at how much the dog resembled Dolly. She picked the puppy up and placed it on her lap, talking to it, scratching its adorable head. Outside the dining room, she heard footsteps approaching. Samantha and the puppy both looked up.

To see Dalton MacLaine enter, escorting an alluring blonde.

****

His aunt entered the room five minutes too late to witness the full awkwardness of the situation. Dalton would deal with her later. Right now he was too busy wanting to strangle Samantha.

"I see we've all met," Mary said to the group. Dalton

saw the subtle look she gave Samantha.

"All but the puppy, I believe. Just brought her home today," he announced, not about to let Samantha ruin any more of his day.

Next to him, Hillary asked, "Have you named it yet, darling?"

They turned to see the puppy cozily settled on Samantha's lap.

Dalton frowned at having to look in her direction. "No, I haven't."

He called for Gloria to rid the canine from the room.

The salad plates were served entirely too slowly for his taste. He very much wanted to eat and then retire, leaving his fine dinner companions to themselves—all but Hillary. He did have plans that included her being naked in his bed.

"So, Mary, do you plan on being present when Clay's baby arrives?" It was his best attempt to sound nice. It came off fake even to him.

"Yes, Samantha and I both do."

He felt like puking. "Good. I'm sure Jessica will appreciate that."

"Dalton, your home is beautiful," Samantha spoke. It was the first thing she had said, other than her name to Hillary.

Looking at her directly for the first time, he answered, "Thank you."

Dinner plates were brought to the table, along with wine and champagne.

It killed Dalton to see Samantha in his home, seated at his table. The old adage of pouring salt in the wound sprang to mind. For years he had imagined her living under this very roof, dining with him, living with him as his wife.

Situated across from him, Samantha's beauty was flawless. Those gorgeous blue eyes of hers still fascinated him—the sight of them gnawed at his core, making him wonder *what if*. She wore a simple white dress and had her hair loose down her back. Her natural skin tone and graceful poise were a sharp contrast to Hillary's tanned skin and flirtatious demeanor.

"What is it that you do, Samantha?" Hillary asked.

Samantha set her fork down and tucked her hair behind her ear—something she did when she was nervous. He could read her like a book.

"I—"

"She's an author," Mary blabbed. "Writes romance."

Hillary threw her bleached blonde hair behind her, laughing. "Not erotic, I hope."

Dalton saw Samantha's blue eyes light up with humor. "No, not erotic. Just simple romance."

"But doesn't erotic pay better?"

Dalton wished Hillary would shut up. After all, his aunt was sitting next to him.

Finishing her glass of wine, Samantha sighed. "I don't know. I hadn't really thought about that." Dalton could see her thinking. His heart actually pained a bit, knowing her present living conditions. He wanted to advise her to write about sheets and cum so she could afford the new roof and windows she needed for her dilapidated house.

Then he recalled Young Jasper. And all the lies.

"Where did you get the puppy, Dalton? Catahoulas are a rare breed."

"The lady next to me on the plane was a breeder. She gave me a good deal," he lied. Something in him snapped. He was ready to end this charade.

"I saw an old friend today," he remarked. He looked from Mary to Samantha. "Young Jasper's back in town."

Samantha only slightly flinched, but he couldn't mistake hearing her sharp intake of air. Dalton watched her downcast eyes. He also watched Mary glance at her, worriedly. So his aunt knew about that, too. Interesting.

Dalton rose from his chair. "Well, ladies, it's been lovely. Please tell Jessica I'm thinking about her. Gloria will show you out." He offered Hillary his arm and left the room.

****

"Mary," Samantha pleaded. "I think I'm going to throw up."

"Oh dear, let's go." She led Samantha down the hall, in the opposite direction from the one taken by Dalton and Hillary. "There's a room right off the kitchen."

Bile rose in Samantha's throat. Coated with rejection

and resentment, the fluid tasted bitter and foul. Dalton mentioning Young Jasper's name was beyond acrimony. She'd been distraught at having to see him, but the vengeance he'd extracted with Young Jasper's name was pure malice.

"Sam, I'm so sorry," Mary apologized. She led her into a spacious guest room.

Racing for the toilet, Samantha flipped up the seat and dropped to her knees, hovering over the commode. Thoughts raced through her mind: the memory of Young Jasper and his cruel hands, the harm he had intended to reap upon her, Dalton and the calculating glances he'd just shot her across the table.

Vomit spewed from Samantha. Projectile, it blasted into the toilet.

Done, Samantha covered her face with her hands and cried. "I still love him, and I hate myself for it."

Choked with emotion, Mary helped her to her feet. "I know. I know you do."

Samantha tore her hands from her face, shaking her head. "I didn't do it, Mary. I didn't sleep with Jasper. I would never—"

"I know, Sam. And one day Dalton will know, too. He's just too hurt to see it now."

"You, you know?" Samantha stuttered and sniffed. "About what happened?" She wobbled a bit, the nausea settling.

Her voice was stripped of judgment. "Jessica told me, a few summers ago."

Overwhelmed, Samantha's eyes shifted to the floor, then to the adjoining room. A huge canopy bed, garlanded with white linens and half a dozen pillows on a plush milky comforter goaded her. Tormenting thoughts of *what if* haunted her mind. For all the midnight snacks she would never have, she closed her eyes and let the tears flow, remembering the candid conversation she and Dalton had had about her desire for a canopied guest room close to the kitchen.

"Let's go, Mary. I can't stay here any longer."

****

The next morning, Samantha rode Beau atop the mountain ridge, within the boundary of the new pasture, keeping the lodge in sight. She spurred him into a fast lope, following the impulse to ride fast and furious in an attempt to blow off the pent-up steam lingering from last night. Both the rhythmic movement of the horse beneath her and the ice-tipped wind nipping at her helped to numb her jangled nerves.

Dalton still believed she had slept with Young Jasper that summer five years ago. His accusation of cheating burned inside her like acid, eating away the calm she was seeking.

Envy like she had never known twisted inside her at seeing Dalton smile and flirt with another woman. The blonde was so opposite of herself. Long, tan legs that didn't stop, mouth-watering cleavage, and a sexual confidence Samantha was sure Dalton found arousing in the bedroom. The way he had supported the small of her back as they left the room stung her, and it pissed her off all the more that she allowed it to consume her.

She slowed Beau to a walk along the ridge. They ambled their way through the scattered rock boulders.

Last night, Mary and Jessica had both apologized repeatedly to her. They had only meant to fix things, and their efforts had fallen far short of mending the relationship the two of them craved so badly between her and Dalton.

Samantha needed to focus. Dalton was lost to her. He'd been gone from her life for some time now. Nothing was going to mend their relationship, because they didn't have a relationship. And words bound inside a book didn't count. She knew that. That was precisely why she had written the damned thing in the first place. To forget. To move on.

The blustery wind on the mountain caused the blue bandana knotted around Samantha's neck to flutter, and Beau's sedate walk became a side-stepping jig. His neck arched and ears pricked forward. He smelled something. "Easy, Beau." She patted his neck.

A rock tumbled loose in front of them and plunged down the hillside. Beau halted, snorting. "It's okay," Samantha tried to reassure him, but he continued to fidget, finally rearing, striking the air in front of him. "Beau," she hollered, but it was too late. She had already been plucked from the saddle.

****

One more outburst from that puppy, and Dalton was going to pull his hair out. Not sleeping well, he awoke to the sound of a gurgling growl and found his leather boots chewed, ground into a pulp by the innocent face of the hound peering at him.

Flinging back the covers, he jumped out of bed, cursing. He knew what his next move was. "As of today, pup, you've got a new home." He bent down and snatched the mangled boots. "Hope you like Kentucky."

Carrying the squirming puppy through the front door of Twin Rivers, he looked for his aunt and uncle. He found them in the living room, conversing with Minus.

"Got a delivery," he announced. He let the puppy leap out of his arms.

All three stared at him.

His aunt rose. "Well, if you've come to say you're sorry, you'll have to wait. Samantha's out riding." Her tone was snippety, to say the least.

"That's not why I came."

Mary sighed. "Well it should be."

The displeased look his uncle flashed him from across the room was lethal.

Disgusted, Dalton shook his head. "Fine. Which way did she ride?" He'd tell Samantha himself about the puppy and explain that it needed a home.

They shrugged. They didn't know.

John rumbled, "She said she wasn't leaving the surrounding pasture."

Dalton turned sharply on his heel, stalked to the barn and saddled Oliver. The horse was fast on his feet and trustworthy, being half kin to Samantha's stallion.

Prowling for signs of a horse and rider, Dalton walked Oliver so the puppy could keep up. He knew Samantha wouldn't be hard to find. There were few places where a rider couldn't be seen from the lodge. Knowing where to search, he headed for the top of the ridge.

A blue speck tossed in the wind near a group of aspens, flittering down the mountainside, limp. Trash? The puppy ran ahead of him, happy to have something to fetch.

As he rode along the trail, Dalton decided to make amends with Samantha. As long as she remained friends with his aunt, and godparent to his future nieces and nephews, a grudge would only worsen things on the family front.

Seeing Samantha again had brought it all back. He still desired her. He would never admit it but he did still love her. No one had ever filled the void she'd left in his heart. Even Hillary, last night, had been sent home early. There was no comparison between the two, and he wasn't one to compromise.

The energetic, nameless pup bounced down the hill, carrying the retrieved item. Dalton dismounted, and the puppy brought it to him.

Samantha's bandana.

Dalton knew she didn't go anywhere without the darn thing. Mounting his horse, he cued Oliver into a gallop. He scanned the mountaintop, seeing no sign of her or her horse. He brought his horse to a halt and listened. The wind whipped, rustling the trees and billowing his jacket around him.

Then a frantic whinny caught his attention. He steered his horse toward the sound.

"Don't!" he heard Samantha beg. "Don't hurt him!"

Beau's front legs were hobbled and bleeding. Young Jasper jerked the horse by the bridle.

He had something clasped in his hands, Dalton couldn't tell what, but he could tell the man intended to harm the stallion with it.

"It's you or him. Make a choice," Young Jasper threatened.

Samantha stepped forward. "Me." She nodded to the horse. "Let him go."

Young Jasper did as she requested, freeing the horse. Violently, he jerked Samantha towards him and grabbed a fistful of hair. "Remember this?" He forced her to look at the object he held next to her face.

Dalton inched forward to better his view. Young Jasper held a sharpened hook pick. If this was a lover's quarrel, it was one for the storybooks, because the conversation they were having was definitely heated. And for Young Jasper to have harmed Samantha's horse, the situation was clearly out of her control.

"All too well," she spat.

Laughing, Jasper said, "I almost had you that day."

Samantha reached to smack him, but Jasper caught her arm and twisted it behind her. She screamed in pain.

Young Jasper dropped the weapon and delivered a smack across her left cheek, throwing her head back. Composed, she turned to him, her lip broken and bleeding.

"Dalton thinks we were lovers. You know that?" he bragged.

"All too well."

He smacked the opposite side of her face.

"You foiled my plans for Dalton, you little bitch. I planned on running Twin Rivers into the ground. That way Dalton would never have anything—kind of like me. For years, I was in his shadow. 'Dalton this, Dalton that.' Everyone always loved Dalton. They never saw me."

"So all the injuries, the mountain lion..."

Young Jasper nodded. "Uh-huh. It was all me. The growl was recorded, but real. Glorified traps did the rest. Smart, huh?"

"Not smart enough." Dalton strode out from behind the boulder. He crossed his arms, letting the man see he had nothing to fight with.

Young Jasper yanked her close. Samantha's eyes pleaded for understanding.

Yes, Dalton understood everything now. Samantha was his, had been his all along.

"Hey Dalton. Glad you could join the party. Samantha and I were just up here enjoying ourselves."

"Yeah, I can see she's really into it. Say, didn't you have a thing for her tits?"

Thrown off course, Young Jasper's eyes darted in thought. Dalton's right hand shot to his back pocket for the knife he carried. He yelled for Samantha to duck and threw the blade, nailing Young Jasper deep in the thigh. He lost his hold on Samantha and hunkered, cursing them both as Samantha raced to Dalton, crying. He embraced her, keeping an eye on Young Jasper. In her ear he breathed, "Sam, I'm sorry. I'm so sorry I doubted you."

****

On the front porch of the lodge, the five of them watched the squad car pull away with Young Jasper in the back seat. Dalton stood behind Samantha, his arms around her shoulders. "I'm never going to let you out of my sight again."

Samantha chuckled. "Fine with me. I never wanted to leave in the first place."

Next to him, Minus winked while John and Mary smiled knowingly.

"Well, we'd best head to the hospital," Mary spoke. "Jessica called to say the twins are on the way."

"Twins?" Samantha asked, a chill fleeting through her.

"It's a surprise."

Dalton turned Samantha in his arms and took in her dazed expression. "Why is that so shocking?" he asked.

"Somebody I once knew said there would be twins in my life."

"Well, they guessed right."

Minus cleared his throat. "When you're not looking, you find what you need the most."

"Yes," Samantha agreed, looking up to Dalton. "Great love shows up when you aren't watching."

Dear Reader,

I hope you enjoyed reading Samantha's and Dalton's story. After taking several trips out west, I feel I captured the true essence of Montana ranch life. In my travels, I came across numerous individuals who rallied me in my effort for authentic research. I want to thank them for all their support.

Residing in a small Kentucky town, I live on a two-hundred-acre Quarter Horse farm. I hold an RN degree and nurse at a local hospital and outpatient clinic. Some mornings you can find me working on my laptop, immersed in characters, a view of the horse pasture just over my shoulder as inspiration. Other mornings, I'll be dressed in scrub uniform and out the door after the last horse is fed and watered. I love to write and have a bad habit of using my fictional world of heroes and heroines as an escape, for vacations are rare occurrences.

Thank you for taking this journey with me. My website is www.sloanseymour.com. I would be delighted to hear from you.

Sloan

Thank you for purchasing
this Wild Rose Press publication.
For other wonderful stories of romance,
please visit our on-line bookstore at
www.thewildrosepress.com.

For questions or more information,
contact us at info@thewildrosepress.com.

The Wild Rose Press
www.TheWildRosePress.com